TEARS OF THE

EMERALD PRINCESS

REECE LEWING

"Tears of the Emerald Princess" is an original work of fiction written and published by Reece Lewing. Names, organizations, and events—other than those publicly recognized trademarks—are products of the author's imagination. Any resemblance to people, institutions, and events are entirely coincidental.

No part of this book may be reproduced in any way without written permission of the author.

Cover designed by Reece Lewing.

Chapter 1

As he ran along the narrow jungle path, Brad Townsend remembered how getting out of hostile territory was more difficult than getting in. He had experienced such situations many times during his two tours of duty flying helicopters in Vietnam. Now, fifteen years later, he was once again behind enemy lines. But this time, circumstances were different: there were no Phantoms for air support, no gun ships to lay down cover fire, and no rescue chopper to whisk him out of harm's way. To make it back to the safety of the Thai border, he knew he would have to rely on his physical and mental strength—and a helluva lot of luck.

His perspiration-soaked khaki shirt provided little protection from the two 35mm Nikons that pounded the left side of his rib cage with each stride. Sucking air, he felt that he could not go much further. Reaching down deep inside to keep his legs moving, he was not about to let mere pain and exhaustion keep him from completing his mission.

The full moon broke through the clouds, touching off a barrage of artillery as Vietnamese spotters took advantage of the evening light to direct fire on Khmer rebel positions. The explosions seemed to walk closer and closer.

Following the lead of his Vietnamese companion, Townsend quickly left the trail for the cover of the jungle. He stumbled through the thick foliage for several yards before fatigue finally overcame him. Hitting the ground with the full force of his two hundred ten pounds, he surrendered a painful grunt. Mustering what little energy he had left, he rolled over on his back and stretched his weary limbs. His head throbbed and his body ached all over. At that moment, he felt worse than any of the three times he had been wounded in combat. He began to question whether his plan was really worth all the misery he was experiencing. But as his pain became soothed by his inactivity, and his strength started to return, he got that notion out of his mind. A little sacrifice now for a future of wealth and easy living was a small price to pay, he reasoned.

"You ok, Captain Brad?" whispered the voice in a heavy Vietnamese accent.

"Yeah, Jimmy. I'm fine. How about you?" Townsend

responded softly to his friend, Jim Lee.

"I am ok," he answered, happy that his American friend had asked.

Townsend had just begun to relax when the cracking of small arms fire roused him from his rest. He sat up and listened, trying to determine how far off the shooting was. It was difficult to judge the direction of the sound in the jungle, but he knew the fighting was getting nearer. He felt helpless without a gun, but remaining unarmed was essential. He had carefully created the identity of a photojournalist, down to the false ID and forged company expense forms. Even the cameras were marked PROPERTY OF LIFE MAGAZINE, just in case he fell into the hands of either side. The Thai-Cambodian frontier was crawling with foreign reporters covering the war and its refugees. Both the Khmer rebels and Vietnamese regulars usually released those correspondents they came into contact with as long as they had the proper identification and were free of contraband. If caught armed, the fate of the violator was usually a bullet in the back of the head.

Jim Lee tugged on the leg of Townsend's trousers. "We go now, Captain Brad."

Townsend gently rubbed his ribs, assessing the extent of damage. "How much further?"

"Only four or five more kilometers...we must hurry."

Responding to the urgency in his friend's voice, Townsend jumped up and collected his cameras. He did a half-squat, cracking both knees, before falling in behind his guide.

They had been on the trail almost an hour when Jim Lee stopped abruptly. He motioned for Townsend to take cover.

Townsend immediately complied. "What's wrong?" he whispered between breaths.

"Someone ahead. I heard voices."

"Who do you think they are?"

"Not sure." Jim Lee turned his head around slowly, scanning for sound. "Sound like Vietnamese. You stay here and I find out."

"I'm going with you," Townsend answered.

"No. It is best I go alone. I will be ok."

Townsend was somewhat surprised at the forcefulness of Jim Lee's voice. "Well, be careful," he cautioned.

"If I don't come back, Thai border straight ahead across river."

"Don't talk like that," Townsend commanded, putting his hand on his friend's shoulder, emphasizing his concern.

Jim Lee smiled. He grasped Townsend's hand and then slipped into the darkness.

Townsend placed his wrist in a narrow beam of moonlight that penetrated the trees and checked the time. Only two minutes had passed since he last acquiesced to this nervous compulsion. Jim Lee had been gone forty minutes, but it seemed like hours. Fidgeting with his watch, he had never been one for waiting. He was concerned about his Vietnamese friend.

He first met Jim Lee when his friend was eight years old, a shabby looking kid hanging around the base trying to get money to help support his family. When asked his name, he gave an answer that sounded like he was saying Jim Lee, so that became his name. Townsend called him Jimmy. While some of the other soldiers gave the kid a hard time and shooed him away, Townsend paid him to shine his boots, clean his hooch, and to do odd jobs. He was a hard worker who always went above and beyond to please the man he came to idolize. In return, Townsend made sure he was taken care of, and taught him to speak decent English. He once brought his thirteen-year-old sister to the base to marry his mentor. Townsend politely declined and sent them both away with ice cream, but the teasing from his fellow soldiers lasted for weeks.

Tired of sitting around, Townsend decided to go looking for his friend. Just as he was moving out, he heard a rustle in the underbrush.

"Captain Brad...Captain Brad!"

"Over here, Jimmy," he answered with a sigh of relief. When he came into view, Townsend patted him on the back. "You all right?"

"I ok," he panted.

"What's the story?"

"There are about sixty refugees getting ready to cross river. We can go over with them."

"Then let's get moving."

They pulled out and made their way through the dense underbrush to the crossing site. When they arrived, the refugees had already started across the river. Tire tubes, sticks tied in bundles, and anything else that would float dotted in the moon's reflection on the water.

Townsend removed his boots, tied the strings together and hung them around his neck. He then placed his cameras in a waterproof bag and followed Jim Lee into the river. As he waded out, the cool water rising against his hot, sweaty body felt good.

A young mother with two small children strapped to her back began struggling in the light current. Townsend swam toward her as fast as his tired body would allow. They submerged and came up several times before he could get to them. Finally, he was able to reach out as they were going down again. He unfastened the children and cradled them with his left arm. Jim Lee swam over and rescued the exhausted mother.

Halfway across the river, automatic rifle fire from the rear strafed the water. The popping of the guns was almost drowned out by the cries and screams of the scared and wounded. Return fire from the Thai side commenced, catching the helpless swimmers in a deadly crossfire.

Small splashes danced around Townsend as bullets hit the water. Instinctively, he pulled the children he was carrying closer to his chest. He could feel the fear in the rapid beats of their little hearts.

A small boy floating face down bumped into Townsend. He turned the body over. There was a baseball-size hole in his abdomen. Townsend felt sick. He was then overcome with anger. "Jimmy," he shouted as loud as he could. "Tell the people not to cross here. Get them to drift further down the river."

Jim Lee quickly translated the order into Vietnamese, repeating it over and over. Those still alive obeyed.

Suddenly, Townsend's face grimaced in pain as a bullet tore into his right shoulder. He struggled to maintain control in the water. The extra weight of the children made it difficult to swim, but he knew he had to keep going.

After ten minutes of agony, he managed to make it to the opposite bank. He crawled a few meters into the jungle, still

4

clutching the children, before his strength gave out and he collapsed.

He came to a few minutes later with Jim Lee softly patting his face with a damp cloth.

"You ok, Captain Brad?"

He looked around. "I think so."

"Looks like you wounded again," Jim Lee said with a smile of relief.

"Yeah...but this time, no purple heart," he responded before passing out again.

Chapter 2

Townsend eased the Ford sedan to the curb in front of the modest white frame house. He pushed the shift lever in park. The engine idled as he leaned over to the passenger window for a better look at the residence. After a few moments, he decided he was at the right place. He checked his watch: 7:42 a.m. He switched off the ignition and exited the car, gently shutting the door to avoid disturbing those who were taking advantage of the quiet Saturday morning to sleep in.

His stomach began churning as he approached the front door. It had been seven years since he last saw his old army buddy. He wondered if that special closeness they had shared while serving together in Viet Nam would still be there. His finger shook slightly as he pressed the doorbell button beneath the brass plate that identified the place as the Taylor residence.

A minute passed before a sleepy, petite blonde appeared at the door. She cupped her hand to her forehead to protect her squinted eyes from the early morning sun. "Yes?" she said, not immediately recognizing the tall mustached man on the other side of the screen.

"Suzy, it's me, Brad."

She focused her blue eyes on his face. "Brad," she shouted in a delayed reaction. She opened the door and threw her arms around his neck, pressing her head against his chest. She hung on to him in that position for nearly a minute without saying a word. Finally, she looked up at him with tears rolling down her cheeks. She released him and wiped her eyes with the collar of her housecoat.

"Oh, Brad, I'm sorry. Come in." She tried to fix her uncombed hair with her hands. "I must look like a mess."

Townsend smiled. "No. You are as beautiful as ever, Suzy."

She blushed. "I can't believe you are really here. Have a seat and I'll get Jeff."

"Don't wake him."

"It's all right. Time for him to get up anyway," she reassured him as she disappeared from the room.

No sooner had Townsend sat down than Taylor, clad only in his boxer shorts, came rushing into the living room.

Townsend stood up and extended his right hand to shake,

but Taylor bypassed it and gave his old friend a big hug instead. The two men patted each other on the back, both tying to fight back the tears of happiness which threatened to appear. Townsend's earlier thought whether the closeness was still there was answered.

"Let me fix some breakfast for you boys," Suzy offered, breaking the silence. She walked into the kitchen, still wiping the tears from her eyes.

Taylor released his friend. "Sit down, Brad...sit down." Townsend took a seat on the sofa. "Boy, it sure is good to see you again."

"It's good to see you too, Jeff."

"How long has it been?"

"Seven years," Townsend answered. "I was leaving for Singapore. This is the first time I've been back to the States."

"Seven years," Taylor repeated. "That seems so long ago. A lot of things have happened since then. I..." he tried to speak but the lump in his throat would not allow it. He turned his head so Townsend could not see the tears returning to his eyes.

Townsend sat quietly, waiting for his friend to regain his composure. He wanted to say something to comfort Taylor, but could not find the right words. The silence was awkward for him. He knew from correspondence with Taylor's parents and Suzy that he was still having a hard time adjusting after his discharge from the army. He could sense that the scars of war were still sore for his friend. He had dealt with his own pretty well, but Taylor and many others he served with were continuing to experience the mental anguish the VA doctors and counselors were calling post-traumatic stress disorder. "That damn war," he whispered aloud.

"I'm ok now, Brad. I'm just glad to see you," he said apologetically.

Townsend smiled. "Hey, where's Scotty?"

"He's spending a few days with Suzy's parents. They are going to Disneyland and up Big Sur to San Francisco."

"Sounds like a lot of fun. How's he doing?"

The question seemed to perk up his friend. "A lot better. He still has asthma and those allergies, but that heart surgery he had two years ago has made him a lot stronger."

"I'm sure glad to hear that. The last picture I saw he's the

7

spitting image of his old man. I know you and Suzy are very proud of him."

"Yeah. He's a real trooper. He never complains. Hey, he will be eight in two months."

"Time sure passes fast."

"Brad, I really appreciate the five thousand dollars you sent. It sure helped with the medical bills."

"Don't mention it. I know you would have done the same for me."

Hearing his best friend say that made him feel good. "You know I would."

Townsend leaned back. "Besides, I've been doing all right. The company takes good care of me and there's not much to spend my money on over there."

"Who are you working for?"

"I'm still with Royal Premier Petroleum."

"Flying choppers?"

"Yes...and small jets too. But I prefer the choppers."

All the talk about flying got Taylor's interest and, for a few brief moments, he was able to put his troubles out of mind. "I'll bet your job is a lot of fun, isn't it?"

Townsend shrugged his shoulders. "The flying and traveling are fun, but it gets routine and boring sometimes...especially when I have to deal with some of the big wheel assholes. How about your job?"

"I'm the day dispatcher for Cal-Southern Trucking. The money's not so hot, but it's not a bad job. I work part-time in security at a sporting goods warehouse...twenty hour per week. It's mostly just sitting on my ass. But I'm not complaining. I need the money. I still owe about twelve thousand bucks in medical bills alone."

The two chatted until Suzy walked in. "Chow time," she announced, thinking the old army buddies would like her choice of words in announcing breakfast. Townsend and Taylor looked at one another and laughed as they followed her into the kitchen.

The aroma of pork sausage and freshly brewed coffee dominated the air. "Smells good in here, Suzy," Townsend complimented her.

"Yeah, Honey," Taylor added.

She glanced over at her husband. It had been a while since he had called her that. She liked hearing it again. "I've fixed you boys a special breakfast," she said, motioning for them to sit down. She walked over to the counter and returned with two plates containing fried eggs, grits, sausage, and biscuits. She placed them on the table imitating the style she used when working at the officers' club at Fort Benning. "I know how you Southern boys like your grits," she said in an exaggerated Southern drawl.

Townsend looked over at Suzy. He noticed she had been watching him as he ate. "These sure are good biscuits."

"Thank you. I remember how you used to love homemade biscuits."

"What do you mean used to? I still do. The problem is I hardly ever get them. Over there, all those people think about is fish and rice. There was this cook on one of the offshore rigs—I think he was from Mississippi—who fixed good biscuits. Whenever I had to fly in a crew, I would go by his galley and he would give me a dozen or so of those big cathead water biscuits to take with me. I'd eat on those things for days," he smiled at the memory. "Unfortunately, he retired about a year ago. I think I went through a sort of biscuit withdrawal afterwards," he laughed. "None of those foreign cooks know how to make anything that tastes that good. Hell, they don't even know what grits are!"

"That's their loss," Taylor remarked as he lifted a fork full of the fine ground corn to his mouth.

"Are you on vacation?" Suzy asked.

Townsend paused before answering. He wanted to make sure he chose his words carefully. "Actually, I'm here to finalize a business deal I have been working on. A lot of money stands to be made on it. I'll tell you about it later." He noticed by their facial expressions he had piqued their interest. He turned to Taylor. "What are you two doing tonight?"

Taylor looked at his wife. She lifted her eyebrows and took a sip of coffee. "Same as always...watching television, I guess."

"I want to take you and Suzy out for a night on the town. We will start with thick, juicy steaks, a few drinks, and maybe even a little dancing. What do you think?"

Taylor looked over at Suzy again. He knew by the look on

9

her face that she was dying to go. Because of his jobs and their money problems, he rarely took her out. He felt guilty about not doing more for her, but she never complained. He was not about to deny her this opportunity. "Sure. It will be just like old times."

Suzy's face lit up. She reached over and placed her hand on her husband's. He squeezed it gently and smiled.

After breakfast the three friends spent the rest of the morning and the early afternoon catching up on what had been going on in their lives. They joked, laughed, and reminisced about old times. Both Suzy and Taylor noticed how just the appearance of Townsend had brought them closer together, evidenced by their continuous holding of hands.

It was after seven p.m. before Suzy was able to run her bath. She tested the water with her foot—very warm—just the way she liked it. She slipped in, resting her head on the back of the tub. The heat from the water penetrated her fair skin and soothed her trim body. She was glad that Townsend had come. Spending time with Jeff would be good for him—and her.

She closed her eyes and began thinking back to the time when she first met Townsend at Fort Benning. She was in college and had taken the waitress job at the officers' club to get through her last year of school. He was a first lieutenant recently back from his first tour of duty in Viet Nam. He liked to come into the club and tell stories of his combat experiences to fellow officers, many of whom had never been out of the States. Though viewed as somewhat cocky, he was well-liked and respected by his peers as well as his superiors. After all, he was a genuine hero. The three rows of campaign ribbons he wore were proof of his distinguished service. Even more, he looked like a hero—at least in the eyes of a twenty-year-old woman who had little experience with men. He was tall, with broad shoulders, a handsome mustached face, and sparkling hazel eyes. His wit and humor added to his personal magnetism. Everyone seemed to be attracted to him. There were few times when he had to pay for his own drinks in the club.

It was Townsend's aura of confidence that first attracted her to him. He was so independent and self-reliant—characteristics sometimes fatal to junior officers. She was surprised when he asked her out, and even more surprised at herself when she accepted. She had heard of his reputation with women from some of the other waitresses, but she did not let their hearsay change her mind. Although she had dated several men, including soldiers at the base, she had never been to bed with anyone. She had always been able to handle them, saving herself for that special one.

Suzy expected her first date with Townsend to be another wrestling match, or at least a battle of wits. But he surprised her. They had dinner and went to a movie. He was a perfect gentleman throughout the evening. When he walked her to the door of her apartment, she was a little disappointed when he kissed her on her forehead, said goodnight and left.

Over the next five months every spare moment they could get was spent together. They went flying, sailing, and fishing. He taught her how to ride a motorcycle, to water ski, and, eventually, how to make love. Then, as suddenly as it began, it ended. He told her that he loved her but they were getting too serious. He tried to convince her that she would only get hurt. But she did not believe him. She asked him to move in with her, no strings attached. He refused. She found out a week later that the reason he broke things off was he would be doing another tour in Viet Nam and did not want to make a commitment and then leave and possibly never return. He had already seen too many young widows and could not stand the idea of her being one. A soldier who was a mutual friend later told her that he had a feeling that he would not return from the upcoming tour. She and Townsend remained good friends, but everyone who knew them could see they loved each other.

A few weeks after they split, Townsend brought his new copilot to the officers' club and introduced him to Suzy. His name was Jeff Taylor. He had a lot in common with Townsend: tall, good-looking, with a great sense of humor. Suzy and Taylor hit it off immediately. They dated for two months before he asked her to marry him. The shadow of Townsend was still in her heart, but she said yes. Townsend was best man. Six weeks later, the two most important men in her life, other than her father, were shipped out to Viet Nam. Since it was Taylor's first tour, she made Townsend promise to look after him and bring him back alive. He agreed.

The bath water began to cool, bringing Suzy out of her daydream. She quickly finished her bath and went into the bedroom to dress. She dropped the housecoat on the bed and walked over to the full-length mirror. With her face up to the glass, she examined herself closely to see if any new lines had sneaked in since she last checked. None had. Her eyes moved down. The breasts were still just as firm as always. From the side they were pointed and stuck straight out. Townsend used to call them snow cones because of their conical shape. Next, was the belly. The front view didn't look bad. But from the side it stuck out a little further than she liked. She could work it down, she assured herself. Finally, she eyed the legs, inspecting the front, sides, and rear. They were thin and shapely. Next to her eyes, she felt they were her best physical feature. So did Townsend. She recalled how proud he was walking beside her at the beach, knowing that men and women alike were admiring her shape. Having successfully passed inspection, she felt she could pass for twenty-five, ten years younger than her actual age.

After brushing out her hair, she dusted with bath powder and chased that with a modest dabbling of her favorite perfume—Chanel Number Five—used only for special occasions. She stepped into a pair of black bikini panties, slipped on panty hose, and pulled up a black half-slip. She opted against a bra. The dress she selected was a black satin with silver sequins bordering the low neckline and sleeves. She last wore it eight months ago at a dinner party celebrating the fortieth anniversary of her parents. She checked the mirror several times, making the necessary adjustments, then slipped on her black high heels before giving her reflection a final smile of approval.

Townsend and Taylor were in the living room listening to rock and roll oldies when Suzy walked in. Townsend was the first to see her. "Wow!" he said, causing her to blush.

Taylor turned around. "Damn, Honey. You look like a movie star!"

She strutted to them, turned and wiggled her ass at them as she walked around the room doing a Mae West imitation. "Ok, big boys. I'm ready." She took a man on each arm and led them to the door.

Chapter 3

After the promised steak dinner, Townsend persuaded his two friends to go dancing. The parking lot was full when they arrived at the Normandy Bar and Grill. Saturday nights featured a Forties-style band that attracted a regular crowd of swing era music lovers. Townsend circled twice before finding a space. As they got out of the car, they were greeted by the lively beat of "In the Mood."

"Sounds like the place is jumping," Suzy teased as they neared the entrance.

"I hope you're wearing your dancing shoes," Townsend responded with a quick wiggle of his hips.

They paused inside the doorway to allow their eyes to adjust to the dark. Their vision was further obscured by the thick cloud of cigarette smoke that hung in the air. The place appeared to be one great big party. Young and old packed the small dance floor. Some jitterbugged, others twisted, and many just moved their bodies in rhythm with the music. Those seated at tables surrounding the dancers patted their feet and offered verbal encouragement to those gyrating to the music.

Townsend scanned the room for an empty table. Unable to spot one, he turned to Taylor. "Wait here and I'll find a place to sit." He then disappeared into the crowd.

Taylor was suddenly hit by a rush of anxiety. He had developed an aversion to strangers, especially a group this large. Two years had passed since he had been in a bar. It was a time he had just as soon forget. He was hitting the bottle heavily then, trying to drink away his financial problems and perceived inadequacies as a husband and father. Any other woman would have left him. But Suzy was not just any woman. She hung tough and finally persuaded him to enter a VA hospital detox program to dry out and receive counseling. He still drank on occasion, but with greater control.

A couple of deep breaths made him feel better. He leaned over and kissed Suzy's head.

She looked up and smiled. "What's that for?"

He pulled her close. Even in the dark he could see the twinkle in her eyes. "You," is all he said.

Townsend walked up. "There's a table over there," he

pointed. They followed him to the far side of the bar. Taylor pulled out the chair for his wife. Suzy gave him a grin of approval at this thoughtfulness as he gently guided the chair under the table.

"How did you find this place, Brad?" Suzy asked.

"I used to come here a lot before I started working overseas. It's a popular hangout for pilots. I stopped in last night to see if it was still here. I was surprised to see it has hardly changed."

Taylor looked around. "Nice atmosphere," he said, referring to the framed photographs of aircraft and other aviation memorabilia that filled the walls.

"Yeah," Townsend nodded his head in agreement. "The owner was a fighter pilot in World War Two." He pointed to a spot above the cash register. "See that swastika? It's the actual tail skin from an ME-109 he shot down during the Normandy invasion."

"Impressive souvenir," Taylor answered. "Do you still have your souvenir, Brad."

"Sure do." He took a key chain from his pocket and placed it on the table. Attached to the chain was an intact projectile from a Soviet-made AK-47 assault rifle. "I take it with me everywhere I go. It's my good luck charm."

Suzy picked up the key chain and examined the spent bullet. She rubbed the slightly flattened tip with her finger. "Why is it lucky?" she asked in a curious voice.

"He was shot with it," Taylor informed her.

Suzy looked surprised. "Was this when you were in the hospital?"

"No. That was the third time I was wounded."

"What happened," she pressed.

"Well, we were evacuating wounded from a fire fight near An Loc. We had just lifted off when we came under small arms fire. I felt this thud in my left side just below my armpit." He pointed to the spot. "I looked down and saw a patch of blood. Jeff took control of the chopper. I reached down and felt part of the bullet sticking out of my side. I yanked it out and stuffed a handkerchief in the hole," he demonstrated with his hand. "When we got back to the base, a nurse cleaned and bandaged the wound. I flew a mission the next day."

Suzy had a stunned looked on her face. "Are you serious?

You pulled the bullet out of your side?"

"It really happened, didn't it, Jeff."

Taylor nodded. "Strange, but true. I was there."

"The doctor said I was lucky. Had it continued straight it would have hit my heart. That's why I carry it around with me...to remind me how close to death I have been. It helps keep me humble," he smiled.

"We used to call him 'Old Ironside' after that. The flat spot on the slug was caused when it hit his rib," Taylor added.

Suzy shook her head in disbelief. "Where's the waitress? I need a drink."

Townsend waived his hand until he caught the attention of a tall, buxom redhead dressed in a skimpy cocktail outfit.

"What would you like?" she asked as she leaned over the table and wiped the top with a damp cloth.

"I'd like a whiskey sour...with Crown," Suzy answered without hesitation. It was a drink that Townsend introduced her to years ago.

"Do you have Coors?" Taylor asked.

The waitress nodded.

"Make it two," added Townsend.

The waitress repeated the order, looked Townsend straight in the eye for a moment, then walked away.

Taylor turned to his wife. "What are you grinning about?"

"Brad." She answered.

"Me? Why?"

"Same ol' Brad. I saw you staring at the waitress' boobs when she leaned over."

Taylor looked over at Townsend. They both laughed. "What's wrong with that?' her husband asked. "She had them right in his face."

Suzy shrugged her shoulders. "Nothing, I guess. It's just the way he looked...as if he wanted her to know he was looking."

"I did want her to know. I couldn't hurt her feelings."

"You're terrible," she said, playfully tapping his arm with her fist.

A few minutes later, the waitress returned. She placed the drinks on the table, exposing her cleavage to Townsend once again. "What do I owe you?" he asked.

"Six-fifty," she answered in her low, sexy voice.

He handed her a ten. "Keep the change."

"Thanks." She leaned down and gave him a provocative smirk. "Would you like anything else?"

Townsend grinned, knowing that Suzy and Taylor were awaiting his response. He moved his eyes over her long, shapely body, pausing at the two large breasts bulging from the low neckline of her blouse. "Maybe later, baby. Check back in a little while," he answered in a flirtatious tone.

All three watched her walk away. Townsend and Taylor looked at each other, then they turned to Suzy.

"I didn't say a thing," she shrugged.

Taylor held up his beer. "Well, I'd like to propose a toast. A man could not have a finer wife and a better friend than I have here with me. I love both of you." They touched their drinks in unison and each took a sip.

They had finished several rounds when Suzy suddenly stood up. She tugged on her husband's arm. "Come on, Jeff, they're playing "Smoke Gets in Your Eyes." Let's dance."

Taylor did not like to dance unless he was tipsy. "Not now, baby," he politely begged off. "You and Brad go ahead."

Suzy turned to Townsend. "All right, Brad. I know you like to dance." Ignoring his protests that he would rather wait until later also, she grabbed his hand and led him to a small opening on the dance floor. Not accustomed to more than two drinks, her inhibitions were lowered. She closed her eyes and rested her head against Townsend's chest. Her body felt relaxed as she followed his lead.

Taylor watched patiently as his wife and best friend moved slowly to the music. Suzy looked radiant. She was by far the most attractive woman in the place. And Townsend, tall and fit, was the picture of poise and confidence. It did not bother him that he was her first love, or that he was the only other man she had been with. They were in love then, and it was the war that kept them from marrying. He knew that somewhere deep inside, they still had feelings for one another, but did not feel threatened by this knowledge. Suzy was a good, loyal wife and Brad was a great friend. He considered himself lucky to love and be loved by two good people like them.

Townsend escorted Suzy back to the table. "Your turn old boy," he instructed.

Suzy leaned down and kissed her husband on the cheek. "Please, honey. I requested the band to play "Harbor Lights." Remember how we used to dance to it at Fort Benning?"

Townsend nudged him. "Go ahead, Jeff. I see someone I need to talk to."

"Okay." He drained his beer and joined Suzy, who was already on the dance floor. She took his hand and led him to an open space. He put his arms around her. She responded by pressing her body close to his. It had been a long time since he had held her like that. He had almost forgotten how good she felt. She was right: the song and the feel of her body did bring back memories of Fort Benning and his army days in Georgia.

After finishing the dance, Taylor saw Suzy back to the table, then went to the restroom. When he returned, a heavy-set man was bent over Suzy trying to put his arm around her. She kept pushing it off.

"Get your hands off her," Taylor demanded.

The guy looked up at him. "Get lost. Me and this babe are gonna dance."

Taylor felt the blood of anger rush to his face. "Get your fat ass away from this table before..." he stopped himself.

The other main straightened up. "Before what?"

Taylor did not respond.

"Who the hell are you?"

"I'm her husband, asshole."

He sneered at Taylor. "Big deal." He bent back down and put his arm on Suzy's shoulder.

Taylor grabbed the larger man's wrist and twisted it behind his back. He applied enough pressure to cause the larger man's face to grimace. "Next time, listen."

A crowd started to gather around. Townsend saw what was happening, but stayed back. He realized Taylor had to handle the situation himself. If needed, he was ready.

"Let go of my arm," the man groaned.

"First, you apologize to my wife."

"Hell, no."

Taylor jerked the arm higher. "Now apologize."

"Ok, ok. I'm sorry, lady."

"That's better." Taylor released his arm. "Now get your ass away from us."

The man held his left shoulder as he turned to leave. Suddenly, he spun around and took a swing at Taylor. The blow grazed Taylor's right cheek. Before he could straighten up, Taylor connected with a right cross to the jaw that sent the larger man across a table and on the tile floor. He was out cold.

Townsend pushed through the crowd. "Great punch, Jeff. Now let's get out of here."

"Why?" Taylor asked, rubbing his hand. "He started it."

Townsend patted him on the shoulder. "I know. But that was the owner's son. They'll probably call the cops."

"So, let them call the cops," he responded in defiance of all present. In his adrenalin-heightened state, rationality was absent. He was ready to take on any would-be challengers. The fight ended too soon. Forced to take his fists out of years of reserve, he was not anxious to put them away. He had too much pent-up anger and frustration dwelling inside.

The brief action had a sobering effect on Suzy. She took her husband's arm. "Brad's right, honey. Let's get out of this place."

He saw the proud look on her face. He had defended her honor—and his. He released his fists and put his arm around her.

As they headed for the door, a man walked up to Taylor. "Good going, buddy. That sorry bastard had it coming to him." Hearing those words from a stranger made him feel even better. Townsend, sporting a big grin on his face, followed them out acting as rear guard.

Suzy hung her dress in the closet and slipped out of her pantyhose. When she turned around, she saw that Taylor was stretched out on the bed asleep. "Oh, shit," she said. The dancing, the liquor, the attention she had gotten all night had her worked up and now Jeff was out. She thought about going over and shaking him, but she did not want to take the initiative. She never did. Her feeling was that it was his place. That was the reason their lovemaking was so infrequent. She loved being with him, but she also liked being seduced. Thinking he was done for the night, she got an ice pack from the freezer and placed it on his slightly swollen cheek bone. The cold caused him to open his eyes. Seeing her leaning over him wearing only bikini panties, he pulled her down on the bed and kissed her passionately. She slipped off her panties. They made love for the first time in three months.

Chapter 4

Townsend rolled over on his back and slowly opened his eyes. The smell of fresh coffee penetrated his nostrils, setting off a mild rumbling in his belly. He took a couple of deep breaths hoping the aroma would help clear his drowsiness. As he sat on the side of the bed, he felt the blood rush to his head, pulsating in rhythm with each beat of his heart—punishment for exceeding his limit last night, he thought. He put his hands behind his head and gently massaged his neck. It didn't help much. He pulled on his pants and walked into the kitchen.

"Good morning, sleepy head," Suzy greeted him with a smile.

"What's so good about it?" he mumbled.

She laughed. "So, you have a headache too?"

"I sure do. It feels like my head is going to explode."

"Can I get you something?"

"That coffee smells good...and a couple of aspirins would be nice."

"Sit down. I've got just the thing for you." She walked over to the counter. Townsend flopped down in the chair. He leaned forward and put his head in his hands. The high pitch whirring of the blender further aggravated his headache. A minute later Suzy handed him a glass of thick reddish liquid. "Drink this."

"What is it?"

"It's my special concoction for hangovers...V-8 juice, two eggs, a little gin, vitamin C, and two Extra Strength Tylenols," she announced proudly.

Townsend studied the contents closely.

"Well, drink up," she coaxed.

He took a sip. "Not bad." He put the glass to his lips and drank the entire remedy without stopping.

Suzy smiled. "Why don't you lay back down and I'll bring you a cup of coffee a little later."

He followed her orders and returned to the bedroom. Within minutes he was asleep.

When he woke up a half-hour later, Suzy was standing over him holding the cup of coffee she promised. He sat up on the bed and rubbed his face. She handed him the cup and sat down next to him. "How do you feel?"

"Much better, thanks. The headache is gone."

"Good."

He took a sip of coffee. "You need to market your headache medicine."

"That's what Jeff says."

"Where is Jeff?"

"He went to work hours ago."

Townsend looked at his watch. "I can't believe that it's almost noon."

"You looked so peaceful in your sleep I hated to wake you. After all, you were partying pretty good last night."

"So were you and Jeff as I recall."

She shrugged. "Well, it was a special occasion. It's been so long since we've seen you. It was kind of like the good old days."

"Yes. It was," Townsend agreed.

The smile left her face. She became silent and stared at the floor. Townsend sensed her sadness. He reached over and put his hand on hers. "Come on now. Everything is going to be all right."

As she turned to him, the top of her robe came open exposing her left breast. She noticed him looking before she eased her hand up and closed it. His interest excited her. They stared at each other without saying anything. Simultaneously, their heads started to moved forward. With their lips just inches apart, he suddenly pulled back. "I'm sorry. I forgot myself for a moment," he apologized.

"It's okay, Brad. Nothing happened. I guess I just need a shoulder to cry on," she explained.

"You know you will always have it."

She nodded and placed her head on his shoulder. "I wish things could be the way they were when we first got married. We were so happy then."

"Jeff is a good man. He's had some bad breaks...but things will get better...you'll see," he tried to assure her.

She sat up and wiped the tears from her cheeks. "You are a good man too, Brad. I don't know what we would have done without your help."

"That's what friends are for."

"I never told Jeff about that other two thousand dollars you sent. I thought it would only upset him. You know how proud he is. If the other money had not been for Scotty, he would have never accepted it."

"I know. You did the right thing."

She managed to crack a slight smile. "We sure are lucky to have a friend like you."

"No. Jeff is the lucky one...to have a woman like you."

Her face lit up. His words meant a lot to her. She realized that even though the romantic feelings were still mutual, their future was in the special friendship they shared. She was comforted in knowing that he would be there for her, Jeff, and Scotty.

Chapter 5

After dinner that evening, Townsend joined Taylor and Suzy in the living room. The three sat around and talked. A couple of hours had passed before Townsend felt it was time to tell them about his plan. He waited until what he thought was the right moment. Finally, he looked at Taylor. "I want to level with you about why I am back in the States." He paused, trying to choose his words carefully. "I told you I was here on business. I am...sorta." He played with his watch as he talked. "For the last six months I've been working on a plan that will make me and a few other men rich."

Taylor looked over at Suzy and back at Townsend. "What kind of plan?"

"Well, in movie jargon it's called a heist."

"A heist?" Taylor repeated in a slightly raised voice. He looked at his wife again. Her face indicated she was as surprised as he was. He laughed nervously, unsure whether his buddy was joking. His smile evaporated when he saw the solemn look Townsend was wearing. He knew then he was serious. "What kind of heist?"

"Jewels," Townsend responded without hesitation.

Taylor appeared confused. "But why, Brad? You have a good job and you're making great money. You've got everything going for you..."

"It may seem that way to you, but I'm not happy," he interrupted. I've been in Singapore for seven years. I'm tired of taking orders from some desk jockey that doesn't know his ass from an altimeter. I'm tired of the food and filth, and I'm tired of the cheap women." The last statement caused Suzy to look up. He wished he had not mentioned the women in front of her.

"I want to come back to the States and do the things I want without worrying about money. I'd like to start a helicopter charter service. Then I could fly when I felt like it."

"You can do that without robbing anyone," Taylor remarked.

"You're missing the point, Jeff. I want to enjoy life, have some fun for a change, call my own shots and be in complete control of my life. It takes money to live like that...a lot of money."

"Hell, Brad. Everyone would like to have things that way. But..."

"I'm not just talking. I plan to do something about it. I'm nearly forty. It's time to take it easy. Who knows, I may find the right woman and settle down." He saw Suzy take note of his statement. "Besides, I'm not going to rob a person. I've worked out all the details over the last six months and it's foolproof."

"Yeah, the prison is full of guys who have said the same thing," Taylor quipped.

Townsend overlooked the remark and calmly responded, "Well, do you want to hear my plan?"

Taylor looked at Suzy as if asking for her approval. She said nothing. "I guess it won't hurt to just listen."

Townsend smiled. He leaned forward, his elbows on his knees. "About eight months ago, I flew some company executives to Rangoon for a meeting with Burmese officials to discuss drilling rights. We were there several days, so I passed the time sightseeing. One of the places I visited was a shrine called the Emerald Princess. It was unbelievable. It has one large temple surrounded by several smaller ones. The large spire is gold-plated and rises almost three hundred and fifty feet high," he gestured with his hands. "And the top is covered with thousands of emeralds. The legend says that a beautiful young princess was to be married to a handsome, rich prince from another region. But on the day before the wedding, he fell in battle. When news of his death arrived, the princess became a recluse in her father's castle. She cried everyday for one year. When the tears from her dark green eyes dried, they turned to emeralds. She picked them up and threw them from the window of her bedroom. The villagers below would collect them. They sold the emeralds and used the money to buy food during the famine that was going on at the time. The shrine was built to honor her for saving the people from starvation." He looked at Taylor and Suzy. Satisfied he had their attention, he continued. "There are also diamonds. I've figured out a way to get those stones."

"A shrine is the target?" Taylor interrupted.

"That's right."

"But stealing from a holy site is bad *karma*."

"It's not a religious shrine. And it's not affiliated with

Buddhism. It is more of a tourist draw," Townsend informed them. "There are millions of dollars in gems at the top of that spire. Some of the diamonds are as big as grapes. I have put a lot of time in on this and, with the right people, I can pull it off."

"Three hundred feet up? I hope it's a good plan," Taylor cautioned him.

"It is. I've thought it through time and time again. I have worked out all the bugs and covered all the angles. Do you want to hear how I plan to do it?" He figured that if Taylor heard it, he could convince him to join.

Taylor once again visually checked with Suzy. He could tell she did not like the conversation, but neither of them wanted to hurt their old friend's feelings. "Okay. I'm listening."

"Good," Townsend smiled.

"Suzy, will you bring us a beer?" Taylor asked.

"Yeah," she answered, finally breaking her silence. "I think I will have one myself."

Townsend walked over to his briefcase and retrieved a manila envelope. He opened it and carefully placed the contents on the coffee table in front of them. "Here are the photos of the target."

Suzy returned with the beers. She thought to herself how the two of them reminded her of boys discovering a new game. But she knew what they were discussing was not child's play. It was a dangerous notion that could land Townsend in jail—or worse. She handed out the beers.

"Look at the height of that spire," Taylor said excitedly as he passed the picture over to his wife, now seated beside him on the sofa.

By the time Taylor had finished looking at the photographs, his second beer was empty. Townsend, still on his first brew, gave his extra to his friend.

"How do you plan to get the jewels?" Taylor asked.

Suzy could see that her husband was beginning to get too interested in the plan. She did not like it, but said nothing. She would express her concerns to him when they were alone.

"By chopper," Townsend answered.

"Chopper? How?"

Townsend picked up an illustration covered with lines and figures and spread it over the photographs on the table.

"Simplified, the chopper lowers an explosives man to the top of the spire. He places a blasting belt with small charges at strategic points along the joint, just strong enough to separate the bud holding the gems from the spire, but not dislodge the stones. A harness with a tarp is placed over the spire. The demo guy is then lifted and the charges fired. The bud, which is approximately three feet in length, separates cleanly and is taken to a remote spot where the jewels are removed."

"Where do you sell the jewels?" Taylor asked.

"I already have a buyer lined up."

"What about the chopper?" Taylor persisted.

"That's taken care of too. I'm using the Huey we stashed in Cambodia."

This time Taylor did not return with a question. He leaned back on the sofa and stared ahead with a blank look on his face, as if he was thinking back to his days as a flyer.

"It is still there...just like we left it. The ship is still air worthy. I checked on it myself five weeks ago...with Jim Lee."

A big smile came to Taylor's face. "Jimmy Lee? He's still alive?

"Alive and well."

"What is he doing now?"

Townsend hesitated before saying anything. He was not sure how Taylor would react to his response. "He is working for Van Tat," he finally answered.

The smile immediately left Taylor's face. He jumped up. "Van Tat...the Chinaman," he shouted, his face red with anger. "I thought that dirty son-of-a-bitch was dead."

Suzy noticed his jaw tighten and his fists clench. She was shocked. He was even angrier than the night before. Surprised at how just the mention of a name could set off her husband like that, she walked over and placed her hand on his shoulder. "Jeff. Are you all right?"

He hesitated before answering. "I'm ok, I'm ok," he tried to assure her.

Townsend walked over to them. "I'm sorry, Jeff. I didn't mean..."

"I'm fine now. It's just that...that name...after all these years. I never hated anyone the way I hated that man. I would have killed him with my bare hands if I had been given the chance."

He was referring to the time that Townsend and their crew chief had to restrain him from physically attacking Van Tat.

"I know. So would I, but the timing was wrong."

Suzy, somewhat confused, wanted more information about this man, but thought it best not to pursue things. "Would you like another beer, honey?"

"No. Just let me sit down for a few minutes," he said, trying hard to keep his composure. He eased back on the sofa. Suzy lifted his legs and helped him stretch out. His glassy eyes fixed on the ceiling overhead.

Townsend looked at Suzy. He wanted to say something apologetic, but she turned and positioned herself in the chair next to the sofa facing away from him. Her sullen look told him that she was pissed off. He took a seat on the opposite side of the room, accommodating her desire to avoid eye contact. Occasionally, he would catch her sneaking glances at him. When caught, she would quickly look away. Their little game continued for ten minutes. The silence made them both uncomfortable. Suzy finally gave in. "Who is this damn Van Tat?" she demanded of Townsend.

He looked at her nonchalantly. "That was a long time ago, Suzy."

Jeff did not talk too much about the war with her. Many times, she tried to penetrate the wall he put up, but he said he just did not want to discuss it. She figured it was his way of protecting her. "Come on Brad. Who is he?"

"Go ahead and tell her, Brad," Taylor responded without taking his eyes off the ceiling. "She has a right to know."

Townsend nodded in agreement. He turned up the bottle and held it there until the last bit of foam disappeared into his mouth. He placed the empty on the table in front of him and settled into a storytelling position in the chair. "When Jeff and I were in Nam, we had a little business going on the side. I guess Jeff told you about it?" Suzy nodded her head. "Some people call it black market. But it wasn't really that. Actually, it was more like a delivery service. We used the chopper to carry beer, cigarettes, candy, and magazines to troops at forward outposts or in the field. We made some pretty good pocket money, but we did not stick it to the boys. A buck for an ice-cold beer in that hot sun was a good deal, believe me."

"What about the other officers? Didn't they know what was going on?" Suzy asked.

"Sure, they did. As long as we kept things low key and created no problems, they turned their heads. I think they approved of what we did, although we were breaking army regs. Jeff and I would never do anything that was harmful to the boys. No grass, no drugs, and no hard liquor...those were our rules and they knew this."

Taylor sat up. "Unlike some of those bastards over there dealing all kinds of dope. No telling how many of our boys bought it because their senses were dulled with that shit."

"Where did you get all that stuff?" Suzy asked Townsend.

"At first, we bought it at the various base exchanges. After a while, the demand exceeded our supply. We got some supplies from the Air Force guys who brought things in on cargo planes. But it was still not enough."

"You mean others were using military aircraft for their own purposes?"

Suzy's naivety caused Taylor to burst out in laughter, surprising her as well as Townsend. He smiled at his wife. "Honey, you just wouldn't believe the horse trading, smuggling, and stealing that went on over there. That war made a lot of people rich...especially NCOs. Sure, me and Brad made a few bucks. But we, and many other officers, felt that what we did contributed immensely to morale. We could have made a real big profit off those boys, but that wasn't our intent. We didn't steal or deal in stolen items and we gave a lot of stuff away to those who didn't have the money to buy a cold beer or candy bar. I mean what else could we do? We knew that each time we saw someone, it might be the last time."

"Jeff's right, Suzy. We could have made a killing if that's what we wanted. It came to the point that the troops in the field depended on us for some of the comforts that they could not get otherwise. A cold beer or a cold Coke in the middle of the jungle while reading a letter from home somehow made things a little better."

Suzy soaked in what they were saying. She already knew they were good, decent men. But hearing this story gave her a greater understanding and appreciation of her husband and Townsend. She went into the kitchen and returned with three beers, keeping one for herself.

Taylor took his beer. "Thank you, babe." He downed half the bottle with one large swig. "Go ahead with your story, Brad."

"There was an Air Force sergeant..."

"Al Blaukuss," Taylor interrupted.

"Good memory, Jeff. Anyway, Blaukuss introduced us to Van Tat. From that point on, we had plenty of everything, especially cigarettes. I don't know how he got them. I never asked." He took a sip of beer. "Things were going fine until Van Tat wanted us to start hauling pot in our chopper."

"That slimy bastard," Taylor remarked, his anger mellowed somewhat by the beer.

"What happened?" Suzy asked.

"We refused," Townsend answered. "He threatened to cut off our supplies, thinking that would make us change our minds."

"We knew he would not do that because he was making too much money himself," Taylor added. "We thought that was the end of it. Later, we learned he was using our bird to transfer dope to his contacts."

Suzy looked at her husband. "How?"

Townsend continued. "That weasel had people working for him all over the place...in and out of uniform. He bribed our new crew chief, Patterson. When Jeff found out, he beat the shit out of Patterson and had him transferred to mortuary services."

Taylor grinned, recalling the incident. "It sure made me feel better."

Townsend looked at Taylor and chuckled. "To get back at us, Van Tat planted some dope on our chopper and contacted army intelligence. We got word in flight that the MPs were waiting for us at Tan Son Nhut. We flew the chopper over to Cambodia and hid it in a cave about a hundred clicks—kilometers—from the Thai border. We arranged for some buddies in another chopper crew to pick us up and take us to a site where a bird had gone down a couple of weeks before. We sat fire to what was left of it and radioed a mayday. A rescue chopper picked us up about a half hour later. Back at the base, we reported that we were hit by ground fire..."

"Yeah," Taylor interrupted with laughter. I can still see the serious look on Colonel Sutton's face when he said, 'We better have that area checked out. That's the second chopper we've lost in a month in that spot. The commies must be trying to take that sector.' What a dumb ass."

Suzy shook her head. "You guys are something else. Why didn't you just burn the helicopter in Vietnam instead of flying it to Cambodia?"

"Honey, it may be hard for you to understand, but we just couldn't bring ourselves to do it. She had gotten us through so many tight spots. It just wasn't right to destroy her. We later planned to turn her over to some Thai officers we knew who were going to falsify paperwork to add her to their fleet. We never got the chance. Before we could get back, the communists moved into that area."

"Tell her the name of the ship, Jeff."

"We called her the *Suzy Q*...after you. She had a World War Two type pinup girl painted on her nose."

"You never told me the helicopter was named after me," she said to Taylor. She got up and sat down next to him on the sofa, putting her arms around his waist. At that moment she felt closer to him than she had in a long time.

"Well, we only flew a couple of months with the nose art. Prior to that, we were prohibited from putting any identification on her because of the type ops we were involved in."

"What kind of name is Van Tat?" Suzy asked. It doesn't sound Chinese."

"Ain't nothing right about that guy. I'm sure it's not his real name," Taylor responded.

"What ever happened to him?" she asked Townsend.

"He moved his operation to Bangkok just before the fall of Saigon. He's still there now."

"Probably counting his money," Taylor added.

Townsend did not want to get back on the subject of Van Tat. He looked at his watch. "I guess I'll turn in." After collecting his papers and photographs, he turned to Taylor. "Jeff, I would like to have you with me. Think it over. If you can't, I understand." He felt awkward saying that in front of Suzy, but he felt it was the right thing to do. He did not want to appear to be going behind her back. He respected her too much. After all, she had a big stake in Taylor's decision.

"Ok, Brad," Taylor responded.

"Good night, Brad," Suzy said with a peck on his cheek.

"Good night." He went to his room with the feeling that Taylor wanted to go but would not because of Suzy. At least he was leaving his friend an option.

Suzy lay in bed unable to sleep. She was processing a lot of newly discovered information. She kept thinking about how much Jeff had changed since Townsend's arrival. He was more thoughtful and respectful to her, and she liked this renewed attention. She felt good about him and that made her feel good about herself. It was almost like falling in love again—and she liked the feeling. She moved over next to him. His strong body made her tingle inside. She softly kissed his face and neck until he opened his eyes. For the second night in a row, they made love. Afterwards, with a big smile on her face, she was able to drop off.

Chapter 6

Taylor and Suzy were seated at the table talking when Townsend walked into the kitchen.

"Good morning," they said together.

"Morning," Townsend returned.

"Would you like some breakfast?" Suzy asked.

"No, thanks. Just coffee will be fine." She leaned over and filled his cup.

"You look tired, Brad," Taylor commented.

"I didn't get much sleep last night. There was too much commotion coming from your bedroom." He looked over at Suzy. Her cheeks turned red. He managed to keep a straight face for only a few seconds before bursting out in laughter. Taylor joined in.

Suzy grinned. "You boys are terrible," she said, shaking her head. Taylor put his hand over his wife's.

"Actually, I didn't sleep too well. I kept thinking about my plan. I've got to do it, Jeff. If I don't, I'll always regret it. Besides, I have already invested over twenty thousand dollars."

Suzy and Taylor looked at each other with raised eyebrows. "That's a lot of money," Taylor said.

Townsend took a sip of coffee. "I would like to have you go with me, but I..."

"Who says I'm not going?" he interrupted.

Townsend was surprised by Taylor's words. He really did not expect that response. "I thought..."

"That I would not go? Suzy and I talked it over last night and again this morning. We know it's risky, but the rewards compensate for the risks."

"Are you sure, Jeff?"

"I'm positive," his friend reassured him.

Townsend turned to Suzy. "What about you?" She nodded.

"Last night I could have sworn that you wanted no part of the plan. What made you change your mind?" he asked Taylor.

"Two mortgages on the house, thousands of dollars in doctor bills, and a worn-out car...not to mention creditors breathing down our necks. I'm working my ass off just trying to make ends meet. I don't know how much longer I can go on like this. It has affected my relationship with Suzy. We were taking one another for granted...just existing, not living. But since you have been here, she and I have gotten along better than we have in years. My share will give us the chance to make a new start...to give Suzy and Scotty the kind of life they deserve."

Townsend understood what he meant. "What about your job?"

"I have three weeks of vacation due. I've already made arrangements for someone to fill in for me at CAL-SO. A college kid down the street is going to take care of my part-time job at the warehouse," he said, proud of his resourcefulness.

"When did you do all this?"

"This morning while you were still in bed."

Townsend was impressed. He reached over and shook his best friend's hand. "It looks like I've got my co-pilot. Now we need a chopper mechanic and a demolitions man. Any ideas?"

Taylor thought for a moment. "What about Henry Salazar?"

"Salazar would be perfect," he responded enthusiastically. He was a first-class mechanic and he can be trusted. Do you know how to contact him?"

"Yeah. He works for a small aviation service in Houston. He calls every couple of months."

Townsend's face showed his excitement. "Do you think he will come in with us?"

"You never know until you ask. But I think he will. Remember how he was always coming up with schemes to hustle a buck? Why don't we give him a call and find out?"

"Not on the phone. I don't trust telephones. We'll fly down tomorrow and talk to him in person."

"Fly down? Just like that?" Taylor asked.

"Sure. Why not?"

It was Taylor's turn to be impressed. Townsend always had a classy style. "Ok."

"What about a demo guy, Jeff?"

Taylor shook his head. "Bill Berry is the only demo guy I can think of...but he blew his brains out last year," Taylor reported sadly.

"An explosives job?" Townsend asked.

"No, a pistol in the mouth. Another delayed casualty of war."

"Oh," Townsend uttered softly.

"Henry can probably help us there. He has a lot of contacts

34

in Texas."

"I hope so. We only have two weeks to get this job done and get back." He finished his coffee and got up from the table. "I have to make a few calls."

"The phone is next to the rubber plant in the living room," Suzy directed him. After Townsend left the room, she leaned over and whispered, "Do you think we are doing the right thing?"

"Sure. Brad knows what he's doing. He has everything worked out. If I didn't believe this would work, I would not go," he assured her.

She moved her chair next to his and laid her head on his shoulder. He placed his arm around her waist and they sat quietly enjoying the comfort of touching one another.

A few minutes later, Townsend walked back in. "The reservations are made. We leave for Houston in the morning on the 8:10 flight. I also rented a chopper for this afternoon."

"What for?" Taylor asked.

"So you can get in a little air time. I imagine you are a little rusty, aren't you?"

"Yeah, I guess I am," he answered with a surprised look on his face.

After they left, Suzy mixed a gin and grapefruit juice and curled up on the sofa—a little ritual she performed when something was troubling her. The idea of Jeff flying again worried her. Five years had passed since he had been in a helicopter. He was flying for a local television station. The job lasted only three months before he got fired for flying too near a building in downtown Los Angeles. It was back when he was still drinking heavily. Afterwards, he swore he would never get into another helicopter. Now here he was, about to fly once again. She didn't care much for the idea, but it was part of the plan she agreed to go along with. Knowing that Townsend was in the seat next to him made her feel better. She settled back and tried to enjoy her drink.

Sweat beaded on Taylor's forehead as he listened to Townsend going through the pre-flight. Sitting at the controls brought back unpleasant memories of his last flight. Thinking about the building that came out of nowhere gave him chill

35

bumps. He had not expected his return to the cockpit to cause such anxiety.

"Ok, Jeff. Everything checks. Fire it up," Townsend instructed.

Taylor switched on the ignition. The blades turned slowly several revolutions before speeding up and settling into a steady spin. The vibration of the aircraft and smell of exhaust fumes did not help his queasy stomach. He started to feel sick.

"Take her up, Jeff...Jeff." Townsend reached over and shook his arm. "Are you all right?"

"Oh...yeah...I'm fine," he answered, trying to appear calm.

"Take her up."

Taylor's hand shook as he gripped the stick to lift the helicopter. He felt like jumping out and puking, but his pride would not allow him to look weak in front of his best friend. Townsend realized what was going on, but pretended not to notice his nervousness. He did not want to embarrass him.

"You will do fine," Townsend tried to convince him. He was unaware of Taylor's close call with the building. "Just ease the throttle and gently lift her. I'm right here if you need me."

Taylor followed his friend's instructions and slowly raised the chopper off the pad. The beads of sweat turned to a steady stream of drops that fell into his lap. At two hundred feet he advanced the throttle and headed east toward the desert.

"I see you haven't lost your touch," Townsend commended him.

He strained to crack a slight smile. "Everything just seemed to come back to me," he answered proudly. After a few minutes in the air, his earlier symptoms were gone. His confidence grew stronger with each mile. Flying over the southern California landscape, he felt freer than he had in a long time. He looked over at Townsend. "Thanks."

Townsend responded with a thumb up. Words were not necessary. He knew what he meant.

Chapter 7

Henry Salazar secured the cowling on the single engine Cessna and closed his toolbox. He checked his watch: 11:40. For six hours he had labored nonstop to get the job out by noon. That task complete, it was time to deal with the hunger pangs that had plagued his belly the last two hours. He wiped the grease from his hands, walked over to his locker and took out a small brown paper bag. Straddling an oil-stained wooden bench, he looked down at the wrinkled bag. He knew its contents without opening it. His sister Maria always packed the same lunch: two bologna and cheese sandwiches, a bag of jalapeno flavored tortilla chips, and a Winesap apple. He never ate the fruit but took it anyway to please his older sibling who insisted it was good for him.

After washing the meal down with a small thermos of black coffee, he went out to the beat-up sixty-five Ford van parked in the shade next to the hangar. Producing a screwdriver from his overalls, he placed it in the hole where the rear handle use to be and, with a simultaneous twist and pull, opened the dented door. He tossed the apple to the side, adding it to the pile from preceding days, and climbed in on the tattered mattress in the rear of the vehicle. He slipped a half empty quart of mescal from under a worn army blanket. After a strong swig, he eased back and stretched out. Having had only a couple of hours sleep the night before, it was not long until he found himself enjoying the fantasies of REM sleep.

He had just gotten to the best part of his dreams—lying on the beach at Ixtaco with a beautiful bikini clad local—when he felt a tug on his boot. Not ready to wake up yet, he ignored it. They were about to make love under the summer moon. He tried to preserve the action in his mind, but a second, more severe pull on his leg caused an abrupt cessation of his erotic imagery.

"Dammit," he mumbled. Still drowsy, he rolled over and propped himself up on his elbows. Upon seeing his disturber, he thought he was still dreaming. He shook his head to clear his vision. "It can't be..."

"Well, it is. In the flesh."

Salazar sat up quickly and grabbed Taylor's hand giving it a long, brisk shake. "I can't believe you are really here, Captain," he said excitedly.

Taylor smiled. "It's been a long time, Henry. What five...no, six years since I last saw you in person."

"Too long."

"You're right. Hey, I'm with another old friend of yours."

Salazar leaned forward with a curious look on his face and peered out of the van.

"*Hola, amigo!*"

He recognized the voice immediately. Townsend used to practice his Spanish with Salazar and that was his standard greeting. "Captain Townsend!" He slid out of the van and performed an encore of his earlier vigorous handshake.

"You're looking good, Sergeant."

"You too, sir."

"Sir? That army shit ended years ago. Call me Brad."

Hearing this made Salazar feel more like an equal than the subordinate he had been during their army days. He always respected Townsend. Not only had his pilot saved his life on more than one occasion, but he always treated him as a man and a good soldier—and Salazar was very proud of his army service. "Ok, Brad." He reached in the van and pulled out the bottle. "I think this calls for a drink."

Townsend checked out the label. "You still drinking that poison? It's a wonder you aren't blind," he joked.

"My mescal? That's what keeps me in shape," he emphasized with a hard blow to his chest. He handed the bottle to Townsend.

Townsend put up his hands. "After you, *amigo.*"

Salazar turned the bottle up and took a hard swig. "Ahh," he growled. He wiped his mouth with the back of his hand and offered the bottle to Townsend again.

Townsend studied the clear liquid for a moment. "What the hell?" he shrugged as he lifted the bottle to his mouth. "Wow, that shit is lethal," he coughed.

"Come on now, Brad. It can't be that bad," Taylor remarked. He took a long swallow. "Damn, Henry. Are you sure this didn't come out of that Cessna's fuel tank?"

Salazar laughed. "You flyboys better stay with your Bourbon and beer." He took another healthy sip. "Remember that shit we used to make in Nam when we couldn't get the real stuff?"

Townsend nodded his head. "How can I forget? That rot gut nearly ruined my stomach."

The three men spent the next half hour talking about old times. Salazar enjoyed his new civilian status with Townsend and Taylor, but knew they had not traveled all the way to Houston to reminisce about their army days. After a few more sips, his curiosity demanded attention. "What are you guys doing so far from home?" He passed the bottle to Taylor.

Taylor fixed his eyes on the last few drops of mescal. "Well, you might call it a business trip." He looked over at Townsend for the explanation.

Without hesitating, Townsend responded. "I'm getting a team together for a job and I need a chopper mechanic...and you are the best."

Salazar beamed at the compliment. "What kind of job?"

"I'll put it this way: it's hard work, it's overseas, and it's dangerous. If things do not work out right, it could mean prison or, worst case scenario, death."

Salazar grinned, thinking that Townsend was joking. The smile quickly disappeared after the look on the faces of the other men told him they were serious. His eyes got big. "You guys are going back to Nam, ain't you?"

"Close," Townsend answered. "Cambodia."

Salazar thought for a moment. "POWs?"

Townsend shook his head. "No. I wish we were. But I don't have any information on the whereabouts of any of our boys still held over there. This mission is for money...lots of money." Townsend was about to explain when Salazar's supervisor walked up.

"What the hell's going on here? I don't pay you to sit around and chew the fat. Now get your lazy ass out of that beat-up piece of shit and get back on old man Farley's plane."

Salazar's face was red with both anger and embarrassment as he climbed out of the van. He sensed Taylor and Townsend's awkwardness for him. Any other time he would have ignored his supervisor's words, as he had many times before. But this time was different. He had been humiliated in front of friends he admired and respected. Although difficult, he fought the urge to cuss out the inconsiderate bastard he worked for. "Mr.

Rizzo, you told me yesterday that when I finished with Mr. Farley's Cessna that I would be off the rest of the day. Well, it's ready. I started on it at five o'clock this morning and this is the first break that I've had."

"You've breaked enough," Rizzo bellowed. "Now get back to work." He turned to Townsend and Taylor. "You bums carry your asses. This chili picker has work to do."

Taylor was about to set the big mouth straight when Salazar rushed over and punched the larger man in the face, knocking him to the concrete. He could put up with the bullshit from Rizzo, but he was not about to let anyone talk to his friends that way.

Rizzo lay sprawled out a few seconds before sitting up and shaking his head. He rubbed his jaw as he moved his eyes to each of the men standing over him. "Just stay where you are," Salazar warned him. "If you get up, I'm going to knock you on your fat ass again. You've been on my case nearly every day for the last eight months. I've put up with your crap to keep from making trouble. But you or no one else is gonna talk to me that way in front of my friends."

"You're fired, Salazar."

"That's the best thing I've heard you say all week." He turned to his buddies. "Wait here a minute." He walked to the hangar.

Rizzo sat silently on the concrete, still rubbing his jaw. With Townsend and Taylor standing over him, he thought it best to stay where he was. It was a wise decision.

Salazar returned carrying a large, grease-stained toolbox. As he walked past his former boss, he looked down and snarled, "Let's get out of here before I give this pig what he really deserves." He loaded the box in the rear of the vehicle and slammed the doors. Townsend and Taylor followed him to the driver's side. He climbed onto the ragged seat and tightly gripped the steering wheel, trying to control his anger.

"Are you all right," Taylor asked.

He nodded. "How much did you say that job pays?"

"Let's go somewhere and talk about it," Taylor responded.

"Ok. I could use a cold *cerbeza*."

"That sounds good. Lead the way. We'll follow."

Salazar started the engine and pulled beside Rizzo, who was

just getting up. He spit at his feet. "Asshole." He stomped the accelerator, leaving Rizzo surrounded in a cloud of white smoke.

As the vehicles drove away, Rizzo shot them the finger. "I better not see you bastards again," he threatened once they were out of hearing range. "Damn," he said as he gently touched his jaw.

Townsend pulled into the gravel parking lot next to the van. Salazar was waiting at the entrance of the hostile looking structure. "Got your switchblade?" Taylor joked, as they got out of the car.

Townsend laughed. "Hey, Henry. I like the name," he called out, pointing up to the light that spelled out GOLDEN BURRO LOUNGE in gold neon.

Salazar smiled as he nodded in agreement. "Every time there's a shooting, they change the name. A few months ago, it was the Golden Eagle. Before that, it was the Golden Panther. It don't look like much, but the longneckers are only a buck, and they're ice cold."

"I hope they don't change the name tomorrow," Taylor mumbled as they entered the dark lounge.

Salazar walked over to the bar. "*Tres cerbezas*, Reuben," he said, holding up three fingers. The bartender placed three Carta Blancas on the bar. Salazar paid and handed out the beer. "Let's sit over there where we can talk." Townsend and Taylor followed him over to a table in the corner. The three positioned themselves so they could see anyone who approached. It was a quirk that Townsend had picked up in Asia.

Salazar leaned over. "Now tell me about this job. What do I do?"

Townsend reconnoitered the room: six men and a woman seated at the bar, two men at the pool table, and a man and woman feeding coins into the jukebox. He looked at Taylor as if seeking a sign it was safe to talk. Satisfied everything was all right, he took a sip. "I love this Mexican beer," he said, smacking his lips for emphasis. He rested his elbows on the table and leaned forward. Taylor and Salazar did likewise, forming an intimate huddle. "Henry, what I'm about to tell you

41

cannot leave this table."

Salazar nodded his head several times. "Ok. You can trust me."

Townsend knew Salazar was a man of his word. "Like I told you earlier, what we are going to do is illegal. I want you to know that up front. After hearing what I have to say, if you decide that you want no part of it, just tell me. We'll sit here and drink beer and shoot the shit about our time in country. We will still be friends and brothers. I only ask that you keep everything said to yourself. On the other hand, if you decide to join us, which I hope you will, you'll be a wealthy man. That is, if everything goes according to plan."

"So, let's hear this plan," he insisted.

Townsend straightened up in his chair and sucked on his beer. He leaned forward again and began explaining his plan. Salazar listened intently. The only time Townsend paused was when the waitress brought more beer to the table.

An hour and three beers later, Townsend finished his pitch. "Well, Henry. What do you think?"

Salazar chugged the remainder of his beer. "I'm in," he said without hesitation.

"Are you sure?" Why don't you think about it overnight and give me your answer in the morning?"

"Hell, Brad. I don't need time to think it over. I'm ready. He reached across the table and clenched Townsend's right wrist.

"Welcome to the club," Taylor said enthusiastically as he slapped him on the back. "We've got the best damn chopper grease monkey there is. Now if we can get a demo man, we will be ready to roll."

"Do you know anybody, Henry?" Townsend asked.

"Bill Berry is the best."

"Bill's dead," Taylor informed him.

"Billy's dead?" Salazar made the sign of the cross and took a strong sip. "I can't believe he would make a mistake and blow hisself up."

"He didn't. He committed suicide last year," Taylor said sadly.

Salazar shook his head. "It don't seem right. All the action he saw and he ends up killing hisself. That war is still killing us." He and Berry were best friends while in country, but had

42

lost touch the last couple of years.

Taylor put his hand on his friend's shoulder to console him. "Seems like just when you start getting your shit together, the ghost of Nam claims another comrade and undoes the healing. Then you just have to start all over again."

Townsend listened to Taylor's words. He knew that his friend was still exorcising demons from Southeast Asia. Anyone who ever served there was—in one way or another. He had found it easier than most vets to relegate those unpleasant experiences to the subconscious. Thousands of hours of civilian flight time had given him the opportunity to deal with them. They were still a part of who he was, but he refused to allow them to haunt him. "Do you know of anyone who can handle explosives?"

Salazar looked up. "Yeah. I know a guy. His name is Broussard. Paul Broussard. But I don't know if you want to fool with him. He's *loco*," he accentuated by pointing to his head. "But he knows juice. He received several commendations, including a Silver Star. From what I heard, his medals were the only thing keeping him from a bad conduct discharge."

Townsend analyzed Salazar's words. The last thing he needed was an unstable juice man. But at this stage of the game, he had no other option. It wouldn't hurt to at least talk to the guy, he reasoned. "How do we get in touch with him?"

"He lives in New Orleans. I met him at the VA hospital there," Salazar answered.

"Do you think he would be interested?"

"*Si*. If he smells enough *dinero*." Mixing English and Spanish was a sign that he was starting to feel his alcohol.

"Do you know how to get in touch with him?" Taylor asked.

"*Si*. I have his number."

"Give him a call and see if we can visit him tomorrow. We'll drive over," said Townsend.

Salazar shook his head. "It's best we drive over unannounced, *mis amigos*. If I call, that will give him time to think that something is up. He is always scheming," he said, tapping his finger to his head. "If he ain't dead, he will be home."

"Ok. Then we drive to New Orleans in the morning. Be

ready at 0600, Sergeant Salazar."

Salazar smiled and saluted. "Yessir, Captain Townsend."

Townsend lifted his right hand to his eyebrow and returned a weak salute. He looked at his watch, then turned to Taylor.

"You ready, Jeff? I've got some things to take care of."

"I'm ready."

The two men shook Salazar's hand. "See you in the morning, Henry," Townsend reminded him. On the way out, he stopped the waitress and slipped a ten-dollar bill in her hand.

"*Gracias*," she acknowledged with a flirtatious smile.

Taylor was glad to get out of the bar. He enjoyed the drinking and that scared him. Those beers went down way too smoothly. He had come too far with Suzy and Scotty—and himself. Driving back to the motel, he kept those thoughts to himself. He did not want to worry Townsend. It was something he would have to deal with on his own.

After Townsend dropped him off at his room, he called Suzy to tell her how much he loved her. Hearing her voice had a calming effect on him. He stretched out on the bed and immediately fell asleep.

Chapter 8

Salazar was waiting in the front yard when Townsend and Taylor arrived the next morning. Without hesitation, he tossed a small nylon bag in the back seat and quickly climbed in behind it. "Let's go."

Townsend pressed the accelerator. "What's the rush?"

"It's Maria. She's on the warpath."

Taylor laughed. "From the way you hopped into the car, I thought some irate husband was after you."

"No. Just Maria. When that Indian in her comes out, she can be real mean."

"What is she so mad about?" Townsend asked.

"Ol' Rizzo called her last night and told her that he fired me. He said he wasn't going to hire me back this time."

Townsend looked back at him. "He's fired you before?"

"Yeah. Three times. But he always calls back in a couple of days to rehire me. That asshole can't find anyone else who will put up with his shit. Besides, there ain't a better mechanic around...at least not at what he wants to pay. I always get a raise for going back," he said proudly.

"Where did you tell Maria you were going?" Taylor asked.

"To visit some friends. I told her I would go back to work for Rizzo when I got back, just to get her off my ass."

"When you get back, my friend, you won't have to work for Rizzo anymore," Townsend assured him.

Townsend turned onto I-10 and headed east. He watched the Houston skyline gradually disappear in the rear-view mirror. "Henry, tell me about this guy Broussard. I want to know everything you can tell me about him."

Salazar leaned forward on the front seat. "Like I told you, I met him at the VA hospital in New Orleans three years ago. We were both in the detox unit. He was a little weird, but once you got to know him, he was ok."

"Weird?" Townsend repeated. "What do you mean?"

"Well, it's kind of hard to explain," he paused, trying to find the right words. "He was real secretive...never opened up in the groups. Said he did not trust those damn shrinks...like they were out to get him or something. He was what you call...what's that word?"

"Paranoid?" Taylor offered.

"Yeah. Paranoid. Real paranoid. He didn't trust nobody. But he was smart. He played the game and did what he had to so he could get out."

"But the program is voluntary. If he did not want help with his drinking, then what was he doing there?" Townsend asked.

"He had to. He got into some kind of trouble. The judge gave him the choice of treatment or jail."

Taylor felt his skin crawl as he thought back to his days in detox. They were hell. But not as bad as drying out in a cell, he figured. "I don't blame him for not going to jail. I think I would have died."

"When did you last hear from him?" Townsend continued.

"About three weeks ago. He calls five or six times a year...usually drunk...wanting me to visit him. I've gone a few times, usually after that old fart Rizzo fires me."

"Do you think he's the right guy for this job?"

"Yes. He's the man," Salazar stated confidently. He really knows his explosives, especially plastics. He told me about some of the gigs he did in Nam and over here."

"What kind of jobs?"

"Construction mostly. He's good, but has a hard time keeping a job because of the drinking. A lot of people don't like the idea of him handling juice while on the bottle. But I've heard he's better with a buzz on than most blasters who are stone sober. Like I said before, he's the man. He loves money and has done a lot of free-lancing."

"Doing what" Taylor asked.

"Some illegal blasting, arson, who knows what else. He don't ask a lot of questions and he can keep his mouth shut."

Taylor looked at Townsend. "Sounds like the kind of guy we need, huh, Brad?"

"Yeah," he answered. But there was still a little red flag in the back of his mind about this guy.

Salazar produced a bottle of mescal from his bag and took a big swig. "I'm going to take a little *siesta*. I didn't get much sleep last night." He took another drink before he stretched out on the back seat.

"A little nap sounds like a good idea," said Taylor. He placed his neck on the head rest and closed his eyes. "Wake me if you need me, Brad."

There was something about Broussard that bothered Townsend. He wasn't sure if it was his drinking or his state of mind. It was just a gut feeling. He had six hours of driving to think about it.

Chapter 9

Sarath Anderson scribbled a short entry in his worn leather-covered notepad and slowly hung up the phone. He leaned against the edge of his metal desk and began tapping the gray Formica top in a slow, hollow cadence—an unconscious reaction to the call he had just received: another murder. There was a time when he would have jumped up and raced to the scene of the crime. But after thirty-two years on the force, the last eight as a homicide inspector, he found it increasingly difficult to get excited over another dead body. At times, he felt guilty about having such an attitude. But that feeling came and went. Tonight, guilt was absent. He turned to the small table behind his desk and fixed himself a cup of tea. He wasn't lazy or derelict in his duty. On the contrary, he was a damn good cop and, unlike many of his colleagues, an honest one. But there had been too many killings lately, mostly drug-related, and the cumulative psychological effects of dealing with the carnage was starting to get to him. Each day he found it harder to get motivated. His wife called it burnout. She said he needed a vacation. Whatever it was, he felt the urge to turn in his badge more than once during the last year.

He eased back in his chair and calmly sipped his tea. It was one of the few activities that soothed his nerves, a trait he inherited from his English father. The hot liquid immediately brought the desired results, shifting his thoughts back to the job he was sworn to do. He quickly emptied the cup, savoring the last few drops in his cheek before swallowing. He was temporarily recharged.

A light rain greeted him as he stepped outside the station. He pulled the collar of his overcoat tight against his neck and looked around for his driver. Upon spotting his white sedan a half block away, he made a quick gesture with his head. By the time he had taken the dozen steps outside the entrance of police headquarters, the car was at the curb with the passenger door open. He climbed in and provided directions to the driver in his calm Thai voice.

Anderson remained quiet as the police car raced through the narrow streets, occasionally dodging an unyielding pedestrian who defiantly challenged the right-of-way of the speeding vehicle. As he watched the reflection of the flashing blue lights pulsate off the wet buildings, his mind wandered. He recalled a newspaper story he had read the day before. It concerned an elephant at the Bangkok Zoo killed by poachers for its tusks. He had seen the proud bull many times while visiting the zoo when his children were small. He wondered what kind of person could slaughter such a majestic creature that brought so much joy to people of all ages. As an animal lover, he believed there was a kind of innocence about animals, even large ones, and misuse of them by the hand of man disgusted him. His jaw tightened at the mental image of the grieving cow standing over her fallen mate. He wasn't sure whether his anger was directed toward the killer of the noble beast, or at himself for feeling more sorrow over the death of an animal than something as precious as a human life. Perhaps his wife was right. Maybe he did need to take some time off.

The rain had let up by the time he reached his destination: an aging four-story apartment building. He was met by two uniformed officers as he got out of the car. Without delay, he entered the building and climbed the stairs to the second floor with his three subordinates close behind. Maintaining a brisk, deliberate pace, he exited the stairwell and followed the room numbers of the dim hallway until he reached 207.

Anderson knocked on the door and identified himself. There was no answer. He tried the handle. The door was unlocked. He called out again. Still, there was no response. He moved to the side of the facing and gave the door a strong push. The unmistakable odor of death greeted him, causing him to grimace as he held his breath. The stench seemed to take refuse in his nostrils. He and the others quickly dug out their handkerchiefs in an effort to filter out the sickening smell. He drew his service revolver and took a deep breath. His heart rate increased as the adrenalin sent his body into a heightened state of alert over the potential danger waiting inside. Most men of his position would send in a police officer of lower rank to test the waters, but Anderson did not think that way. He was in charge and he would lead. It was his duty, and the other officers respected him for that kind of leadership.

He eased into the dark room, his pistol cocked and ready. Groping in the dark, he located the light switch. He crouched

49

into an action stance and flipped on the light. The room was unoccupied. He signaled his men to spread out as he moved cautiously toward the rear of the apartment, his finger taut against the trigger.

The smell was almost unbearable as he walked into the bedroom. His dark eyes fixed on a young woman lying on the made-up bed. Her neatly brushed long black hair covered her shoulders and the pillow upon which her head rested. The eerie glow of her white satin gown in low light sent a chill down Anderson's back. At first glance, she seemed to be resting. As he moved nearer, he recognized the pale, swollen look of death. He leaned down for a closer inspection: she appeared to be Vietnamese. So young and beautiful. What a waste, he thought. He carefully eased down the hammer of his weapon and returned it to his hip holster.

The youngest uniformed officer walked in and saw the body. He dropped his service revolver on the floor and covered his mouth with both hands. Unable to control his gagging, he rushed toward the toilet.

"Not in there," Anderson said forcefully, concerned about protecting the integrity of possible evidence. "Go outside to do that."

The rookie officer tore out of the room, complying with the orders of his superior.

Anderson turned to the other officers. "Anything in the other rooms?"

"No, Inspector," another uniformed officer answered respectfully.

"Call the medical examiner. Then check on your partner...and do not let anyone in or out of this building."

"Yes, Inspector."

Anderson leaned over the body. "What do you make of this, Pryang?" he asked, referring to the dark marks on the victim's neck. He often questioned his driver, allowing him to practice his deductive reasoning skills. The seasoned veteran saw potential in his young associate. Unlike his last three drivers, Pryang was dependable, competent, and, as for as he knew, free of graft. He felt that one day he would make a good detective, an asset greatly needed on the force.

Pryang walked over to his mentor. He tried to appear

unaffected by the body, but he knew Anderson sensed his uneasiness. His eyes scanned the body. "Looks like bruises, Inspector," he offered.

"I can see that, Pryang. How do you think they got there?"

"She was strangled," he shot back.

"Why do you say that?"

Pryang positioned his hands just above her throat, turning the fingers toward his body. "The marks match those of the hands. It appears she was strangled from behind."

"Any other observations?" Anderson continued.

He examined the body closer. His eyes got big. He pointed to the antecubital area of her left arm. "Those look like needle marks!"

Anderson nodded in agreement. "You are very observant, Pryang. Perhaps I'll make a detective of you yet."

The younger man smiled with pride under his handkerchief. "Thank you, Inspector."

Anderson noticed that his young subordinate looked a little faint. "Why don't you watch the front door of the apartment. The medical examiner will be arriving soon."

Pryang appreciated the suggestion. "I will be there if you need me."

After he left, Anderson explored the room hoping to find something that would help his investigation. He poured the contents of the victim's red vinyl purse onto the nightstand: a hairbrush, makeup, and a small bottle of perfume. There were no documents to tell him who the dead woman was. A search of the closet and dresser turned up nothing useful. As he walked to the other side of the bed, a small object on the floor caught his eye. It was a book of matches. He picked it up on the edges with the tips of his fingers, taking care not to ruin any fingerprints. Gold letters against the red background identified its origin as the Mekong Club. He knew the place. It was a hangout for Vietnamese and Cambodian expatriates—a rough joint frequented by drug dealers, gunrunners, and assorted murderous scum who would slit a throat for the price of an ugly whore or a bottle of cheap American whiskey.

He looked over at the body, then back at the matches. Something didn't sit right with him. He searched the other rooms in the apartment. There were no cigarettes or ashtrays.

He was curious as to what a used book of matches from a place like the Mekong Club would be doing in her room. The apartment's furnishings and her personal belongings offered nothing to link her with the seedy bar. Perhaps they were placed there to be found—or maybe it was not a lead at all, he thought. In any case, he had begun investigations with less.

He moved to the foot of the bed and stared down at the corpse. The onset of anger blocked out whatever apathetic feelings of burnout he had experienced earlier. He silently promised the dead woman that he would find the one responsible for her death, just as he promised his deceased daughter, Achara, who died under similar circumstances two years earlier. After a reverent bow of the head, he went outside for some fresh air.

Across the street a shadowy figure stood motionless in the unlit alley, patiently observing the increased traffic in front of the victim's apartment building. Avoiding detection by those gathered on the street, he maintained his vigil until the ambulance pulled away with the body. He then turned and melted into the damp early morning darkness.

Chapter 10

Dark clouds formed in the distance over New Orleans. By the time Townsend and his partners hit the city limits, a light rain began to fall.

The sound of the windshield wipers brought Taylor out of one of the many catnaps he took during the trip. "Never fails," he mumbled as he sat up.

Townsend looked over at him. "What?"

"Seems like it rains every time I come to New Orleans. No matter what time of year it is, it just seems to rain. We'll probably see at least one wreck before we turn off the interstate."

"Speaking of turning off, you'd better wake Henry."

Taylor leaned over the seat and shook Salazar several times before he came around. "Get up, Henry. We're in New Orleans."

Salazar slowly roused. Once up, he reached in the athletic bag and produced the bottle of mescal. He held it up. "You guys want a shot?" Both men declined. Salazar took a long drink and then carefully returned the bottle to the bag. "Get off on Poydras and turn back toward Canal. Broussard lives on Royal at the edge of the French Quarter."

Up ahead the flashing lights of an emergency vehicle signaled a three-car pile-up. Taylor looked over at Townsend. "What did I tell you?" he boasted. Townsend cracked a smile and nodded, acknowledging his friend's correct prediction.

Chapter 11

Paul Broussard opened his eyes and rubbed the sleep from his bristled face. It was approaching noon, his normal time of stirring. Not one for wasting time on his back, he rolled out of the antique poster bed and pulled on his pants. As far as he was concerned, the sack was good for only two things: sleep and sex. He was through with one and not in the mood for the other, despite having a warm, willing body curled up under the sheet. He lit a cigarette and greeted what was left of the morning with a chest-rattling cough, which was repeated with each drag. A quart of Chivas down to the last three fingers awaited him as he entered the kitchen. He filled his mug, tore off the end of a loaf of hard French bread and settled out on the balcony with his breakfast. He was ready to see what the day had to offer.

Like every morning for the past four years, Gloria LeGrande was awakened by the guttural hackings of her Emphysemic companion. She waited until he left the room, then slipped into her nap-worn terry cloth robe and matching pink slippers. She tossed back her bleached blonde hair and made her way to the bathroom. Waiting for the sink faucet to provide her with warm water, she studied the pale gaunt face for any uninvited wrinkles that may have appeared overnight. Satisfied none had, she gently washed with moisturizing soap, dabbed dry, then worked in a light coat of skin conditioner for added measure. Her mother always told her that a pretty face was a woman's best friend, and that she would do well to take care of it. She wished she had taken the advice sooner. Although still attractive when made up, a decade of hard living made her look older than her twenty-five years.

She brushed her hair in slow, mechanical strokes as she stared blankly into the mirror, her mind reflecting on earlier times and places. The image in glass before her offered a nonjudgmental confidante with whom she could share unspoken intimacies.

On this day, her thoughts were of her childhood. As an only child of loving parents, she lived a charmed life. It was a world punctuated with dance lessons, piano recitals—her mother maintained that all proper young ladies must play—and shopping at Maison Blanche department store on Saturdays. But most memorable was the spacious two-story Victorian home near the university. Century old oaks shaded the meticulously landscaped one-acre lot in the heart of the Garden District. Every spring hundreds of people would pass the house to experience the blooming of the dogwoods and multicolored azaleas. The estate was the young girl's symbol of love and security.

Unfortunately, on this day she was unable to block out the unpleasant years that followed the tragic death of her father. He was killed in an automobile accident caused by a drunk driver three weeks before her fourteenth birthday. Her world began to fall apart. Unable to accept her father's death, her mother fell into depression and started drinking heavily. In less than two years, they lost the house and were forced to move into a small apartment near the *Vieux Carre*. Her mother's drinking got worse. She began bringing home men she met in bars. The closeness they once shared deteriorated.

During the summer before her junior year in high school she was raped by one of her mother's boyfriends. She never told her mother or reported the crime to police. At that point, she no longer felt clean and her self-esteem never recovered. She dropped out of school and starting drinking and using drugs. For five years she repressed the traumatic incident, with the help of a combination of alcohol and various mind-altering substances.

She knew Broussard casually from running into him often in the Quarter. Their friendship began early one morning when she found him drunk and disoriented on Bourbon Street. She helped him home. Later that day, he invited her to move in and she accepted. Broussard was not a passionate man, but he did not make a lot of demands on her. She felt comfortable enough with him to confide about her rape. He was the only person she had ever told, and just letting it out and the compassion he showed her was very therapeutic for her. She gave up the drug use and cut back drastically on her drinking. Recognizing that she had a good head on her shoulders, Broussard encouraged her to go back to school. Once she got her GED, he paid for her licensed practical nurse training at the local vocational school. She graduated with honors and went to work at Veterans

Hospital. Broussard was not the easiest man to live with, especially when he was drinking, but he was not controlling and allowed her to come and go as she pleased.

While out with Broussard one evening, she recognized the man who raped her. He was a mean bastard who beat her mother and was always causing trouble in Bourbon Street bars. Ignoring her pleas not to confront him, Broussard walked over to him and they had words. She did not hear what was said, but a few days later the rapist was found dead in a French Quarter alley. She often wondered whether Broussard had anything to do with his death. She never asked. It didn't matter. He would not be hurting anyone again.

A series of quick blinks ended her trance and brought her back to the present. She felt angry. If only daddy hadn't died, things would have been so different, she thought. As she had done so many times before, she promised herself that one day she would get her house back. She would make up with her mother and start over. The past did not matter. Frustrated, she slammed the brush against the wall and stormed out.

The smell of stale beer and rotting garbage accented the humid air as Broussard sat in his lattice-bordered perch overlooking Royal Street. Quietly sipping his Scotch, he tapped his foot to the sound of a single clarinet bellowing an old blues melody that echoed through the paved valley flanked by old brick buildings. Below, tourist buzzed in and out of retail shops reminiscent of bees hopping from flower to flower in search of some special nectar. He loved the Quarter; the sights, the sounds, even the smells. It was home. It was his world.

Gloria walked out on the patio and stood behind him a while before making her presence known. Broussard was very moody, especially after first getting up. He might lash out at her or just simply ignore her as he often did. Easing her hands down to his shoulders, she decided to chance it. Receiving no objection, she gently massaged his neck, moved slowly to the traps, down to the deltoids, then back up. She repeated the sequence over and over.

Their relationship was unusual. He was a loner guided by an internal locus of control that forced him to contain his feelings. She was a kind and caring extrovert, not afraid to express her emotions. Although they shared the same bed, they were not lovers, at least in the usual meaning. The infrequent occasions in which they shared carnal intimacy were initiated more in a response to libidinal demands than by passion—at least on his part. He occasionally abused her verbally, and sometimes physically, when he had too much to drink. But there was something about him that allowed her to remain with him in their co-dependent lifestyle.

He reached up and placed his hand on hers. "Thanks," he whispered. She smiled with the thought that it was going to be one of his good days. She untied the sash and let the robe open, hoping to interest him in getting back into bed. As she leaned down to hug him, there was a knock at the door. She ignored it and moved to his side to give him a better view of what awaited him just for the asking. He worked his eyes up her long, shapely legs, past the patch of neatly-trimmed light brown pubic hair, and paused at her erect nipples. "You gonna get that?"

"I'd rather not," she responded in the soft voice of a temptress.

He knew what she had in mind but he was not interested at the time. "Maybe later. Better see who it is."

The frown on her face signaled her disappointment. It had been nearly three months since he had last indulged her desires. Due to her earlier negative experiences, she was not particularly fond of sex, but her pent-up needs begged for release. With a quick jerk of the sash, she removed her nakedness and stormed off, her frustration enhanced.

She opened the door. There were three men. "Yes?" she said with a tone of anger in her voice.

The shortest of the men stepped forward with a big smile on his face. "Hi, Gloria."

She glanced at the other two men and then back to him. "Hello, Henry."

"Is Paul here?"

She looked over at Townsend. Their eyes locked momentarily. "Yeah. He's out on the balcony," she said, gripping the neck of her robe with her left hand protecting her well-endowed cleavage. "Come on in." She cut her eyes at Townsend as she led them out to Broussard.

"Some people here to see you," she announced.

Broussard turned around. "Henry Salazar," he called out loudly. He stood up and extended his hand. "How goes it, *Bandido?*"

"Good, Paul. Real good. I'd like you to meet two of my old buddies from Nam: Brad Townsend and Jeff Taylor."

Broussard shook their hands. "Have a seat," he said, motioning to three wrought iron chairs. "Would you like something to drink? I've got Scotch, but I'm a little low on Bourbon. I can send Glory down the street to get some. Oh, this is Gloria, or Glory, as I like to call her."

Gloria glared at him. If he wants liquor, he can get off his ass and get it himself, she thought.

"So, what will you guys have?"

The three men declined his offer. For the next hour, they talked about their service in Viet Nam. Broussard did not care for officers, but Townsend and Taylor seemed all right. Still, he was curious as to why they had come. He knew it wasn't to talk about the past. He figured it was time to get to the point. "So, what brings you to the Big Easy?"

Salazar looked over at his companions. Townsend and Taylor remained silent. He picked up their cue to proceed. "Actually, we're in town on business."

"Yeah?" What kind of business you guys in?"

Salazar looked over at Townsend who nodded for him to continue.

"Uh...well, we're looking for a demo man."

Brossard's face lit up. He turned to Townsend, aware that he was the one calling the shots. "What for?" Townsend looked at Gloria and back to Broussard. "It's all right. You can talk in front of her."

Townsend leaned back. "On second thought, I would like something to drink. Coffee will be fine," he said, sending the message to Gloria to get lost.

"Yeah. I could use a cup," said Taylor, picking up on Townsend's hint.

"Make that three...with a little of tequila, if you have it," Salazar added.

"Glory. Go fix some coffee. And here, get me a refill," Broussard said as he shoved the cup at her. "There's a new bottle on the refrigerator."

She snatched it from his hand and gave Townsend a cold look as she went inside. She and Broussard did not get many visitors and when they did, she did not like the idea of being cut out of the conversation.

Townsend pulled his chair closer to Broussard. "Before I go any further, I want your word that what I'm about to say will not leave this table if you decide you do not want in."

Broussard stared hard into Townsend's eyes and took a long drag from his cigarette. He leaned forward. "Ok. You have my word. Now what is this big plan?"

As Townsend began to speak, Gloria returned with a fresh charge of Scotch and took position behind Broussard. "Coffee's brewing," she announced.

"I'm waiting to hear your plan," Broussard reminded him.

Gloria cast a triumphant grin to let Townsend know she was not so easily disposed of.

"She's not going to say anything, are you, Glory?" Broussard said as he applied pressure to her hand resting on his shoulder.

She shook her head, trying not to show her discomfort. A slight grimace betrayed her.

Townsend was impressed with Gloria's composure. He looked at her and acknowledged her victory with a smile. "Ok." He leaned toward Broussard and began an overview of his plan, providing only the details necessary at that stage.

Gloria listened intently as Townsend spoke. There was something about him that she found attractive. She wasn't sure if it was his confidence, mannerism, or that he just seemed to have his shit together—a rarity in most men she had been around. The fact that he was also good looking was something she tried not to think about.

Broussard remained silent throughout the presentation, his only movements were an occasional drag of his cigarette and the raising of the cup to his lips.

After he was through, Townsend rested back in his chair. "Well, what do you think?"

Broussard looked first at Salazar, then Taylor. He finished off his second cup of Scotch, creating a little suspense with his delay in responding. He propped his feet up on the glass table-top. "I like it. A lot of details are missing, but I can do it," he said confidently.

"Good," Townsend returned as he collected his materials. "I've got some things to do. While I'm gone, make a list of the items you will need. I'll be back in a few hours."

Broussard quickly sat up. "When does this go down?"

"We leave for L.A. day after tomorrow. From there, we will catch the flight to Bangkok." He read the surprised look on the faces of Broussard and Gloria. "It has to be then. Is that going to be a problem?"

"Uh...uh...no," Broussard stuttered. "But what about the plastic, tools, uh, a passport?"

"That will all be taken care of. I have camera equipment out in the car. We'll bring it in and do the passport shots right here."

Broussard was impressed. "You do have the details worked out, don't you? Who's doing the passports?"

"I'm going to do them myself. I have some blank ones," Townsend answered.

"Don't do that. It's too risky. I know a guy over in Algiers who can do them," Broussard suggested. "He's done hundreds."

"I don't know," Townsend balked. "I don't want any more people involved..."

"Don't worry," Broussard assured him. He doesn't have to know anything. Just tell him I sent you and pay him a hundred bucks for each one. He can be trusted." He looked at Gloria. "Glory, bring me something to write with."

Townsend turned to Taylor for advice. "What do you think, Jeff?"

"He may have a point. Some airport people look at those things pretty close. If this guy has done a lot of them, then he must be doing something right."

Gloria returned with pen and paper. Broussard rubbed her hand, making up for the earlier discomfort he caused her. "Thanks, baby." He scribbled on the paper and handed it to Townsend. "Take this note to that address. Do you know where Algiers is?" Townsend nodded.

"Good. The man you want to see is Antoine. Don't tell him anything you don't want him to know."

"Why don't you just come with us?" Taylor asked.

Broussard chuckled. "I don't go to Algiers."

60

Townsend figured there must be a story to go along with his statement. "Well, let's go ahead and take the pictures. We don't have much time," he reminded them.

"Come on, Henry. Let's get the camera," Taylor volunteered.

Townsend tossed him the keys. He leaned back in the chair and sipped his coffee. Broussard excused himself, leaving him alone with Gloria. "You make good coffee," he complimented her, trying to make conversation.

"Thanks," she answered.

"What do you think about the plan?"

"I think it's dangerous."

Townsend emptied his coffee and placed the cup on the table. "Perhaps, but the rewards..."

"More coffee?" She cut him off.

She did not appear too interested in talking to him. He took the hint. "No, thank you." She then walked back inside.

Taylor and Salazar returned and set up the camera and lights. After photos of each man were taken, they quickly packed up the equipment. Townsend turned to Broussard. "I guess we had better get going. We have a lot to do."

Broussard got up from the table as the three men started to leave. "Hey, Henry. Why don't you stay. We can have a few drinks and you can fill me in on what's been going on."

Townsend figured Broussard wanted to try and pump Salazar for information. He didn't realize that he already knew as much as Salazar did. "You can stay if you like, Henry." As he turned around, he caught Gloria staring at him.

"I'll show you out," she offered as an excuse for her looking at him.

During the short trip to the door, Townsend's eyes were fixed on the form that filled out the robe in front of him. He figured there was a fine body hidden under that tattered cloth. When she stopped to turn the knob, he almost walked into her. He felt her eyes on him again as he passed through the door.

Going down the stairs, Taylor nudged him with his elbow. "That babe was sure checking you out."

"You noticed that too?"

"Yeah. Several times. I wonder what she had on her mind?"

Townsend cracked a big grin. "Who knows?"

They cleared the congested traffic of the French Quarter and

61

crossed the Mississippi River into Algiers. Taylor looked up at the dark clouds that covered the city in showers once again. Townsend knew something was bothering him.

"What's on your mind?" Townsend asked.

"Broussard."

"What about him?"

"I don't like him and I don't trust him," Taylor responded without hesitation.

"Neither do I. But at this stage of the game, we've got to go with him if we're going to do this. I don't know of any other demo man and there isn't time to look for one."

"He looks unstable. Did you see him squeeze his old lady's hand? No telling what kind of shit she has to put up with."

Townsend was angered just thinking about Broussard's treatment of Gloria. He didn't realize that Taylor had picked up on the incident. "Do you want out?"

Taylor was surprised by the question. "Hell, no. I've come this far. I'm going to see this thing through. It's a good plan. Besides, you need somebody to watch your six."

Townsend reached over and patted him on the shoulder. "I'm counting on you, buddy." His words made Taylor feel better. "T-N-T?" he asked, recalling the moniker given them in Nam from other soldiers that was a play on their initials, but also a reference to their explosiveness.

"T-N-T," Taylor responded, with a touch of their fists.

Chapter 12

Anderson fixed himself a cup of tea and began wading through the stack of watch reports and intelligence summaries that made up his daily routine. It was not his favorite part of the job, but it was important. Over the years he had received many leads from pages such as those in front of him. As he stared at the white sheets of paper, questions about his latest homicide case interfered with his comprehension of the material before him. Six other killings over the past ten months were similar. Each victim had bruises on the neck and needle marks on the arm. None showed any signs of struggle and all were lying nude on the bed, as if asleep. This case was a little different. The victim was dressed in a gown—a small, but troublesome, point to Anderson.

Shortly after initialing his last report, he was handed the medical examiner's report. Turn around time was normally several days, but as a favor to Anderson, who was an old friend, the doctor expedited the autopsy. Anderson opened the file and began reading. It confirmed what he already knew: the young woman died from strangulation. She had a high level of heroin in her system and had engaged in sexual intercourse at or near the time of death. Like the other victims, there was a small puncture on her neck caused by what was thought to be a long nail on the little finger of the murderer's left hand. Anderson privately referred to the strangler as the "fingernail killer."

He closed the file and added it to the stack. He shut his eyes and slowly rubbed his temples with his fingertips, a practice he employed in hopes of generating some fresh ideas. No other cases in his career had caused him as much frustration and feeling of ineptness as these murders. There were other homicides he never solved, but these were different: a cold, calculating serial killer was on the loose in his city. He was determined to bring that animal to justice. Until then, his flirtation with retirement would have to wait.

Chapter 13

It was nearly midnight when Townsend and Taylor got back to Broussard's place. Gloria answered the door wearing a halter-top and jeans cut off slightly below the back pockets. Her hair was put up with a red ribbon and her makeup was well done, making her appear much younger.

Townsend's eyes surveyed the trim body, moving slowly from her full breasts, down to her flat stomach, coming to rest on her creamy thighs. Stunned at her beauty when fixed up, he found it difficult to believe she was the same woman he met only hours earlier. It was at that moment that something inside him seemed to click.

Gloria could tell by the expression on his face that he liked what he saw. A slight blush came to her face. She felt good about herself for the first time in a long while. "You coming in?" she teased.

He looked up quickly. "Uh...uh, yeah," he stuttered, a little embarrassed at being caught with his mouth agape.

"Paul and Henry are in the kitchen," she said as she turned and led the way. The bottoms of her buttocks appeared and disappeared under the frayed denims with each step. She felt Townsend's eyes on her tight ass. Her rare instance of being the object of flirtation forced her to fight the urge to giggle.

Townsend sensed something was up the moment he walked into the kitchen. "What's wrong?" he asked Salazar.

Salazar looked over at Broussard, then lowered his head without speaking.

"What's the matter, Broussard?" Townsend asked.

"There ain't nothing wrong. In fact, everything is fine." He took a sip of Scotch. "There's just been a small change in plans, that's all."

Townsend looked over at Taylor and back to Broussard. "What kind of change?" he asked with a hint of anger in his voice.

"Glory is going with us."

Townsend stared at Gloria who had positioned herself behind Broussard. "What the hell are you talking about? There is no way we can take her. The plans are already made. I've got the plane tickets and the passports are almost done." He threw

64

the tickets on the table. "We proceed as originally planned."

Broussard took a long drag on his cigarette and blew a heavy stream of smoke. "Well, if she don't go...I don't go."

Upon hearing his ultimatum, Taylor tightened his fist and moved toward Broussard. Townsend stepped in front of him and motioned him back with his head. "Damn it, Broussard. I thought we had a deal. I hold a man to his word."

Broussard tried to play it cool. He knew he was an inch away from a good ass whipping. "I plan to do exactly what I said I would. I just want Glory to be with me. I can't work without her." Townsend did not realize it at the time, but he was telling the truth.

"You son-of-a..." Townsend felt the anger overcome him. He slammed his fist down on the table and walked out on the balcony. Taylor was right behind him. "What now, Jeff?"

"I say let me beat the shit out of that dirty bastard. I never trusted him anyway."

Townsend leaned his forearms on the railing and looked out over the French Quarter. Taylor left him alone with his thoughts. He stood there staring for a couple of minutes before turning to Taylor. "She will have to go with us."

His response surprised Taylor. "What?"

"We will have to take Gloria. He is serious about it."

"You're going to give in to that son-of-a-bitch? I don't believe my ears."

"There's no other option, Jeff. He's got us by the balls. It's too late to find someone else and that piece of shit knows it. Besides, he knows too much for us to leave him behind."

"But Brad..."

"Think about it, Jeff. She goes or there is no plan."

Taylor remained silent for a minute before answering. "I guess you're right. But I don't like it."

Townsend touched the shoulder of his friend. "Neither do I, Jeff." They went inside and sat at the table.

"Ok. She can go. But there are conditions," Townsend informed them.

"What conditions?" Broussard asked.

"I'll get her a ticket and a passport, but she splits your share of the take, not ours."

"Done. That's what I had in mind anyway. What else?"

"She is your responsibility. If anything happens to her, it's on your head solely for taking her along."

Gloria walked over to the table. "Just a minute. You are talking about me like I was some kid. Well, I ain't no kid. I can take care of myself," she interjected.

Townsend eyed her body, making sure she saw him. "I'm sure you can. But where we are going is not a picnic. It's hot, dirty, dangerous, and..."

"Agreed," Broussard cut in. He extended his hand to Townsend and they shook. Gloria leaned down and hugged Broussard, more to spite Townsend than to comfort her keeper.

Salazar went into the kitchen and returned with five small glasses. "I'd like to prepare a toast to my *amigos*...and *amiga*." He carefully filled the glasses from a fresh bottle of tequila. "To our good health and wealth," he toasted. They touched glasses and downed the shots.

Townsend turned to Gloria. "I need to take a picture of you for the passport."

"Ok."

"You might want to slip on a blouse and fix your hair."

"What's wrong with my hair?" she shot back.

"Nothing. It looks good. But for a passport, a conservative look is more appropriate."

Satisfied with his answer, she went into the bedroom. While she got ready, Taylor and Salazar retrieved the equipment once more and set it up in the living room. A few minutes later she appeared wearing a flowered cotton dress. "I'm ready!" she announced.

Townsend was again pleasantly surprised at her appearance. He wanted to tell her how nice she looked, but instead he instructed her to sit down and face the camera. With the soft lights complimenting her fair skin and handsome facial lines, Townsend realized there was something to his attraction to her. He did not welcome the feeling, but it was there. She was the wrong person at the wrong time, he thought.

Townsend took more photographs than he needed, allowing him to study her beauty. She appeared to like the attention, unaware that her eyes revealed more than just casual feelings for the man taking her picture.

"Ok. I'm finished," he informed her. As she headed for the

bedroom, she turned back after hearing her name. It was Townsend. "I said you look real nice, Gloria."

She cracked a polite smile. "Thank you, Brad." She then continued to her room.

Townsend did not say much as he and Taylor drove back to Algiers for Gloria's passport. Taylor knew that his friend had the woman on his mind but decided not to say anything to him about her. He trusted his buddy's judgment.

Taylor surveyed the area as Townsend parked the car in front of the Pirates' Cove Bar. It was almost two a.m. and people were still milling around on the street. "This place gives me the creeps."

"I've seen worse," Townsend responded. Keep your eyes open just the same."

They exited the car and went up the outside stairs of the bar. Townsend knocked on the door. After a minute, a man's face appeared in the crack of the door anchored by a heavy-duty safety chain. "Back so soon?"

"Yeah. Got another job, Antoine," Townsend answered.

The obese man unhooked the chain and let them in. He stepped out on the landing and looked around, making sure no one was watching the place. Satisfied that it was clear, he walked back inside, locked the door and re-hooked the chain. "You can't be too careful around here. So, you need another passport?"

Townsend nodded, as he handed Gloria's photo to Antoine. He studied it a moment. "So, Broussard is taking his woman? I should have known. One of them does not go very far without the other. Can't say as I blame him. That is a hot little piece of ass."

Townsend did not appreciate the comment, but let it ride. "So, is this going to be a problem?"

"Problem? No. In fact, I am almost finished with the others. If you like, you can have a drink down in the bar while I work on this one. It won't take long...and it will save you a trip coming back."

Townsend looked at Taylor. "Sounds like a good idea to me. Ok. We will be downstairs."

As they entered the bar, all eyes in the place seemed to be on them. Townsend felt the hair up on the back of his neck. Maybe Jeff was right, he thought. They found a table in the corner and ordered a couple of beers.

Townsend noticed that a woman playing pool kept looking at him and smiling in between shots. He returned the smile a couple of times. A few minutes later, a lanky, scruffy-looking man walked over to the table.

"Hey. Have you been staring at my old lady?" he asked Townsend.

"Who's your old lady?"

"The blonde in the jeans at the pool table."

"I've been watching the pool game, but I wouldn't say I was staring at her."

"Well, I don't like guys checking out my woman."

Townsend took a sip of beer. "Look, I don't know you or your woman, and I don't want any trouble. I just want to sit here with my friend and enjoy my beer." Townsend was pissed that the man would come over and confront him. But he figured the guy knew most of the people in the place. He did not like those odds so he controlled his desire to punch him.

Satisfied with his explanation, the man returned to his friends at the pool table. They looked over at the table and laughed.

"That guy was just looking for a fight," Taylor informed his friend.

"Yes, I know. And I would be happy to accommodate him, but we would have to fight all the guys in this joint."

"Yeah...and half the women too. Some of them look more dangerous than the men." They both laughed.

After they finished their second beer, they decided to go and check on the passports. When they were leaving, the woman who had been looking at Townsend earlier followed him with her eyes as he passed. As he went out the door, he looked back to see her boyfriend scolding her.

Antoine had just completed the last job when they arrived. Townsend looked at the passports and then passed them to Taylor for his opinion. Satisfied they would work, Townsend paid Antoine and wasted no time in heading for the door. Antoine tried to engage him in small talk in order to pump him for information, but he passed. He was eager to get out of the neighborhood.

As they approached the car, the man Townsend spoke with earlier, along with a half dozen of his friends, confronted him. "I saw you smile at my woman when you left. I told you I don't like men looking at my woman. I think I'll just take a piece of your ass."

Townsend calmly produced a forty-five automatic from under his shirt. "How about a piece of this, big mouth?" He cocked the pistol and leveled it between the man's eyes.

The man, clearly shaken, put up his hands and slowly walked backwards without saying a word. When he got over to his friends, they had a quick discussion before going back into the bar.

Townsend turned to Taylor, who also had a surprised look on his face. "Let's get out of here."

Driving off, Taylor shook his head and chuckled. "You never cease to amaze me. Where the hell did that gun come from?"

Townsend laughed. "Like Antoine said, you can't be too careful."

Chapter 14

Anderson was in deep thought as he leaned back in his chair with his eyes closed. Although he tried not to get too worked up over this investigation, there were aspects about it that kept lingering in his mind. The last thing the city needed was another serial killer. He had worked on a number of these type cases and he hated them. They took a heavy toll on everyone involved. He began to go over the facts in his head again as he had so many times already. True to his creed, a good cop would have no peace until the murderer was apprehended.

He opened his eyes to find Pryang sitting in a chair next to his desk. "How long have you been there?" he asked his driver.

"Just a moment or so, sir. I did not want to interrupt your concentration."

"What is it, Pryang?"

"Inspector, I have some information about the case."

"Have you been poking around again, Pryang?"

Pryang lowered his eyes to the floor. "Yes, sir...but on my own time," he quickly informed his superior.

Anderson often humored his driver by listening to his novice investigative notions, but he was not in a facilitating mood. "What have you today, Pryang?"

Pryang sensed from the tone of his mentor's voice that it was not the time to have his ideas critiqued. "Sir, it can wait until later. I did not mean to disturb you." He got up and turned to leave.

Anderson realized he had dampened his subordinate's spirits. "Just a moment. Let me hear what you have to say."

Pryang was worried that his information might not be important enough to get him out of this anxiety-producing situation. He sat and clasped his hands in his lap.

"Come on, Pryang. Tell me what you have," Anderson demanded in a slightly irritated voice.

"Sir, I have been canvassing the area of the last murder in hopes of turning up a witness...or at least some clues. I found a woman who says she saw a man loitering in a doorway across the street from the hotel before and after the arrival of police officers."

"A man was seen standing in a doorway on a rainy night. Is

70

that what you came to tell me? Pryang, I..." he was about to scold the young man for bothering him, when he realized he was only trying to help. He recalled being in similar situations when he was a young officer. "What else do you have?" he asked in a softer voice.

Pryang relaxed slightly in response to his tone. "The woman did not use the word standing, sir. She was very adamant about the fact that he was watching the events at the scene of the crime investigation. He would move in and out of the light so as not to be observed. But he seemed to be very interested in what was going on in the hotel. Sounds suspicious, would you say, sir?"

"Perhaps he was just getting out of the rain," Anderson offered to initiate their game of deductive reasoning.

"But he was there for over three hours. He could have left after the rain stopped," Pryang countered. "And what about his not wanting to be seen?"

"That was the supposition of your witness. Of course, he could have been a criminal or fugitive and did not want to risk being stopped on the street and apprehended."

Pryang could not offer an immediate explanation. "I do not know, Inspector. I just have a feeling about this shadowy figure." He was disappointed that Anderson did not receive his information with more regard.

"You are a good officer, Pryang. Your enthusiasm and dedication are not unnoticed. Continue to search for the truth and do not be afraid to speak your ideas. Thank you for sharing your information with me."

The young police officer felt better after hearing Anderson's words. "Was it worthwhile?"

"That remains to be seen. I will need to give it more thought. It could be significant," he added as verbal encouragement.

Pryang stood, slightly bowed his head, and exited the office, content with his contribution to the case.

Anderson leaned back in his chair again and closed his eyes. He wanted to incorporate this last bit of data into his thought processing.

Chapter 15

It was early afternoon when Townsend got up. He followed the smell of coffee into Taylor's adjoining room. "That smells good," he informed his friend.

"Help yourself. There are some pastries on the dresser."

He poured a cup and took a bite of donut. "Mmm, this is good. Damn, it's almost one o'clock. Why didn't you wake me?"

"I figured you needed the rest. Brad, you have been driving yourself pretty hard."

Townsend appreciated his friend's concern. "Thanks for looking after me."

"Well, that's what you brought me along for."

"True. But I also wanted you with me for other reasons."

"Yeah...like what reasons."

Townsend hesitated in answering, trying to find the right words. "I trust you and I know I can count on you. But, Jeff, I am more confident with you...more complete."

Taylor was surprised, but honored by his words. He always viewed Townsend as the epitome of self-confidence, as evidenced by his success in everything he attempted, from sports to flying. "Thanks, Brad. I really appreciate you saying that. I think we complement each other."

"We do. But if we don't get going and tie up all the loose ends today, then we will not be going anywhere tomorrow."

Taylor nodded in agreement. "I guess we better start by checking on Salazar and the others. Did you get things lined up on the other end?"

"Yes. I called before hitting the sack this morning. Everything we need will be waiting for us in Bangkok."

"Including a big piece of shit," Taylor added, referring to Van Tat.

"Yes, a real big piece"

Gloria met them at the door. She had on make up and her hair was fixed. Townsend noticed the top two buttons of her blouse were undone, providing a teasing glimpse of her breasts. "Good morning, boys. Come on in." She led them into the kitchen.

"Where are Henry and Paul?" Townsend asked.

"They're still asleep. They stayed up late telling war stories and shooting tequila."

Taylor looked at his watch. "It's almost three o'clock. You know we only have today to get packed and tie up any loose ends. We leave out in the morning," Taylor reminded her.

"Don't worry. We will be ready," she assured them.

"When Paul gets up, tell him we placed his order," Townsend informed her. He turned to leave.

"Are you going?" she asked, sounding disappointed.

"There's nothing to do around here."

"We could talk...get to know one another better. After all, we are going to be spending some time together."

Townsend looked over at Taylor. "Jeff and I need to go to the store and pick up some things. You can come with us if you like."

A smile appeared on her face. "Ok." She stood up and was ready to leave before she realized what she had said. "On second thought, I better stay here. Paul and Henry will be hungry when they get up. I will need to fix them something."

"Are you sure?" Townsend asked. She nodded. Townsend sensed her disappointment. "Can we pick up anything for you?" he asked her.

"No. I'm fine."

At the door, Townsend turned and looked back at her. "Gloria. I'm counting on you to make sure Paul is packed."

She liked hearing him say her name. "Don't worry. We will be ready," she said with a smile.

"We should be back a little later this evening. I want to go over things one more time."

Taylor waved. "Bye, Gloria."

"Bye, Jeff." She closed the door and went to the kitchen. As she sat at the table sipping her coffee, she reflected on what had transpired. She appreciated Townsend's apparent confidence in her. Maybe he was a pretty good guy after all, she thought.

The evening went smoothly. Townsend went over the plan and the procedures for the trip to Los Angeles the next day. Broussard was surprisingly alert and cooperative. His desire to work on an explosives job outweighed his usual obstinacy and sarcasm. He even went easy on his drinking.

Before closing the meeting, Gloria added a little unsolicited humor when she innocently asked, "Why not just rent a helicopter instead of having to repair one that may not be able to fly?"

The four men just looked at one another, fighting the temptation to burst out in laughter. Finally, Townsend answered. "The paper trail would be big...too many documents to trace us and too many witnesses. We would be arrested before we could leave the country."

"Oh," she commented without realizing how silly her question really was.

As midnight approached, Townsend felt comfortable with the team's progress. "Let's call it a night and get some rest. We have a long day before us. I appreciate everybody's attention and input. The flight leaves at 1:15p.m. I will be here at 10:00 a.m. Paul and Gloria will take a taxi together. The rest of us will take separate taxis...just as an extra precaution." He looked around to see if there were any comments. No one spoke. "Ok. Get some rest."

On the drive back to the hotel, it started to rain. "I hope she will be ok," Taylor commented.

"Who?" Townsend asked.

"Gloria. She was staring at you most of the night. You mean you didn't notice? Broussard sure did."

"Yes, I noticed. But I tried not to make eye contact with her. I saw Broussard catch her looking several times. You don't think he would do anything to her like we saw before, do you, Jeff?"

"I don't know. With guys like that you just can't tell. But I doubt he would do anything with Henry there."

Chapter 16

The afternoon flight to L.A. was uneventful. Broussard got loud a few times, but Gloria managed to keep him in check. Salazar, not exactly crazy about flying, sipped from his ever-present mescal bottle to keep away the jitters. Midway through the flight he was feeling no pain. When tipsy, he often got in an amorous mood when attractive women were around. The flight attendants, being professionals and good sports, politely laughed off his continual advances. Townsend rested with his eyes closed, alternating his thoughts between the plan and Gloria. Taylor just stared out the window, thinking how nice it would be to see his wife again.

Chapter 17

Suzy was waiting at the gate when the plane arrived. Spotting her husband, she ran up and planted a long, passionate kiss on his lips. "Oh, I've missed you, honey."

"I've missed you too, baby."

She turned to Townsend. "Hello, Brad," she said as she gave him a hug and pat on the back.

"Hello, Suzy."

"Who's that woman who keeps looking this way?"

Taylor turned. "That's Gloria. I'll explain everything when we get home."

"Boy, she sure is staring a hole in you, Brad. Better watch it. I think she wants your body."

Taylor put his arm around her. "Well, I want yours. Let's get my bags and go home."

Townsend smiled. "I'll talk with you later, Jeff."

"Ok, Brad. You know how to reach me if you need me."

Townsend acknowledged with a nod.

"Aren't you going to stay with us, Brad?" Suzy asked.

"No. But thanks for asking. I need to keep an eye on this bunch. We can't afford any unexpected surprises at this point."

She looked at Broussard and Salazar who were obviously intoxicated, then glanced at Gloria. "Yeah. I see what you mean. Can we drop you somewhere?"

"That would not be a good idea. I don't want you involved in any way."

"He's right, Baby." He turned to Townsend. "I'll see you tomorrow morning about ten." He looked at Suzy and pulled her closer. "Make that noon," he grinned.

"Ok. Take good care of him, Suzy."

She smiled. "Don't worry. You watch out for that blonde."

He laughed. "I will."

After they left, he met briefly with Broussard, Gloria, and Salazar. "I have rooms reserved at the Airport Inn. When you get there, remember to use the name on your passport. We need to get use to these fake names." He handed Gloria a ten-dollar bill. "This is for your cab fare. Once you collect your luggage, go to the motel. Henry and I will follow along a little later. I don't want all of us to arrive at the same time. Try to maintain as low a profile as possible. If you want something to eat or drink, order room service. Put a do not disturb sign on the door and we will meet tomorrow. If you have to make contact with me, use a house phone. Don't use the phone in your room. Any questions?"

"Do you think all this cloak and dagger stuff is really necessary, Townsend?" Broussard asked sarcastically.

He gave him a hard look. "Yes. I do."

Broussard shrugged. "Whatever you say, sir," he said with a mocking salute. He retrieved his luggage and walked off. Gloria got her bags and followed after him.

"That is one *loco* bastard," Salazar said to Townsend.

"You're right, Henry. I want you to help me keep an eye on him. He could jeopardize everything, including all of us.

Around midnight Townsend turned off the television and walked out on the balcony for some fresh air to help him think. He noticed Gloria leaning against the railing outside her room a few doors away, looking down on the pool area. "Can't sleep?" he asked, as he eased over to her.

"No."

"Neither could I. What about Broussard?"

"He drank half a bottle of Scotch and is out cold."

"I was going down to the bar. Care to join me?"

She was surprised by his invitation. "Sure. I could use a frozen margarita."

"That sounds good."

"What about us being seen together?"

"I'll risk it."

"You like risks, don't you?"

"Sure," he smiled. "Don't you?"

"Sometimes." She looked deep into his eyes. At that moment she wanted so much to kiss him, but fought the urge.

He picked up on her mood. He placed his hand gently on her back. "Let's get that drink."

A handful of people were scattered throughout the bar. Most appeared to be travelers drinking alone in a strange city. Townsend escorted Gloria to a table in the corner. It was dark and cozy, just the kind of place for a quiet drink and a probing conversation, he thought.

"I want to thank you," he said to Gloria.

"For what?" she asked, puzzled by his statement.

"Looking after Broussard on the flight and getting him settled in the room."

"Oh. It just seemed like the thing to do."

The waitress came over to the table. "Can I take your order?"

Townsend looked at Gloria. "Two lime margaritas?"

"Frozen," Gloria added.

He waited until the waitress left before continuing the conversation. "I know you put up with a lot from him. I don't see how, or why you do it."

She cracked a slight smile at his concern. "Sometimes, I don't either. He can be really nice when he wants to be. You don't like Paul, do you?"

"No, I don't," he answered without hesitation.

"What about me?"

This time his response was not so forthcoming. "Well..."

"Six dollars," the waitress informed him as she placed the drinks on the table.

The interruption allowed him a brief moment to consider his response to Gloria. He handed the waitress a ten. "Keep the change."

"Thank you," she answered.

He took a sip of his drink. "Hey, this is good. How is yours?"

She tasted her drink. "It's fine."

"What were we talking about?" he stalled.

"I asked you what you thought about me. You strike me as an honest guy, Brad. Tell me the truth," she pressed.

Townsend took a long sip of the frozen drink. "Let me put it this way, my first impression of you was not very favorable. I guess it was because I associated you with Broussard. To be honest, I don't know enough about you to form an unbiased opinion. But the more I'm around you, the better I like you."

She got higher marks than expected. "Maybe by the time this is all over, we will be good friends."

"My turn," Townsend informed her. "What do you think of me?"

She gripped her drink with both hands and touched it to her lips, sampling the salt on the rim with her tongue. "Are you sure you want to know?" she teased.

"Yes."

"My first impression of you was that you were an arrogant son-of-a-bitch."

Townsend smiled. "And now?"

"Too soon to tell." They both laughed.

They talked and sipped margaritas until the bar closed at two a.m. Afterwards, they walked slowly back to their rooms trying to delay the end of their evening together. At her door he eased forward as if to kiss her. She maintained her position in anticipation of the touching of their lips. He turned away instead. "I guess we had better turn in."

"Yeah. I think you're right," her disappointment evident in her voice. She turned and opened the door.

"Good night, Gloria."

"Good night," she returned as she disappeared into her room.

Townsend wanted to kiss Gloria's beautiful lips, but he knew that he made the correct decision. Starting a romance at this time could be dangerous, he rationalized. He went back to his room and took a cold shower.

Chapter 18

The next afternoon Townsend met with the group in his motel room to go over travel arrangements to Bangkok the following morning. With the exception of Broussard and Gloria, who were to travel as a married couple, everyone would arrive at the airport separately. No contact with team members was to be made there, during the flight, or at the Thai airport. He wanted to lessen the likelihood of their association being discovered in the event future complications arose.

Broussard was very quiet and attentive during the meeting. His lack of lip concerned Townsend. He wondered if he knew about Gloria joining him for drinks the night before. As the meeting broke up, he managed to get Gloria off to the side and ask her to meet him again at the bar later that evening. She agreed.

It was after eleven when Gloria found Townsend sitting in the same dark corner of the bar. "Hello," she greeted him in a soft voice.

"Hi." He stood and pulled out a chair for her. "Thanks for coming."

She sat down to find a lime margarita waiting for her. "You must have been pretty sure I would come," she said with an impish smile.

"Well, you said you would meet me. I took you at your word."

She took a sip of her drink. "So, what did you want to see me about?"

"I just wanted to check to see if everything is all right with Broussard."

"What do you mean?" She knew that was not the reason he asked to meet her—or at least the only reason. He could have done that at the meeting earlier. She suspected that the same thing that had been in her head was also in his, and that was the undeniable fact that something was at work between them. Still, she was unsure how to proceed.

"Broussard seemed too calm at the meeting today. He usually has some smart-ass remarks to make about everything. But he was pretty quiet."

"He's okay. He can be serious when he has to be. In fact, I think he is a little intimidated by you. You have that way about you, you know."

"Oh, really?" he laughed.

"Yes, you do."

"But you think everything is ok with him?"

"He's fine. Say, is that the only reason you asked me to meet you here? I thought it was because you enjoyed my company," she joked.

He searched for the right words. He couldn't come right out and tell her he wanted to spend some time with her to help him sort out the feelings he was experiencing. The attraction was mutual, he knew that. But he felt kind of vulnerable. "I do enjoy your company, Gloria. And as I said last night, the more I get to know you, the better I like you."

Somewhat disappointed with the direction of the conversation, she lifted the margarita to her lips and sipped on it while she figured out a response. She had hoped that his words would be more encouraging, that he would confess his attraction to her, perhaps even voice his desire to take her to his bed and make love to her. But she also felt vulnerable and the fear of rejection kept her from suggesting they go to his room. "Oh, I see," is all she could come up with.

Townsend sensed her disappointment. He reached over and gently touched her hand. "Maybe when this thing is over...we..." he stumbled for the right words.

He did not have to say more. A smile appeared on her face. She understood what he meant—not that it helped soothe the passion inside her that was about to explode. She put her hand on his. "We'll see," she offered. It was her way of protecting herself.

"Finish your drink and let's go. We have a big day before us tomorrow."

She nodded in agreement. "I'll take care of Paul. I won't let you down, Brad," she assured him.

"I know you won't, Gloria."

They finished their drinks. He walked her to the room she shared with Broussard. The awkwardness from the night before was absent as they traded "good nights." They shared a friendly hug and he went to his room. There were two cold showers that night.

Chapter 19

Han Anderson knew something was troubling her husband. On his days off he usually worked in the garden or caught up on his chores around the house. But today he just sat in front of the television and stared at the screen. She knew it was best not to disturb him.

Over lunch he broke his silence. "Han, I think you are right."

"About what, Sarath?"

"I believe I am burn out from my profession. I think I am going to retire after closing the case I am working on."

His announcement surprised her. She knew the case was weighing heavily on his mind, but he loved his work. "Are you sure?"

"Yes. I no longer find the work as challenging as I would like. The murder, drugs, and prostitution have corrupted the job. It is no fun anymore. I remember when I could not wait to get up and go to work. But that feeling is gone. It not right for me to feel this way and still remain as part of the force."

Han listed attentively. "Maybe it is just this case. Perhaps once it is solved, things will be better."

"I do not know."

She got up from the table and wrapped her arms around her husband's neck. "I support your decision whatever it is."

"You always have. And that is one of a thousand reasons why I love you."

She pressed her head against his. "I love you too."

Chapter 20

Everyone arrived at the airport as prearranged and boarded the aircraft without incident. Townsend made a quick visual check of his team as he made his way along the aisle. As he passed Gloria, their eyes locked momentarily. They traded smiles, signaling that things were ok between them.

He fastened his seat belt and closed his eyes. Once airborne, sleep would be nice, but he kept assessing the various steps of the mission in his mind. An occasional thought of Gloria would interrupt the process, and he would have to start all over again.

The seventeen-hour flight allowed the team members to catch up on sleep, go over the plan again and again in their heads, and ponder their future upon completion of the mission. An occasional movie helped break the monotony of being confined in a large silver tube cruising through the air at six hundred miles per hour.

Chapter 21

Townsend was the first through customs. His rationale was that if his fake passport was detected, the others could claim they lost theirs or it had been stolen and could use the roundtrip ticket to return home. He was confident everything would be fine in spite of the churning in his stomach. All eyes were on him as he waited in the customs inspection line. When his turn came, the agent made a quick search of his bag, then stamped his passport. "Enjoy your stay in Thailand, Mr. Lawrence."

"Thank you," Townsend responded.

As he waited for the others, Townsend noticed he was being watched by an Asian man wearing dark glasses. He did not try to conceal his interest in the American.

A few minutes later Taylor walked up. "Well, that wasn't so bad." Townsend did not answer him. He sensed something was wrong. "What's up?"

"See that guy in dark glasses?"

Taylor casually glanced over. "Yeah."

"He's been checking me out."

"You sure?"

"Well, he's still staring."

Taylor looked again. "Think he's a cop?"

"I doubt it. He's too sleazy looking. Besides, if he was, he would have already come over."

"What do we do?"

Townsend thought a moment. "See that the others collect their bags and get on to their hotel rooms. I don't want our friend there to see all of us together."

"Do you want me to go with them?"

Townsend shook his head. "No. I want you to cover my back...just in case."

As Taylor turned away, the Asian man casually walked over. "Captain Townsend?"

Townsend was surprised by the reference to his former rank. "I'm Townsend."

The Asian dipped his head slightly. "Please allow me to introduce myself. I am Mr. Chang. Mr. Van Tat sends his respects. I am here to pick you up."

"Oh, yeah. So how is the Chinaman?"

"Good," Townsend returned sarcastically.

Chang's smile turned to a frown at hearing his employer referred to in what he considered a derogatory term. He quickly rebounded with a smile. "Mr. Van Tat is doing well, thank you."

"Will you be traveling alone?"

"No. I have someone with me. He will be along shortly."

"Are you Van Tat's chauffeur?" Townsend asked, making small talk while he waited for Taylor.

"I occasionally drive for Mr. Van Tat...among other things," he added with a smirk.

"Yeah, like what?"

Chang held his grin but did not answer.

Townsend felt bad vibes coming from the Asian. He figured that if he worked for the Chinaman, he was dangerous and not to be trusted. Van Tat was the sorriest excuse for a human being he had ever met. He was a user and surrounded himself with the same kind of people. Anything for a buck was his credo. He was evil, but a necessary evil for now, Townsend rationalized.

"Is this your companion?" he asked as Taylor approached.

"Yes."

Taylor looked at Chang and then to Townsend as he walked up. "Is everything ok?"

Townsend nodded his head. "This is Mr. Chang. The Chinaman sent him to pick us up."

"Yeah?" How is the old bastard?"

The smile melted from Chang's face. He was starting to tire of their disrespect for his employer. "As I told Captain Townsend, Mr. Van Tat is doing well. He is waiting."

As they headed for the car, Chang turned to Taylor. "I did not catch your name."

"I didn't throw it," he said sarcastically.

The three men remained silent on the trip from the airport to their destination. Townsend had signaled Taylor not to say anything in front of Chang, so he just stared out at the city, quietly reflecting how much it had changed since he furloughed there during the war. There was more traffic and the street corner whores seemed younger. But it was still crowded, dirty, and smelled as bad as it always had and probably always would, he thought. Bangkok was definitely not one of his favorite places.

Chang pulled the limousine up to the drive leading to a large house surrounded by a wrought iron fence. Two guards stood at the entrance, each with a nine-millimeter semi-automatic pistol strapped to the hip. They gave a quick glance and waved the car through the gate. As the automobile stopped in front of the house, another armed guard was posted at the front door. Taylor leaned over to Townsend. "Looks like the Chinaman is as popular as ever."

Chang held the car door open until his passengers got out, then gently closed it. "This way, gentlemen."

The guard opened the door. Townsend and Taylor followed Chang inside to the study. Taylor checked out the opulence of the place. The room was furnished with antique English furniture and numerous pieces of high-quality Chinese porcelain. Fine oil paintings hung on all four walls. "Wonder where the Chinaman stole all this stuff?" Taylor said out loud.

"No telling," Townsend answered.

"Gentleman, please make yourselves comfortable. Mr. Van Tat will be with you shortly," Chang informed them.

While Taylor stretched out on a settee, Townsend, an aficionado of fine art, milled around the room studying the objects of art. He was especially drawn to the paintings. Although no authority, he was savvy enough to know that the items in the room were worth a large sum.

Taylor noticed his friend deep in thought staring at an oil painting. "What are you thinking about, Brad?"

"I must admit that I am impressed with the things in this room. Some of the paintings are probably worth hundreds of thousands, perhaps more. That is, if they are real. And if they are, no doubt they are stolen. I can't see Van Tat spending money on fine works of art like these. That tasteless bastard lacks the class to appreciate these things."

"Ain't that the truth. His idea of art is a carved ivory opium pipe."

"Yeah," Townsend chuckled. "Oh, by the way, Jeff. Take it easy when we meet the Chinaman. I know how you feel about him. But in order to complete the job, we need to be on as good of terms as possible with him."

Taylor sat up. "You know I can't stand that piece of shit...and I trust him even less."

"Same here. That's why we need to watch each other's sixes with him. Now, will you control that temper of yours?"

Taylor gave him a little nod. "I'll try. But I'm not going to take any crap from him. In fact, the less contact I have with him, the better."

"Thanks, Jeff. I knew I could count on you. T-N-T?"

Taylor smiled. "T-N-T," he repeated as they touched fists."

A slightly built, middle-aged Asian man entered the room followed by Chang. Dressed in a white linen suit, he reminded Taylor of a skinny version of Charlie Chan. He touched his open palms together, raised them to his chin, and gave his head a slight nod. "Captain Townsend. So good to see you again. I trust your flight went well." Neither man offered his hand to the other.

"Yes. It was fine."

Van Tat turned to Taylor. "Oh, Captain Taylor. It has been a long time. It is a pleasure to see you."

You lying bastard, Taylor thought. He knew Van Tat was about as happy to see him as he was to see the Chinaman—and that was not at all. He felt like slapping the fake smile off Van Tat's face, but true to his promise to Townsend, he held his tongue and his fist. "It has been a while, Chinaman," he remarked. His refusal to address him by his name was his way of denying Van Tat respect. Taylor knew he did not like being reminded that he was half Chinese.

Van Tat pretended to overlook his remark. He was irked but not insulted enough to let a few little words stand in the way of what promised to be a lucrative business arrangement. He reasoned he could repay Taylor's insolence later.

Townsend sensed the uneasiness in the air. "Van Tat, I didn't know you were such an art lover," he remarked in an attempt to change the mood.

Van Tat turned to him and smiled. "These are a few things I have acquired through my business transactions," he responded modestly.

"Real nice," Townsend continued.

"Thank you. Now, gentlemen, shall we discuss the matter at

hand?" He motioned for them to take a seat. "May I offer you some refreshments?" Both men declined.

"Were you able to get the things I asked for?" Townsend asked.

"Yes. Everything has been taken care of as you requested."

"The truck, the juice, the papers...all the supplies?"

"As I said, everything is as you wanted. I think you will be pleased by the efforts of my associates," he insisted.

Taylor fought the urge to walk over and knock the smug look off Van Tat's face.

"Good. Then we will leave in the morning."

Van Tat leaned back in his chair. His faced turned from a smile to a look of concern. "I thought you would be leaving in two days."

"Is that a problem? You said everything was ready."

Now it was Taylor who leaned back smugly in the chair. He knew Townsend moved things up to throw off any plans for surveillance or interception Van Tat may have planned.

Van Tat was aware of the reason for the change. He respected Townsend's craftiness. "There is no problem. Everything will be ready."

Townsend glanced over at Taylor. His buddy acknowledged his small victory with a nod. "Ok. Let's discuss the plan."

Chang entered the room with a pot of tea and cups. "Are you sure you would not like a cup of tea? It is one of my special blends."

"No. Let's just get on with it," Townsend insisted.

The three men spent the next two hours going over details. Townsend provided only the information necessary for Van Tat to hold up his end of the arrangement. He was not about to let him in on all the details. After the meeting, Chang drove them to their hotel.

That evening Townsend called everyone to his room for a meeting. He had them arrive at different times in order to lessen suspicion in the event they were seen. Broussard and Gloria were the last to arrive.

He motioned for everyone to take a seat around the table. "The room has already been checked for bugs, so we can speak freely. I called you here to go over the next phase of the plan. I talked with our contact. He assured me that everything we need has been provided." He pulled out a map. "Tomorrow we will travel to this village on the Thai-Cambodian frontier." He pointed to the site on the map. "We will pick up our vehicles there along with supplies and travel documents. The following morning, we cross over into Cambodia disguised as a Red Cross team taking food and medical supplies to refugees. We will encounter Cambodian soldiers and probably Vietnamese soldiers as well...not to mention rebels. Both sides of the fighting usually respect the Red Cross, but sometimes steal food and medicine for themselves. As I have stated before, there are risks. But the rewards should more than make up for them."

He surveyed the faces of his team members. There were no signs of anyone having second thoughts. He traced a wavy line on the map with his finger. "We will follow this route to where the chopper is stashed. I figure the trip will take about six to eight hours if everything goes well. Once there, we will start to work on the chopper." He looked at Salazar. "Henry, this is when you really start to earn your money."

"Don't worry, Brad. If she is in the shape you say, then just give me a few hours and I'll have that baby running just like she did in Seventy-two," he responded confidently.

Taylor slapped Salazar on the back. "As for as I'm concerned, Henry, you're the best in the business." Salazar smiled at the vote of confidence.

"Jeff and I will help," Townsend added. "Broussard, while we are working on the chopper, you can prepare your juice."

"No problem," Broussard returned.

He looked at Gloria. During the meeting he minimized his eye contact so the others would not pick up on his growing feelings for her. "You will be our sentry and on stand-by to assist with the chopper or the juice." She acknowledged her duties with a slight nod of the head.

"We will fly along this route to Rangoon. The action has to take place at night. I figure it will take one hour forty minutes to get there, about ten minutes over the target, and another hour and forty minutes to get back...if every thing goes as planned. That leaves no more than five to eight minutes extra to play with. We should be able to dislodge the gems in about two hours with all of us chipping. Afterwards, we ditch the bird and drive back to Bangkok. Any questions?"

"Isn't it going to be hard to take off the tip of that temple in the dark?" Gloria asked.

Townsend handed her some photographs of the shrine taken at night. "That place is so lit up, it's like daytime."

Gloria handed the photos to Broussard. He took a quick look and placed them on the table. "Like I said, no problem."

"Are we going to have any guns for protection?" Salazar asked.

Townsend shook his head. "We can't be armed. Remember, we are traveling under the Red Cross flag, without permission, of course. We can't take any chances. If we're found with guns we would probably be shot on the spot. Anything else?"

"Yeah. Where are those refreshments you promised?" Taylor reminded him.

Townsend went into the kitchen and returned with a buffet cart filled with meat and cheese. "Help yourselves. The bar is over there."

While relaxing, they went over some of the finer points of the plan. After a couple of hours kicking around all options and contingencies, Townsend felt confident that everyone was on the same wavelength. As the conversation turned to war stories, Gloria walked out on the balcony. Townsend used the excuse of making a head call to get away from the others. When he finished in the bathroom, he slipped out to the balcony. Gloria had her back to him, leaning on the balcony railing. "What are you thinking about?" he asked her.

"Oh, nothing. I was just looking at all the lights of the city."

"It's not like New Orleans, is it?"

"No. She turned around and faced him. "I was hoping you would join me."

"Why?"

She took a sip of her drink. "You mean you don't know?"

He paused before responding, trying to find the right words. "I have a pretty good idea."

"It's difficult, isn't it?"

"What? The plan?"

She giggled. "No. Trying to hide your feelings."

He was not sure what to say. "Uh..." he started to answer.

"I know because I am going through the same thing myself."

Her feelings were no surprise to him, but her verbalization of them was. He figured the liquor loosened her tongue. "Yes. It is difficult. Damn difficult. But that is the way it has to be for now. At least until this thing is over and we get back to the States."

"I don't know if I can wait that long." She moved closer to him with their eyes locked.

"You've got to," he said softly.

She put her arms around his neck. "I'll try. But I want you to do one thing for me."

"What?"

"I want you to kiss me. I've got to know."

He looked back to see if anyone was around. Satisfied they were out of sight, he pulled her closer. As they explored each other's mouths, he felt her knees weaken. She let out a heavy sigh as he pulled away. "Well?" he asked.

She labored to focus her eyes. "What?"

"Do you have your answer?"

"What do you think?" she teased.

He thought for a moment. "I think I need to get back inside." He walked away, leaving Gloria and her palpitating heart in the Bangkok night.

Townsend entered the room and fixed a drink. Broussard and Salazar were too busy bullshitting and pickling their livers to notice he had been gone. But when he looked at Taylor, he knew his friend was on to his brief rendezvous with Gloria.

Gloria returned a few minutes later. The men were just sitting around drinking and talking about things other than the plan. She fixed another drink to heighten the buzz she was already feeling. For the next hour she played a little game with Townsend in which she would make eye contact, then quickly break it before the others noticed. The more she drank, the less concerned she was whether anyone saw her. Now, Townsend was the one looking away, not her.

Taylor stayed behind after the others went to their rooms. "Something's up, Brad. What is it?"

"What do you mean?"

"Come on, buddy. Don't give me that. I know you too well. Something is troubling you and I don't think it's the job. It's the girl, isn't it."

Townsend leaned back in his chair and took a deep breath. He was not surprised at Taylor's astute perception. He nodded.

"I thought so."

"There's..." he faltered searching for the right words. "There's just something about her that attracts me. I don't know what it is. Hell, Jeff, I didn't even like her when we first met her. But now...there's something there."

"I guess so, like those big tits, fine legs, and firm ass. There's something there all right...not to mention it has been a while since you've had some."

"No, no. It's more than that."

Taylor shook his head in disbelief of what he was hearing. "Damn, man. Are you telling me you're falling in love with her?"

"No. I don't think it's that either. It's hard to explain." He got up and opened another beer. "It's like I feel a closeness to her...like I understand her. I can't explain it. But I do know that I like being around her."

"That feeling must be mutual. She couldn't keep her eyes off you tonight."

Townsend realized he and Gloria had not been as careful as he thought. The possibility that Salazar and Broussard also noticed bothered him. "What about the others? Did they see?"

"I don't think so. They were too busy downing the booze."

Townsend breathed a sigh of relief and took a big swig of beer. "Good." In a way he was glad that Taylor had noticed things. At least now he knew to be extra careful in his behavior with Gloria.

"Brad, you asked me to cover your back and that is exactly what I intend to do. To make things easier, you need to cool it with the babe until this thing is over. Getting involved with her right now is only going to complicate matters. Besides, Broussard is unstable enough as it is. No telling what he would do if he thought you were poking his chick."

"I haven't slept with her," Townsend quickly informed him. "In fact, we have only kissed once...out on the balcony earlier this evening."

"It's not what does or does not happen. It's what he thinks is happening." Taylor stood up to leave. "Anyway, I just wanted you to know."

Townsend got up and hugged his friend. "Thanks, Jeff."

"Just watching out for you, buddy. You have worked too hard on this thing to blow it now by being careless. It's just not like you." He walked over to the door. "See you in the morning."

Townsend had been lying in bed about an hour thinking about the plan and his conversation with Taylor when he heard a noise in the hall. He got up and went to the door. He looked in the peek hole. It was Gloria. He unhooked the door chain and eased open the door. Gloria quickly slipped in. Before he could say anything, she covered his mouth with hers. He reached over and closed the door. After a few seconds, he pulled away. "What are you doing here?"

"I couldn't sleep," she whispered as she went for his lips again.

"Hold on," he said as he put her at arm's length. "You shouldn't be here."

"Why?" No one knows I'm here. Paul passed out over an hour ago," she informed him with a seductive smile.

"Still...look, Gloria. We need to talk. I think we have to..." Before he could finish his sentence, her mouth was on his again. He started to push her away, but the feeling his body was sending overruled this thought. Her hand in his boxer shorts opened his eyes. This time she pulled away. She untied her robe and let it fall to the floor, revealing the trim, shapely body he had fantasized about since he first met her. Now, it was standing right in front of him and, even in the dim light, he could see it was better than he imagined. He pulled her to him and kissed her passionately. Their hearts pounded. He then picked her up in his arms and headed for the bedroom, their lips never parting. Along the way, flashes of rational thought bounced in and out of his brain like a blinking red light. But by the time he got to the bed, all he saw was green.

As Gloria lay next to him, his many nights of unfulfilled desires and pent-up passion overcame him. His better judgment deserted him and his earlier conversation with Taylor vaporized from memory. For the moment, there was no plan, only the here and now.

Chapter 22

Gloria had already returned to her room when Townsend woke up. He checked his watch: 0720. Plenty of time before he was to meet the others at 0900, he decided. He returned his head to the pillow and closed his eyes, thinking back to the night before. A slight smile appeared on his face. He had no regrets about the events that happened. Being with Gloria recharged his batteries and satisfied his curiosity of how it would feel being with her. The distraction he had experienced over the past few days had been eased. The vibrations about her were still there, but would have to remain in check. The plan was back to first priority. Even his earlier apprehension about the day's drive to Aranyaprathet on the Thai-Cambodian frontier had diminished. Strange what residual effects come from the satisfaction of dammed up libidinal energy, he thought. Feeling good about things, he jumped out of bed. A nice hot shower seemed like a good idea.

Chapter 23

Anderson was mentally drained after his meeting with the police chief. Another murder of a young girl occurred the night before and he had been summoned from his bed to provide a briefing of his investigation of the crime. This time the victim was not some whore or poor girl from the countryside. She was the nineteen-year-old daughter of a prominent merchant and civic leader. It had been only twelve hours since she was found, and he was already feeling the heat to catch what the chief called a homicidal maniac. He would get him, he promised himself. But for now, he just wanted to crawl back in bed and get a few hours sleep.

Chapter 24

The team met in front of the hotel where they were to be picked up by taxi. Townsend and Salazar took the cab driven by Chang. Gloria, Broussard, and Taylor rode in the other cab. Townsend arranged the travel arrangements that way to keep Broussard away from Chang. He also thought it a good idea to be in a different car than Gloria.

After traveling a few blocks, the driver looked back at Taylor. "Good to see you again, Captain Taylor."

Taylor did not recognize his old Vietnamese friend at first. Then, it suddenly dawned on him that it was Jim Lee. He leaned up on the front seat. "Jimmy," he bellowed with a big smile and pat on the back. "How are you, old buddy?"

"I'm fine," Captain Taylor," he answered, returning the smile. "And, how are you?"

"I can't complain. Sorry I did not recognize you at first...but it has been fifteen years."

He nodded. "The years have been good to you," Jim Lee complimented him.

"Thanks. You were just a boy last time I saw you. Now, you are all grown. Time sure passes quickly, doesn't it?" Jim Lee nodded.

Their rapport reestablished, the two hashed out the old times as the cab cleared the chaotic city traffic and entered the serenity of the countryside. Taylor noticed Gloria's interest in their conversation, especially when Townsend's name was brought up. He knew that look on her face. God help us, he thought.

Unaccustomed to being up so early, Broussard just slept, occasionally changing his sleeping position in response to the bumps and ruts in the narrow road.

Taylor enjoyed the ride and the conversation as they traveled to Aranyaprathet. Chachoengsao and Prachin Buri, two of the larger towns along the way, reminded him of some of the Vietnamese towns he saw during the war. Except this time, he did not see an enemy behind every face like before. As they crossed the Tha Lang River, he noticed hundreds of people camped along the bank. He looked back until the cab moved beyond sight of them.

Jim Lee noticed his interest. "Refugees," he informed him, breaking Taylor's concentration. "The Cambodian border is less than an hour away."

Suddenly, his mood changed as he felt the unmistakable presence of adrenalin enter his body. He depended on this fluid of self-preservation during his tenure in Vietnam, and now that he was about to return to a combat zone, his body demanded another fix of it to see him through this new tour.

"Are you ok, Captain Taylor," Jim Lee asked in response to the different look on his face.

Taylor did not hear Jim Lee as he stared out the window. His thoughts were not in the vehicle. They were on his past service in the region, along with the fear, anger, uncertainty, and a thousand other things experienced then. For fifteen years he had been insulated from the faces of anguish and terror he had seen at the river. In an instant, the quick shot of reality he just received brought back these feelings as if that period of time was only yesterday. He finally shook his head as if clearing his mind from the disorienting effects of an involuntary snooze. "What?"

"I asked if you were ok."

"Oh...yeah, I'm fine," he politely lied.

Gloria leaned against the front seat. She was also shaken at the sight of the refugees. "Jimmy, what will become of all those poor people back there?"

"Relief organizations will provide food and clothing for them. There will not be enough to eat, but they will not starve to death. If they are lucky, they will be able to join relatives living in other countries...or perhaps even receive sanctuary from Thailand, Malaysia, or some other Asian nation."

"What if they are not lucky," Gloria persisted.

Jim Lee paused a moment before answering. He did not feel comfortable telling her that he spent time in a refugee camp after the fall of South Vietnam to the communists. It was a very dark period in his life. A time in which he spent six months in filth, misery, and being hungry every single day. And a painful time in which he lost two of his four sisters and one of his two brothers. "They will be sent back. And if that happens, most will die or be killed by the butchers who run the communist governments," he finally answered.

"That's awful," she said. Visibly upset, she sat back in her seat and said nothing else until they reached Aranyaprathet.

Taylor noticed the genuineness of her concern. At that point, he began to see her in a more favorable light. Perhaps he was starting to realize what Townsend saw in her, he thought. He glanced over at her and then looked out the window once again with his own concerns to deal with.

Chapter 25

The two cabs arrived at a warehouse on the outskirts of Aranyaprathet. A half-dozen armed guards were stationed outside the building. Chang got out and motioned to the guards. They opened the two large doors and posted themselves at the entrance. Townsend and the others exited their cabs and followed Chang inside.

Townsend surveyed the supplies. Everything he asked for appeared to be there. "Where's the juice?" he asked Chang.

He pointed to a box on the floor.

"Check it out," Townsend instructed Broussard.

Broussard opened the box and closely examined it contents: plastic explosives and charges. "Best Uncle Sam has to offer. This will do the job," he advised.

Townsend was impressed with Van Tat's thoroughness. "The Chinaman did good," he said to Taylor.

"Yeah, looks like it," he responded, equally impressed.

Chang walked over to Townsend. "Does everything meet your approval?"

"So far. But what about the tanker?"

Chang gave his smile of self-assurance. "It is done. See for yourself." He led them over to the truck hosting a large red cross on both sides. Townsend turned the valve. A white liquid flowed out.

"Milk?" Gloria asked.

Townsend looked at her. Determined not to allow his feelings to show, he had on his business face. "Sure. Would you like some?"

She looked surprised. "How is a truck full of milk going to help steal a fortune in gems?"

Townsend decided to let Chang answer. "Tell her, Chang."

The invitation came as a surprise. Perhaps he was gaining Townsend's trust, he thought. He smiled at the prospect at being considered part of the team. He gestured his approval of being called upon with a slight bow of his head. "You see, Miss Gloria, there are actually two tanks inside the large tank. The small tank contains one hundred gallons of milk. The other tank contains five hundred gallons of aviation fuel. When we are stopped—and that will happen—we will be asked to provide samples of our cargo to our inspectors, Vietnamese or Khmer. When the valve is opened, out comes the milk. The valve to the aviation fuel is concealed." As he finished his brief lecture, he flashed another of his smiles that irked Taylor.

"I'd like to punch that shit-eating grin off his arrogant face," Taylor whispered to Townsend.

"So would I. Maybe one of us will get the opportunity later," he answered with a slap to his friend's back. "Ok. Let's start loading this gear." He turned to Jim Lee. "Since you are the interpreter, you ride in the lead jeep with me. Jeff, you and Chang will go behind me in the truck with the food and medical supplies. Gloria, you will ride with them. Henry, you and Paul will bring up the rear in the tank truck. And Paul, remember to pack that juice carefully in the spare tire. Make sure it has plenty of insulation to absorb the shock of the bumpy roads. I figure most of the food and medical supplies will be stolen by soldiers or guerillas long before we get to the chopper." With Chang present, he was careful not to give too much information about where the helicopter was stashed. He knew that the Chinaman's stooge was operating on a parallel agenda. But what he did not understand was the excessive interest Van Tat and Chang showed in the *Suzie Q.* In any case, he planned to be extra vigilant to avoid any pitfalls that would add to the intrigue that already hung heavy in the air.

"I'll take care of it," Broussard assured him.

Townsend liked Broussard's confidence. "Henry, are the tools ok?"

"*Si.*"

He turned to Gloria. "Are you ready to become a nurse again?"

She looked over at Broussard. "Sure. I'm not too rusty. I've had some experience since leaving the VA," she said, referring to the many times she had patched him up following one of his fights or drunken falls. Picking up on Townsend's earlier cues, she avoided prolonged eye contact with him.

"Jeff, how is everything with you?"

"Great. I'm ready to do it."

"Chang. What about you?" Townsend asked.

The Chinese man walked to the middle of the group. "As you can see, I have set up cots for everyone," he motioned with his arm to a corner of the warehouse. "You will be sleeping here with the equipment tonight. Food and beverages are forthcoming. If there is anything you require, please inform me." He bowed his head slightly, then walked away. After a few steps, he stopped and turned around. "Oh, don't worry about your safety. Armed guards will be posted outside...for your protection." He flashed his customary smile before leaving the warehouse.

"One of these days somebody is going to wipe that silly grin off his face," Broussard snarled.

Townsend and Taylor looked at one another for a moment before cracking up with laughter. At first, the others wondered what was so funny, then they also joined in.

"All right. Let's get this work finished then we'll have some refreshments," Townsend suggested.

Chapter 26

Anderson sat at his desk reviewing his notes and going over the evidence once again. There was not much to go on, but he was convinced there was some lead in the few papers that were spread on the desk before him. He picked up the matchbook from the Mekong Club. As he studied it, he began to get a feeling that it was important to the case, or at least in one murder. He could not explain the feeling, but he learned years ago he did not need to. His instincts had come through for him many times. He placed the matchbook back in the manila envelope and sipped his tea. A visit to the Mekong Club would be forthcoming. He leaned back in his chair and closed his eyes, somehow hoping the pieces of the puzzle would start falling in place. He was still confident that he would solve the case, but whether he could do it before another life was taken tore at his gut.

Chapter 27

Townsend walked around and talked with each member of the team. Satisfied that everything had been checked and rechecked, he called everyone together. "It looks like everything has been taken care of. I appreciate the hard work you have done in making the final preparations. Chang should be here shortly with some food and booze. Eat, drink, and enjoy. Just remember that we head out at 0500. Are there any questions?" There were none.

No sooner had he finished than Chang reappeared with the food and liquor. "Gentleman, Miss Gloria, please enjoy." He gave his detested smile, bowed slightly, then left.

Broussard noticed everyone looking at him to check his reaction. "I'm glad he's gone. Looking at him was affecting my appetite."

"Mine too," Townsend added. "Come on, let's eat." Before taking their places at the table, Townsend signaled to the others to check for a bug. After a short search, Taylor held up a small remote microphone concealed in a fruit basket. Townsend figured that Chang placed it there. "No shop-talk. Let's just enjoy our meal," he directed the others.

After eating, they checked their sleeping area for more mics. Convinced there were none, they huddled around their cots to discuss any final concerns. The conversation was short. Everyone had gone over their roles so many times they were tired of thinking and ready to just do it. They broke out the booze and started to relax.

Townsend went outside for some fresh air. The guards kept an eye on him as he sipped on a beer. He didn't like the idea of being watched, but decided against starting anything with them. The plan, as usual, was on his mind.

"What are you thinking about?"

He turned around. It was Gloria. "You shouldn't be out here," he said calmly.

"It's all right. I told the guys I had a few questions to ask you."

"Yeah, like they believed that," he said sarcastically. "I thought we were going to be more careful." He knew by the look on her face that he had hurt her feelings. "Ok. What kind of questions?"

She grinned. "Oh, things like do you want to touch me as much as I want to touch you...or do you want to kiss me as much as I want to kiss you?"

He stared at the sparkle in her eyes, answering her question with a lazy nod. They stood looking at each other without saying a word. He wanted to take her in his arms and taste her lips, but fought the temptation knowing that the guards could see them and would report it. He could not let Chang know his feelings for Gloria because the Asian would surely use this knowledge to his advantage. Instead, he placed himself so they could not see him take her hand. "This will have to do for now. You better get back inside."

She gave his hand a soft squeeze. "Ok."

Just the touch of her sent a feeling of excitement throughout his body. He tried to get back to thinking about the plan, but she kept entering his thoughts.

Chapter 28

At precisely 0500 Townsend and his team climbed in their vehicles and started the engines. Chang walked up to Townsend's truck with another Asian man. "Captain Townsend. Let me introduce Mr. Deng. He will be traveling with you."

"Like hell, he will," Townsend roared. "Now step back. We're about to leave."

Chang maintained his position. "Mr. Deng must go with you. Those are my instructions."

"Instructions from who?"

He cracked his familiar smile. "From Mr. Van Tat. He insists that Mr. Deng accompany you."

"Yeah. And I insist that he doesn't."

Chang was still smiling. "Mr. Van Tat says that if Mr. Deng does not go with you, then there is no mission."

Townsend did not try to hide his anger. "Everything has been planned. I don't need anymore help. The Chinaman knows that."

"Mr. Deng will be very helpful."

"How?" Townsend asked.

"He will be your interpreter once you are in Cambodia."

Townsend looked over at Jim Lee. "I already have an interpreter."

"With all due respect to Mr. Lee, Mr. Deng is very familiar with the dialects of that area. Unless Mr. Lee is from the region, he may not be as effective."

"Is that true, Jimmy?"

Jim Lee nodded. "He could be right. There are many tongues spoken between here and the destination."

Taylor walked over to Townsend. "What's going on?"

"It appears that Mr. Deng here is going with us."

"What for? We don't need him."

"He's going to be our interpreter. That's the way the Chinaman wants it."

"Interpreter my ass," Taylor answered. "He's just another damned spy."

Townsend led him out of hearing range. "Everybody knows that. But don't worry. He's going to get lost along the way," he assured him. Taylor nodded in agreement and returned to his truck.

"Ok, everybody. Get in your vehicles and let's go," Townsend commanded. "Deng you ride with me."

The trip to the border crossing took only ten minutes. The Thai guards made a token visual search of the vehicles and waived them through the gate. They had been paid well to do so.

As the team arrived on Cambodian soil, they were stopped by a squad of Vietnamese soldiers. The commanding officer asked Townsend for his papers. He presented the forged documents to the stoic-looking lieutenant. While the officer examined them, several of his troops gathered around the vehicles. On soldier climbed in the back of the supply truck and began going through its contents. He loaded his arms with a variety of booty and jumped down. Two more soldiers climbed in and grabbed a few items before scampering away. Others began to follow suit. The officer spotted them and barked out an order to them. They walked over to the truck and returned the stolen food. He handed the papers to Townsend and motioned the small convoy to proceed.

Townsend turned to Jim Lee. "Well, that wasn't so bad. For a moment I thought they were going to take all the supplies. Maybe there are some Vietnamese officers with integrity after all." Deng chuckled at his comment.

"What's so funny, Deng?" Townsend asked. The Asian man did not respond. Townsend looked back at him. "I asked you a question, Deng. What was so damn funny?"

Deng leaned forward. "You, Mr. Townsend. I was laughing at you...or rather your naivety."

Townsend gave him a mean glance. "What do you mean?"

"Integrity had nothing to do with why that officer let us pass. He could care less if these supplies made it to refugees. He did it for his own gain."

"What makes you say that?"

"Because he is an employee of Mr. Van Tat."

Townsend was surprised. "Are you saying that guy is impersonating a Vietnamese officer? That could get him a bullet to the back of the head."

"He is a Vietnamese officer. He is on what you call a

retainer."

Townsend looked at Jim Lee and shook his head. "Is there anybody that damn Chinaman doesn't have a handle on?"

"Not many, I'm afraid," he answered.

Deng smiled and sat back in his seat. He enjoyed tainting Townsend's humanitarian idealism.

For the next fifty minutes the three sat without talking. Townsend broke the silence when they encountered a roadblock just east of Sisophon. He slowed the jeep and looked over at Jim Lee. "What do you think?"

Jim Lee studied the men scattered across the narrow road dressed in ragged uniforms. "It does not look good," he responded.

Townsend followed the hand signal of the soldier in front and eased the vehicle to a stop. The leader walked over to driver's side of the jeep and spoke to him in Vietnamese. He kept his eyes on the AK-47 hanging on the soldier's shoulder. Without looking over at Jim Lee, he asked what was said.

"He wants to know where we are going and what our cargo is."

The other soldiers began flanking the vehicles. Townsend counted seventeen—all armed with AK-47s. The symptoms of tension felt like a fist gripping the muscles around his sternum. He knew first hand the destructive force of those automatic weapons if they decided to open up. "Tell him we are on a Red Cross mission to deliver supplies to a refugee camp near Koulen.

Jim Lee translated Townsend's answer. The soldier directed them to stay in the jeep. He walked back to the supply truck, pulled back the tarp and examined the contents. He called out to several of his comrades who quickly ran over. One climbed in the back and began passing out boxes of medicine and food.

Townsend watched in the rear-view mirror as each soldier took a box. He turned to Jim Lee. "Damn, Jimmy. They're robbing us blind. I'm going to see if I can stop them."

Jim Lee grabbed his arm. "Don't do that, Captain Brad. Those men are not like the soldiers we encountered earlier. These men are deserters. They are dangerous and will kill without hesitation."

Townsend felt his heart trying to beat its way out of his chest.

He felt helpless. For a moment, he wished his crew was armed. But his better sense made him realize they would still be outgunned by battle-hardened, desperate men. "What can we do?"

"Just remain here," Jim Lee answered. "The leader will be back."

Taylor noticed Townsend looking back at him in the rear-view mirror. He held up his hand and shrugged, gesturing to his friend what to do. Townsend understood. He moved his head from side to side signaling him to do nothing.

Ten minutes later, the leader came back. He wanted everyone out of the vehicles. Jim Lee translated. The three got out of the jeep. Townsend motioned to the others to follow suit. Once out of the truck, the soldiers searched the cabs.

Townsend had enough. As he approached the man in charge, he heard the disturbing sound of metallic clicks as several of the deserters pulled the slides of their weapons. Townsend stopped in his tracks. The leader held up his hand directing the others to hold their positions. He then motioned for Townsend to come to him. Townsend pointed to Jim Lee to accompany him. The leader nodded.

"Jimmy, tell him that we are on a mission of peace to deliver food and medical supplies to refugees. We also invite him and his men to take whatever they need. But we must reach our destination as many women and children are depending on us to feed them and treat their illnesses and wounds."

The leader kept his eyes on Townsend as Jim Lee translated. He slowly scanned Townsend's team, making brief eye contact with each one. He looked back at Townsend and asked what was in the last truck.

Townsend slowly walked over to the tank truck with the leader following. He pulled out a plastic pail and filled it with milk. He handed it to the leader and instructed Jim Lee to tell him it was for the children. The other soldiers gathered around. The leader smelled the white liquid, then took a cautious sip. He said something to the others in an excited voice that caused them to move in closer.

Townsend turned to Jim Lee. "What did he say?"

Jim Lee cracked a smile. "He said, 'cold milk.'"

Townsend began filling the quart pails and passing them out

to the soldiers. Some of them returned for a refill. Others filled their canteens with the precious juice. After they were sated with milk, the leader gave them permission to proceed. The renegade soldiers picked up their booty and disappeared into the jungle.

Townsend turned to Jim Lee, "I guess it has been a while since they have had milk." He then walked over to where Taylor and the others were standing. "Is everyone ok?" They all nodded.

"For a while, things were looking a little hairy," Taylor remarked.

"You're right about that," Townsend agreed. "Let's get out of here before they get thirsty again." He whispered in Taylor's ear, then gave Gloria a quick smile before heading back to the jeep. As he started the engine he looked back at Deng, who was visibly shaken over the sequence of events. "I guess we finally met someone not on Van Tat's payroll." He put the jeep in gear and pulled out.

Broussard wiped the beads of perspiration from his forehead. "I could sure use a drink," he moaned.

Taylor looked over at him. "So could I, Paul. So could I."

Gloria smiled. "Well, there's plenty of cold milk back there, fellows." They laughed as they headed for their trucks.

Thirty minutes down the road, Townsend noticed in his rear-view mirror that Taylor was flashing his headlights. He pulled over to the side of the road.

"What's the matter, Captain Brad?" Jim Lee asked with concern.

"Jeff is having some kind of trouble with his truck. Stay here and I'll check it out."

As he walked back, he was met halfway by Taylor. "So why did you want me to signal you?"

"It's time for Mr. Deng's nap," he said with a grin.

Taylor smiled. "Oh, I see."

"Raise the hood on your truck so he won't get suspicious." He walked over to Gloria. "You know that sleep medicine I asked you to fix for Chang when we thought he was coming with us?"

She nodded. "Right here in the canteen."

"I think Mr. Deng is thirsty."

"Whatever you say." She passed him the canteen.

He took the canteen and another one and walked back to the jeep. "Jeff is having some engine problems. Looks like we will be here for a while." He passed out the canteens to Jim Lee and Deng. "Drink up." Jim Lee removed the cap and took a swig. Deng followed his lead, taking a big swallow of the doctored water.

Townsend walked back to Gloria. "How long will it take?"

"It should not be long. I mixed it extra strong because I figured Chang to be a sipper."

He returned to the jeep and slid behind the wheel. "Keep an eye out, Jimmy. I'm going to take a nap." He pulled his cap over his eyes and eased down in the seat.

After a couple of minutes of bobbing his head, Deng stretched out in the back seat. Townsend sat up and looked back at him. "Deng," he said as he shook his shoulder. He was out cold. "Help me get him back to the truck, Jimmy."

"What's going on, Captain Brad?"

"We had to give this spy a little nap," he answered as they carried him to the truck. Broussard helped them lift Deng up to Taylor and Salazar who were in the back of the truck. They covered him with a tarp.

"Make sure you can see him from the cab," Townsend instructed them. He turned to Gloria. "Help keep an eye on Deng."

"How much did he drink, Jimmy?" she asked.

"I am not sure. I did see him take about three big swallows."

"He should be out for four or five hours," she estimated. Why don't we just tie him up, then we will not have to worry about him getting away?"

"Because if we get stopped again, I don't want to try and explain a tied-up man in the back of a truck," Townsend informed her.

"Oh. I didn't think about that. Well, if he starts to wake up, we can always pour more down his throat. His swallowing reflex will take care of the rest."

Townsend patted her on the back. "Good job."

"Thanks." She appreciated his recognition. She wished he could provide her with a more satisfying reward. Perhaps later, she thought.

"Ok, gang. Let's get back on track," Townsend announced. "The turn-off should be only a few kilometers ahead on the left. It's not a paved road so be alert. Paul, stay with Henry and keep your eyes open in case Deng wakes up and tries to jump out of the back.

"Sure," Broussard answered. He was beginning to feel like part of the team. He knew that Townsend had Gloria holding his hand to keep him in check. But for the first time, he began to realize that Townsend trusted him and was allowing him to pull his own weight. He felt good in spite of the fact that he was stone cold sober, an unusual condition for him. Even stranger was he didn't want a drink.

Taylor noticed a big smile on Gloria's face. "What's so funny? You're grinning like a possum eating sour briars."

She laughed. I've never heard that saying before."

"I thought you were a southern girl," he teased.

"I am. But I'm from New Orleans, not the swamps," she smiled.

"Oh, I see. You still haven't answered my question."

"What am I grinning about? Oh...I was...eh...thinking about how we took care of Deng."

He looked over at her. "Are you sure that's it?"

She did not answer. He seemed to know that she was really thinking about Townsend. She wondered if he had picked up on the vibes between them. Surely not, she tried to convince herself.

A few minutes passed before Taylor probed again. "He's some kind of guy, isn't he?"

"He sure is," she blurted without thinking. She knew she had screwed up before she finished her sentence. But as she thought about what she said, she realized that he was already aware of her feelings for him. "How did you know?"

"I know Brad very well. He's a good-looking guy. Women are always after him. But he's pretty picky. I can read his signals when he finds someone he really likes."

Gloria blushed. She was flattered by his words. "So, you think he likes me?"

"Oh yeah," he responded immediately.

"Do you think anybody else knows?" she asked with concern in her voice.

"I don't think so. Still, you two need to cool it until this job is done and we get back to the States. There's too much at stake here. We all have to be focused one hundred per cent or else we are going to end up in jail...or worse."

It was not what she wanted to hear, but she knew he was right. She thought she had been doing a good job hiding her feelings, especially since she felt like the emotions built up inside her were about to burst. It was only for a few more days, she reminded herself.

"That's the road, Captain Brad," Jim Lee said as he pointed to the narrow dirt trail up ahead. Townsend looked back and motioned the other drivers to follow his lead. After all vehicles were out of view from the main road, he signaled the column to halt. He walked back to the last truck. Broussard had a pretty good idea what he wanted.

Townsend called Broussard to the side. "Paul, I need your advice about the road. We've got about eighty clicks to go and I'm worried about mines."

"You got a mine detector?"

"Yes."

Broussard carefully examined the trail as he walked past the jeep and disappeared from view. The others got out of their vehicles to see what was going on. Townsend told them that Broussard was checking the condition of the road. The men knew what Broussard was doing, but kept their thoughts to themselves. They did not want to scare Gloria.

Broussard returned forty minutes later. Townsend went out alone to meet him. "What's the story?"

"The road should be ok...at least this part of it. There are fresh footprints and ox shit that leads to a little village about two clicks away. As long as we follow these fresh tracks and ox crap, we should be fine. It appears this trail is used mostly by people on foot and with carts. If there was any chance that there were landmines around, they wouldn't use it and it would be more overgrown."

He patted Broussard on the shoulder. "Good job, Paul."

Broussard gave one of his rare smiles. He felt good at being recognized for his expertise. "You're welcome, Brad."

"Ok. Let's get going."

When they got back to the vehicles, Broussard stopped at the jeep. "I think it would be a good idea if I rode in the jeep so I can keep an eye on the road."

"Sounds like a good idea. Jimmy, why don't you ride with Henry."

Jim Lee knew that Townsend wanted him out of the jeep in the event they hit a mine. He appreciated his friend's concern. "I'll stay in the jeep. You may need me to translate and help with directions."

Townsend nodded his approval. He respected Jim Lee's loyalty.

They made a quick stop in the first village, dropping off a few food and medical supplies in order to maintain their Red Cross guise. After receiving the latest information on road conditions ahead, they were moving again. The next village was about twenty kilometers away. Once again, they dropped off supplies. About five kilometers beyond the last stop, Broussard quickly ordered Townsend to stop.

"What's wrong, Paul?" Townsend asked in an excited voice.

"I don't like the look of things. See how the trail is suddenly overgrown? There hasn't been much travel on it lately. Also, there's a crater about fifty meters ahead. That's from a landmine. This section is mined."

Townsend felt a chill pass through his body. "What do we do now?"

"Where is that mine detector?" Broussard asked.

"In the supply truck." They walked back and Townsend fetched it from the rear of the truck. "Be careful, Paul."

"Don't worry, I will," Broussard assured him. "We'll use this newer trail that forks to the right. Stay here while I make sure it's not booby-trapped." He put on the headphones and disappeared in the foliage. Townsend went back and told everyone to stay put.

After checking his watch several times, Townsend was starting to get worried. Broussard had been gone nearly an hour. He was about to go and look for him when Broussard appeared carrying the mine detector in one hand and a round object in the other. He walked up to Townsend and held out the object. "Here, I brought you a souvenir."

Townsend reached out his hand, then quickly pulled back upon recognizing the landmine. "What the...are you nuts?" he said in a voice a couple of octaves higher than normal.

Broussard laughed. He had never seen the cool Townsend so rattled. "It's ok. I disarmed it."

"Well, get rid of it and let's get out of here," Townsend ordered with regained composure. He shook his head as he walked back to the jeep.

"It may come in handy later," Broussard responded.

Townsend stopped and looked back at him. "Yeah, and it will be our asses if we are caught with it. We would be accused of laying mines."

"I guess you have a point," Broussard conceded. He placed it in the bush and got back in the jeep.

Townsend started the engine and looked over at Broussard with questioning eyes. "So, is the side trail safe now?"

Broussard nodded.

"Are you sure?"

"Yeah," he answered confidently. "You know how I know?"

Townsend shook his head.

"The water buffalo shit is fresh," he laughed.

Townsend looked back at Jim Lee. After a delayed reaction, they also laughed.

"Surely the people in that last village knew the original trail was mined. I wonder why they didn't tell us?" Townsend asked.

"Because they are gooks," Broussard answered, his lingering resentment of Asian villagers coming to the surface. He looked back at Jim Lee. "No offense, Jimmy."

"No offense taken," he answered. "They are gooks."

Townsend turned on to the narrow trail. The other vehicles followed his lead. The little voice of caution inside his head was working overtime. He cut his speed down to ten miles per hour. After an hour, the trail veered back into the main trail. He stopped at the intersection to allow Broussard to check it. Broussard made a couple of sweeps and returned. "It's clear," he reported.

Townsend pulled out his map and conferred with Jim Lee. They agreed their destination was less than twenty-five kilometers away. Townsend felt a little better, but maintained his vigilance as he started on the last leg of the drive.

Taylor eased the truck forward. He looked over at Gloria.
"How's your patient doing?"

She peered back at Deng. "He's feeling no pain," she
reported.

"That's more than I can say," he said as he rotated his neck.

"Stiff neck?" She slid closer to him. "Here, let me massage
it." She reached over and began kneading the back of his neck.

"Mmm. That feels good. You have good hands. You should
be a masseuse."

"I was once," she answered.

"You're a woman of many talents, aren't you?"

She stopped rubbing. "What do you mean by that?"

"Hey, don't get all pissed.   I didn't mean anything
derogatory. It's obvious that you have had some sort of medical
training, and now you tell me you were once a masseuse.

She patted his shoulder. "I'm sorry," she apologized. She
continued the massage.   "I guess I'm just not used to
compliments. In fact, I kind of thought that you didn't even like
me, because of Brad and all."

He looked into her eyes. They radiated her beauty. "To be
honest, I did not care for you when we first met back in New
Orleans. But that is changing. He placed his hand on hers as a
gesture of his sincerity.

Jim Lee tapped Townsend on the shoulder. "This is where
we turn."

Townsend slowed the jeep and turned in to chin high
elephant grass that bordered the trail.   Knowing the final
destination was only minutes away caused his heart to beat
faster.   He fought the temptation to press his boot harder
against the accelerator in order to eliminate the pangs of
anticipation building up inside his chest. As he topped a rise,
he spotted a rock formation that appeared to pop out of the sea
of grass. His jeep seemed to hone in on the spot like a magnet.
He was brought out of his trance-like state by the sound of
Broussard's voice. "What?"

"I said, do you want me to get out and check this area before
we go any further?" There are signs all over the place saying
this area is mined," he repeated.

"No need. Jimmy and I placed those signs there to keep
away the soldiers. The villagers will not come around because

they think these rocks are possessed by evil spirits. The troops are only scared by what they have seen in the past...arms and legs blown off by landmines. Jimmy actually placed some bones around that he found at sites where there were mines. We'll find out soon enough if our plan worked."

Broussard was impressed. Scattering the bones around was something he would have done. He didn't peg Townsend as being that morbid. "I've got to hand it to you, Brad. You have really covered all the bases."

Townsend brought the jeep to rest in a rock-lined nook large enough to accommodate all three vehicles. He got out and directed the drivers where to park. "This is the place," he informed them as they gathered around.

"Where's the *Suzy Q*?" Taylor asked.

"Right over there, Jeff." He pointed to an area of vegetation on the side of a rock. "Behind all those vines and growth is the cave where we left her fifteen years ago."

"Let's go check the old girl out," Taylor suggested, the excitement apparent in his voice.

Townsend walked over to the jeep and returned with a couple of machetes. "Henry, will you get the flashlights from the truck?"

"Sure."

"Now I want everyone to be careful. This area has poisonous snakes," Townsend warned. His words gave Gloria goose bumps. She hated snakes, poisonous or otherwise.

Salazar returned with a box of flashlights and passed them out. After hearing Townsend mention snakes, he also brought two more machetes. He didn't like snakes either.

"Let's take a look," Townsend suggested as he walked to the entrance of the cave. He chopped away a small section of vegetation and slipped inside, the flashlight in one hand and the machete in the other. Upon entering, he checked the immediate area to make sure there were no uninvited reptiles around. Seeing none, he waved the others in. One-by-one they made their way in. Once inside, they trained their lights on the Huey.

With a look of awe on his face, Taylor eased forward to the aircraft and softly stroked her metal skin. He panned his flashlight until he found what he was looking for: the name

Suzie Q painted on the helicopter's nose. "I can't believe it. It's really her," he said with the enthusiasm of a boy finding a long-lost toy.

Salazar walked around the chopper, surveying its condition. "What do you think?" Townsend asked.

"Everything looks fine on the outside. Once we get some light on it, I can check things out closer. I'm anxious to take a look at her power plant and hydraulics. This is really remarkable. Even the tires on the skid dollies are still up," he said, almost as excited as Taylor.

Townsend sensed his delight. "Go ahead and bring in the tools and the generators. Paul, will you give him a hand? Jeff, you and Gloria start bringing in the supplies. Jimmy, help me chop this opening a little wider."

Everyone began the tasks as Townsend ordered. The truck was quickly unloaded and the gear stored inside the cave. Afterwards, they covered the vehicles with camouflage netting to reduce the risk of being spotted from the air.

Townsend called everyone together to make the job assignments. "Paul, get your explosives ready...but work outside...just as a precaution. Henry, go ahead and get started on the Huey. Jeff, give him a hand. Gloria, check out the supplies. See how much food those bandits left us. Jimmy, you take the watch. I'll float around and help out where needed. Any questions?"

"Yeah," Taylor answered. "How about some chow? I'm getting hungry."

"Me, too," Salazar added.

"I'll take care of that," Gloria volunteered.

"Thanks," Townsend said. His smile was all the thanks she needed. "Ok, folks. We know what we have to do, so let's do it. I'll be in the cockpit if anyone needs me." They split up and went to their jobs.

Townsend climbed into the chopper and sat in his old seat. He carefully checked the stick, pedals, and controls. Everything appeared to be in working order. He visually scanned the instrument panel. Things looked all right, but he would have to wait for the power before determining if the gauges worked. He was still surveying the equipment when he heard Gloria scream.

Everyone ran over to her makeshift kitchen to check on her.

Less that a yard from her feet was a snake. It was coiled and appeared to be ready to strike. Salazar jumped back, shuffling his feet as he moved far away. "Stand very still, Gloria. Don't move. Jimmy, bring me a machete," Townsend hollered out.

Jim Lee pointed the flashlight at the reptile. "Be careful, Captain Brad. That is Malayan pit viper...very poisonous."

"Well, it's about to be very dead," Townsend informed him.

"No need for that," Broussard said. He took off his shirt and gently placed it over the snake's head. The snake remained coiled. Broussard reached down and grabbed the thirty-six-inch snake behind the head and lifted it up. He then took it outside the cave.

Gloria ran over and wrapped her arms around Townsend. She was shaking and sobbing. "It's all right now," he tried to reassure her as he softly patted her back.

A few minutes later, Broussard returned. "Did you kill the snake?" Townsend asked.

"No," he answered casually.

"Why not?" Townsend asked.

"There was no point. It didn't hurt anyone."

"But it could have bitten Gloria."

"If it wanted to bite her, it would have. It was just taking a defensive mode. The snake is no longer a threat to anyone. Besides, if you would have taken a swipe at it with that machete, you or Glory could have gotten bitten. I just neutralized the threat. That viper is long gone now."

Salazar walked back over. "You are one *loco* son-of-a-bitch, Paul. But you got one set of balls!"

"Thanks, Henry. I will take that as a compliment." He walked over to Gloria. "Are you ok, Glory?" Still holding on to Townsend, she wiped the tears from her eyes and nodded that she was. He then went back outside to resume his assigned duties.

"Are you all right?" Townsend asked Gloria.

"I'm fine now, thanks. Dinner will be ready in a few minutes," she said, still visibly shaken.

After they had eaten, Townsend called on each person for a report. He started with Salazar. "Will she fly, Henry?"

"I believe the *Suzy Q* will be able to return to the air," he was happy to report. "There is some leakage of hydraulic line fittings, but that is to be expected. Some frayed wiring...no problem. We have enough hydraulic fluid to allow us to bleed the system and replace it. I'm glad I brought that extra electrical wiring. We will need it."

"What about the engine?" Townsend asked.

"I don't see a problem. The rotor gears seem to be fine. She ran when she came in here so she should run now. There is one thing that may be a problem."

Townsend stared at him with concern in his eyes. "What's that?"

"The tips of the blades have some small nicks on them. I didn't see any cracks, but there may be some extra vibration."

"I did that when we were putting the bird in here. I got a little too close to some trees," Taylor explained.

"I think it will be fine. We'll know for sure when we fire her up," Salazar added.

"Good show, Henry. You too, Jeff." He turned to Broussard. "How are things going with the juice, Paul?"

"No problems. I've got enough stuff to do the job...maybe a little extra just in case."

"Well, just be careful. I want you and everyone else to get back home in one piece to enjoy the fruits of our labor. Gloria, how are the provisions?"

"We have enough food, but the medical supplies are pretty low after those thieves took what they wanted. The thing to remember is that nobody gets hurt, then I won't have to worry about what to patch you up with."

"I hope nobody will. Also, I want to thank you for a nice meal. Has Jimmy eaten yet?" Townsend asked.

"Yes. I took him something before we ate," she answered.

A grin came to Townsend's face. "I must say I am really impressed with everyone's competency and dedication. Keep up the good work and let's get this done so we can head back home. I thank you all. Oh, I have one more thing." He opened a metal box. Inside were six forty-five automatics with web belts and holsters. He passed them out.

Taylor removed the clip. It was full. "Where did these come from?"

"They were in a metal box attached to the bottom of the truck chassis made to look like a battery box. We had to appear unarmed before because I knew we would be stopped. But now it's a whole new ball game. We need them for protection. I just hope we don't have to use them."

After they broke up the meeting, Gloria walked over to Townsend. "Is there anything I can help you with?"

He looked around to make sure no one could hear. "Yes, but this is not the time or place."

"Oh?" she said softly.

"I'll settle for you taking the night vision binoculars to Jimmy. It will be getting dark soon. Also, be sure to keep and eye on Deng. Jeff tied him up earlier, but we still need to keep him quiet and make sure he doesn't hear anything." He winked at her and joined Taylor and Salazar to resume work on the chopper.

Townsend was checking the wiring in the cockpit when he heard Salazar began rambling loud in Spanish. He turned around to check out the commotion. Salazar was holding up a small burlap bag that had a white powder falling from it. "What have you got there, Henry?"

"I'm not sure, but I have a pretty good idea. And there are nine other bags too. They were hidden in this panel. It's either heroin or cocaine. Broussard walked over and picked up one of the bags. He put some of the powder on his finger and placed it to his tongue. "Heroin," he informed them confidently before spitting it out.

"Are you sure," Taylor asked.

"It's heroin all right...and very potent."

"It's probably worth a couple of hundred thousand dollars," Taylor estimated. "Now we know why the Chinaman and his men were so interested in the *Suzy Q*."

"You're right, Jeff. He probably had one of his agents place it on board before our last flight," Townsend presumed. "At least we know it wasn't Patterson. He was in sickbay after that ass whipping you gave him."

Taylor smiled at the memory. "Regardless of who put it in there, it was probably meant for our boys. That is just one more reason I can't stand Van Tat...like I needed another reason. I told you that you should have let me kill that bastard when I had the chance."

"What are we going to do with it?" Salazar asked.

"Destroy it," Taylor responded without hesitation.

"No. That was my first impulse, Jeff. But I think we need to hold on to it in case we need to use it as a bargaining chip with Van Tat," Townsend responded.

Taylor looked at him in disbelief. "Are you serious, Brad? We need to trash that shit now."

"Van Tat will not get his hands on any of it. You have my word on that. We can always destroy it later."

Taylor knew his friend had a good reason for keeping the illegal substance, so he did not pursue his objections further. "Ok."

"Let's get back to work," Townsend announced.

By midnight everyone was exhausted. Townsend insisted that everyone get some sleep. Jim Lee was standing the mid watch, so he volunteered to take the morning watch to allow Jim Lee to get some rest. At 0400 he went out to begin his shift. Jim Lee tried unsuccessfully to persuade Townsend that he was not tired, but reluctantly followed orders and went into the cave.

Townsend had been outside about an hour when he heard a rustling sound. He looked around with pistol in hand and spotted Gloria. "What are you doing here?"

"I brought you some hot coffee." She handed him the cup and nestled next to him.

"You should be in there sleeping. But I'm glad you're here. I was really fighting to stay awake."

She put her arm around him. "Is the coffee the only reason you are happy to see me?"

He pulled her close. "You know it's not. But we really do have to be careful."

Have you missed me as much as I've missed you?" she whispered in his ear.

He put his hand on her neck and pulled her head to his, pressing his lips against hers in a long, sensual kiss.

"Whew," she sighed as he broke off the kiss. She rested her head on his shoulder.

They sat quietly enjoying the stolen moments together. Finally, Townsend kissed her on the cheek. "You better get back before you're missed."

"I'd rather stay with you."

"I know. I wish you could."

"You said you were having a hard time staying awake. I could watch and let you get some sleep. I'm wide awake," she pleaded.

"No thanks. I'm ok now. The coffee, and seeing you, really helped. We will make up for lost time later."

She really wanted to stay, but she respected his decision. After giving him a quick peck on his lips, she headed back to the cave. On the short trip, she carefully shined her flashlight on the trail before her. She did not want any more slithering surprises.

At 0800, Townsend was relieved by Jim Lee. When he returned to the cave, the others were already busy with their duties. Gloria handed him a cup of coffee. "Would you like some breakfast?"

"That sounds good," he answered. He walked over to the *Suzy Q.* "How's it going, fellas?"

Salazar looked up with an oil-smudged face. "Great, Brad. The bird is in excellent condition. She just needed some new fluid, grease, some minor repairs, and a lot of tender loving care. We're going to fire her up shortly. I just have to make some last-minute checks."

"Henry is everything we thought he was...and more," Taylor informed Townsend.

Townsend nodded in agreement. "You guys have really been busy. Is there anything I can do?"

Taylor shook his head. Not right now. Why don't you try to get some shut-eye?"

"I'm wide awake now."

"Brad," Gloria called out. "Come and eat."

Townsend patted Salazar on the shoulder. "Holler if you need me." He sat down and Gloria served him toasted bread and canned ham. Broussard walked in and got a cup of coffee. "How are things going with you?" Townsend asked.

"I'm done," he answered.

"Paul, I'm glad you came along."

Broussard was beginning to like the guy, even though he knew that something was going on with Gloria. He and Townsend were opposites in many ways, but he respected his honesty and even more, he trusted him—one of the few people he could say that about. "I'm glad you asked me." He sipped his coffee and walked back outside.

After finishing breakfast, Townsend stretched out on a blanket on the floor. Soon, he was asleep. Gloria folded another blanket and placed it under his head. He was too out to notice.

Townsend was suddenly awakened from his much-needed sleep by the sound of an engine. Expecting the worst, he quickly sat up and produced his pistol as he tried to gather his bearings. His heart raced as his surveyed his surroundings. The rear of a truck appeared in the cave, guided by Salazar's hand signals. He gave his head a couple of quick shakes as if to rid himself of the sleepiness he still felt. His efforts were unsuccessful. Just fifteen more minutes, he thought. But sleep was a luxury he could not afford now. He walked over to the driver's side. Taylor was behind the wheel. "Hey, what's going on?"

Taylor looked at him and smiled. "We're going to tow this baby outside and test the engine," he announced proudly.

"It's ready?"

"We'll soon find out," he answered as he eased the truck back.

Gloria walked over with a cup of coffee in her hand. "Here. I think you can use this."

"Yes, ma'am. Thanks." He reached over and touched her face and showed her the grease smudge on his finger. "How did you get that?"

"Oh, I've been helping Henry work on the helicopter," she answered as she rubbed her cheek.

He chuckled and played a little eye game with her as he took a couple of sips before joining the others to secure the chopper for towing.

Four feet from the nose of the aircraft, Salazar signaled Taylor to stop. He attached the tow bar he fabricated out of steel canopy rods from the supply truck. Once the bar was attached, Salazar stepped back, quickly admired his handy work, and repositioned himself as spotter. "Brad, you watch the starboard side."

"I got it."

Taylor climbed back in the truck and watched the side mirror for instruction. Salazar made sure everything was in position. He then motioned to Taylor. "All right...take it slow."

The *Suzy Q* began to ease out of her lair like a giant insect creeping up on unsuspecting prey. Salazar walked along the side motioning Taylor on until the aircraft reached her makeshift launch site.

Broussard pulled up in the fuel truck. He connected the hose to the fuel inlet and began pumping by hand.

"Just put in one hundred gallons," Salazar instructed. He looked at Townsend. "That should be enough to run it up and take a test flight. The tank was pretty rusty. I cleaned it best I could, but if we have to drain it again, I don't want to contaminate too much fuel. Besides, there is always a chance of fire, and the less fuel the better."

"What about the hose to fill the tank from within the cabin?"

"Done. The pump is already attached."

Townsend stared quietly at the metal bird, studying her lines and appreciating her beauty like a man rekindling an old flame. He thought about the close calls she had gotten him out of. Taylor walked over and slapped him on the back. "What do you think, Brad?"

"I think she's beautiful," he answered, his eyes remaining on his objection of affection of the moment. He ended his gaze and turned around. "What's more, I've got a feeling that she is going to come through for us."

"I know she will," Taylor agreed.

Salazar walked over to the aircraft. He held up four decals. "Hey, we don't want to forget these babies." He then placed them on both sides of the fuselage and tail boom, giving the helicopter markings of the Thai Army.

Seeing another nation's flag on the *Suzy Q* brought a frown to Townsend's face. "Great job, Henry. She looks like the real thing. What about the Burmese markings?"

"Right here." Salazar handed him the decals with the flag of Burma. "We will put them on at the next stop. I also duct-taped an olive drab cardboard panel over the nose art to camouflage it."

"And we removed all serial numbers that can identify the *Suzy Q*," Taylor added.

Townsend was impressed. "You guys are very meticulous. Then I guess it's time to test the engine."

Salazar walked over to where Broussard was still pumping. "How are you coming along?"

"Give me about ten more minutes and I'll be finished."

"You need me to take over?"

Broussard shook his head. "But thanks for the offer." With every task assigned and each kind word received, he felt more a part of the team. He realized he was not an easy guy to get along with, but he could feel himself warming up to the others. They showed respect for his talents and took him for who he was, and he appreciated that.

Townsend's heart raced as he prepared to enter the *Suzy Q*. Pausing to pat her skin, he climbed into the cockpit. He was greeted by the familiar smell of the aircraft—a combination of aviation fuel and hydraulic fluid that seemed to be trapped in the molecules of the metal. His feet instinctively found the pedals as he took the cyclic in his right hand. A flood of memories flashed through his head as he scanned the instrument panel. Taylor's tap on his shoulder brought him out of his daze. "Ready to try this old girl?"

"Oh...yeah. Tell Broussard to pull that truck out of the way and grab a couple of fire extinguishers. He and Gloria can stand fire watch." He noticed the concerned look on Taylor's face. "Just in case," he explained.

Taylor carried out his orders. He took his place in the left seat and put on the headset. Like Townsend, he automatically guided his hands and feet into position.

"Brings back memories, doesn't it?" Townsend asked.

He nodded. "It does. Also seems a little strange."

Salazar entered the rear cabin door and put on the headset. "Ready for the pre-flight."

There was no written checklist to follow, but Townsend and Taylor had repeated the procedure so many times, one was not necessary. Every item checked out, and after all the years, not a single step was missed. The time had come to try the engine. Anticipation hung heavy in the air, both within and outside the fuselage.

Townsend wiped the perspiration from his hands on his pants. He realized the whole mission hinged on the *Suzy Q's* response once he engaged the ignition. Everyone was silent. He held his breath as he reached forward. His heart pounded as he hit the switch. The engine turned sluggishly, belching a puff of white smoke with each rotation. After several revolutions, the engine caught. The entire team cheered as the blades settled into a swishing cadence.

Salazar leaned forward and checked the gauges. "Everything looks good, Brad." Townsend rewarded his confirmation with a thumbs-up. "After I check outside for leaks, let's take her up," he suggested.

"Henry...I thought I would take her up alone, you know, as a precaution."

"Bull shit," Taylor interrupted. "I'm going to ride her here in this left seat."

"But Jeff, if something happens, I will be the only one to suffer the consequences," he tried to explain.

"Look, Brad. I know you promised Suzy you would look out for me. I appreciate that. But you will need another pair of hands if something happens."

"And you need me in case you have to sit down for repairs," Salazar piped in.

Taylor nodded in agreement. "I'm going and that's all there is to it."

"Me too," Salazar insisted.

Townsend anticipated their responses. He was proud of them. "Ok. You both go. Henry, go ahead and do your check outside...and send Broussard over here."

Salazar jumped out and relayed the message. Broussard bent down and made his way to the pilot's window. "Did you want me, Brad?" he shouted over the noise of the engine.

"Yeah, Paul. We are about to take the chopper up for a test flight. I believe everything will be fine. But in case something happens, Jimmy knows what to do to get you and Gloria back to the States. Just trust him and do what he says, ok?"

"Sure." He extended his hand to Townsend. "Good luck." He looked over at Taylor. "Good luck to you too, Jeff."

"Thanks," he hollered back.

Salazar climbed in the back and put on the headphones. "No problems. Let's do it."

Townsend opened the throttle all the way. He trusted his

127

instincts to tell him when he was at the proper operating RPM. When he reached it, he pulled slowly on the collective. As pitch increased, he pushed the left pedal to counteract the torque. He continued pulling in pitch and depressing the pedal until the chopper eased off the ground. A touch of forward cyclic and the aircraft advanced forward with a little shudder that disappeared with an increase in airspeed. The proud war bird was back in the sky again.

Broussard walked over to where Gloria stood watching the chopper gradually disappear from sight. "Are you falling for him?"

The question caught her off guard. "What?" she stalled.

"You heard me. Are you falling in love with Brad?"

She hesitated, trying to come up with the right words to say. "Whh...what do you mean?"

"The eyes. The eyes will always give you away. I know you too well. I hardly know Brad, but the eyes give him away too. There is something about the way you two look at each other. You both try to hide it. But that chemistry is just too strong."

Her eyes teared as she placed her head on his chest. He put his arms around her and stroked her hair. "It's ok, Glory. I just want you to be happy. I know that I have not made your life a pleasant one. But this guy has really put a glow on your face in the short time you have known him. And you certainly deserve something good after all you have been through."

"What should I do?" she asked without looking up.

"I can't tell you what to do. I know what I would do."

She raised her head. "What's that?"

"I'd follow my heart."

She stepped back, surprised at his answer. Broussard was pretty cynical about life, yet she had known him to show a tender heart at times. But he never demonstrated a romantic side.

He smiled. "You looked shocked. Surprised that my heart is not made of stone? Believe it or not, I have been in love."

"What happened?"

His smile gave way to a jaw tightened as he stared in the distance. "She died."

"Oh, Paul, I'm sorry."

"I'd rather not talk about it. That was years ago. The bird

will be back shortly. I've got to get things ready." He started to walk away.

"Paul." He stopped and turned. "Thanks."

"For what?"

She walked over and kissed him lightly on the lips. "For understanding...and being my friend."

He acknowledged with a nod and returned to work.

The chopper glided proudly through the blue sky, flexing its rejuvenated mechanical muscles and slicing through the occasional cloud that floated in its path. The engine hummed and all systems functioned properly. Any doubts the crew had about her air-worthiness were laid to rest.

Townsend looked over at his co-pilot. "Take the stick, Jeff." Taylor eagerly obliged.

"Let's take her through a few maneuvers to see if she is still the gal she used to be."

"Don't worry, she is," Taylor said confidently.

They spent the next thirty minutes doing turns and takeoffs and landings. No problems encountered. Taylor's flying skills were outstanding.

Gloria's heart raced as she heard the chopper approaching in the distance. She ran over and put her arm around Broussard's waist, tightening her grip as the helicopter appeared, and maintaining it until touchdown. Once the blades stopped spinning, Broussard pulled the truck over and began refueling.

Townsend instructed his team to begin loading the gear. He walked over to Broussard. "Paul, top her off and fill those six Jerry cans for the pump Henry rigged in the cabin. When you finish here, pull the truck in the cave with the other vehicles. We'll cover the entrance again. Hopefully, this will buy us some time if anybody comes snooping around."

He motioned to Gloria, who had been watching him since he landed. She eagerly obeyed his signal. He took her by the arm and escorted her a few steps out of sight from the others.

"Oh, Brad, I..." Before she could finish, he held her tightly in his arms and pressed his lips against hers. She was surprised that he would risk their being seen together, but made no attempt to stop him. Not sure when this opportunity may come again, she tried to project all the passion she was feeling into her soft, wet lips. Townsend responded. After what seemed like minutes, he raised his head and placed his strong hands on the sides of her face. As he looked into her eyes, it was then that she realized without doubt his feelings were as strong as hers.

"You'd better get back to work," he said softly. Without comment, she turned and went back to her duties. For the next half-hour she worked in a pleasant kind of trance.

With the equipment stowed aboard the *Suzy Q* and the trucks out of sight in the cave, Taylor performed a last walk around to make sure no incriminating evidence was left behind. They wore gloves most of the time, so fingerprints were not a concern. To be on the safe side, he wiped down the steering wheel and any places on the trucks that might have been touched by bare hands. Confident the cave was clean, he began placing shrubs and camouflage over the entrance.

Suddenly, he heard Jim Lee calling out and pointing. He rushed over to Townsend in the chopper. "We got to get going. Some trucks heading this way."

Townsend got out of the chopper and joined Jim Lee on the top of the rocks. He took a long look in the binoculars, carefully scanning the area. "How much time do you think we have before they get too close for us to take off?"

"Fifteen minute...twenty at most," Jim Lee answered.

"Then let's see if we can do it in ten." He climbed down, followed by Jim Lee.

"Ok, folks. Get in the chopper and make yourselves comfortable. We're ready to go," Townsend announced.

Gloria walked up to him. "What about Mr. Deng?"

"We ought to leave his worthless ass here," he answered.

"Brad, we can't do that!"

He saw her concerned look. "I was just kidding. He knows too much. And if those soldiers find him, believe me, he will sell us out in a minute. Give him another sip of your concoction for the road. Henry and Paul can put him in the chopper."

Jim Lee and Salazar stood by with the fire extinguishers as Townsend fired up the chopper. Satisfied that everything was go, they jumped into the cabin. He wasted no time in lifting off. The extra weight presented no problem. He turned east to pull the two approaching trucks away from the cave. After he saw them turn and head in the direction of the chopper, he dropped down to tree top level to obscure their view.

"Good thinking, Brad," Taylor complimented him. "Looks like they are heading the other way."

Townsend stayed on that course a few minutes before turning and heading west. He handed the map to Taylor. "I figure a little over two hours to Three Pagodas Pass."

Taylor nodded in agreement. "We should make it just before dark. Have you ever been there?"

"Yeah. I stopped there once taking some company executives on a sightseeing tour. It can be hairy at night with all the hills."

"Not half as hairy as plucking the top off a stone shrine."

Townsend looked over at his buddy. "Having second thoughts?"

"Nope," he answered without hesitation. "Just making conversation."

Townsend slapped him on the shoulder, a sign of thanks for his support. "Tell everyone to keep their eyes open. We are coming up on the Thai border."

Chapter 29

Anderson leaned back in his chair and shuffled the crime scene photos. This was becoming a routine he did not care for. He studied each one carefully, still hoping for that clue he knew was there. With his ever-present cup of tea on his desk, he sipped and shuffled. Suddenly, an idea flashed in his head. He called for his driver to get the car.

Chapter 30

Taylor stared down at the ocean of green that lay below, thinking how lucky he was. Lucky that he made it out of that damned war, lucky to have a wife like Suzy, lucky to have a beautiful son, and lucky to have a friend and redeemer of his self-respect like Brad. It was a good feeling—a real good feeling. He looked in the cabin to see how everyone was doing: Salazar and Broussard had joined Deng in a nap, Jim Lee kept his eye on the horizon, and Gloria just sat quietly and smiled at him. He was beginning to understand what Townsend saw in her. Fixed up, she would be very beautiful, he thought. As for her toughness and resilience, he had already seen that. There was definitely something special about her. He returned her smile and went back to studying his map.

"How is everyone?" Townsend asked.

"Fine. The guys are sacked out, Jim Lee is vigilantly eyeing the skies, and Glory...well, she is just sitting there looking beautiful."

Townsend was a little surprised. It was the first time he heard anyone but Broussard call her Glory. He liked hearing his best friend say it. It was a sign he was warming up to her.

"Three Pagodas just ahead," he notified Taylor. "Wake those sleeping beauties."

Taylor signaled Gloria. She nudged Broussard and Salazar. Both men roused right away. Salazar put on the only headset in the cabin. "What's going on, *amigo*?"

Townsend looked back at him. "Henry, we are at the pass. Have everyone keep their eyes open. We don't want to put down in the middle of any surprises. There should only be the fuel truck and one other vehicle. We can't be too careful when dealing with the Chinaman and his bandits."

Townsend circled the two trucks below. Once he was convinced it was safe, he sat the chopper down. He switched off the ignition and reached for his forty-five. After chambering a round, he placed the belt around his waist and exited the aircraft. The fuel truck pulled along side the chopper just a few feet from the path of the blades. Taylor moved beside Townsend with his weapon ready on the hip. Two Asian men got out of the truck and gave Townsend a quick glance. They uncoiled the hose and began re-fueling before the blades stopped spinning.

"A no nonsense bunch, eh?" Taylor remarked.

Townsend nodded. "Take a look around and let everyone know when the coast is clear. Have Henry and Paul untie Deng and put him in the back of that covered truck. We'll tell those guys he got into the first aid box."

"Well, he did," Taylor smiled. "He just didn't know it."

Townsend called the team together while the *Suzy Q* was being fueled. "Ok, gang. We are about to embark on the meat of this whole mission. We need to make sure we are all on the same page and everyone knows his," he glanced at Gloria, "or her part. First, we've got to keep our eyes on those two guys at all times. Under no circumstances are they to get any closer to the chopper than they are now. And there is no reason for them to get inside the bird. Use of deadly force is authorized." His strong words surprised the others. "Each of you has been issued a weapon. From here on, keep it with you at all times." He looked at Gloria. "You too."

She opened her mouth to speak, but stopped after seeing the serious look on Townsend's face. She just nodded instead.

"There has been a change in plans. After we do the job, we are not coming back here. We are going to land about twelve clicks south of here near Sangkha Buri on the Khao Laem reservoir. Jimmy knows where it's at. So that means we are going to need that fuel truck. Henry, replace those Thai flags with Burmese ones."

"Ok," Brad. What are we going to do with them?" he asked, pointing at the Asians with his head.

Townsend turned to Gloria. Do you have enough sleep medicine for them too?"

"Yes. It doesn't take much."

"Good. Then put them to sleep with Deng and take them with you."

"How do I do that?" she asked.

"After we leave, fix something to eat. Put it in their food or drink. If that doesn't work, give them a dose at gunpoint. Just make sure they are out because we need both vehicles." Townsend looked at the trucks. "Henry, when we are finished here, I want you to check the trucks for weapons and radios

134

while those guys are occupied.

"Ok. But why the change in plans?"

"Call it a gut feeling. But it is a contingency I planned for. When I brought you guys into this, I told you I had planned this very carefully and I would do everything I could to get you home alive." He looked at Taylor who knew of his promise to Suzy. "I'm keeping my word." He knew from the looks on their faces they appreciated his concern. "Ok, let's review. Gloria, you are to make sure those guys are out of the picture." She nodded. "Henry, your job is to keep an eye on the Chinaman's men and help Gloria with their *siesta*..."

"I thought I was going along on the chopper," Salazar interrupted.

"Sorry, Henry. I would like to take you but this is a three-man job. We need to fly as light as we can. I don't know how much of that stone we will have to take...besides, you are more important here. And you need to drive one of the trucks."

Salazar felt better after the explanation. "Okay, Brad."

Townsend then turned to Jim Lee. "Jimmy, you are the guide. You've got to make sure that the rest of the team gets to the rendezvous spot. Do whatever it takes, but be there."

"We will be there, Captain Brad."

Townsend smiled. "I know you will, Jimmy. I figure we should be gone just over three hours. Be careful and watch each other's sixes. The Chinaman is tricky and has spies and agents all over this part of Southeast Asia. Any questions?" There were none. "Jeff, make sure they top off the tank. We are going to need every drop of fuel."

"Will do," Taylor assured him.

Townsend's eyes locked on Gloria's for a moment. In those fleeting seconds they passed a silent message of their feelings for one another. "I mean what I said about the pistol. You need to put that belt on."

She teased him by puckering her lips. "I will." She wanted so much to kiss him, but would save it for later.

Chapter 31

The unmarked police car stopped at the front door of the Mekong Club. "Wait in the car," Anderson directed his subordinate. He exited the vehicle and surveyed the surroundings. The doorman made a slight dip of his head and smirked as he opened the door, as if letting Anderson know that he recognized him as a police officer. Once inside, he was met by another man wearing an expensive suit.

"May I be of assistance?" he asked in Thai with a heavy Chinese accent.

Anderson gave him the cold hard look he used during interrogation of suspects. "I want to see the proprietor," he said forcefully.

"He cannot be disturbed at this time."

Anderson flashed his badge. "Just get him."

The man backed up a step and dipped his head in respect. "I will tell him you are here." He quickly disappeared into the shadows.

Anderson scanned the room through the heavy smoke that hung in the dark club, illuminated only by a few multicolor neon signs and the spotlight that cast an eerie aura over the dancer performing on the stage. The place had changed since he was last in several years ago. It used to be a nice nightclub. He and his wife would come in to dance and catch the act of an occasional popular entertainer. It was called the Imperial Palace in those days. He heard the place had gone down hill since the previous owner was found dead of an overdose in his office. There was talk on the street that he was murdered by the club's new owner—a mysterious man who relocated to Bangkok just before the change in ownership.

Anderson was talking with a young woman when an Asian man dressed in white appeared. A look of fear came across the woman's face and she quickly walked away.

"I am sorry to keep you waiting, Inspector. I was completing some important business. I am Mr. Van Tat."

Anderson just glared at him with the same cold stare he gave the other man earlier. Normally, he would not be so disrespectful, but given the reputation of the man before him, he was sending a signal he would not be intimidated, even on the other man's home turf. He pulled a photo from the envelope in his hand. "Do you know this woman?"

Van Tat's eyes glanced at the photo. "Shall we go to my office?" he gestured with a wave of his arm.

Anderson had an uneasy feeling as he followed the man past the bar and through a dimly lit corridor. He was extra vigilant in the event of any unexpected surprises. The thirty-eight revolver against his left rib cage gave him some comfort, but would not be much good if surprised from one of the several doors that lined the hall. Once they arrived at the office, he checked it out carefully before accepting the invitation to sit.

"May I offer you something to drink?"

He shook his head. "I am Inspector Anderson. I am looking for information on this woman." He held up the photograph of a woman lying on her back, obviously dead. "You never answered whether you know her."

Vat Tat leaned back in his chair. "No, I don't believe I do," he answered without looking at the photograph. "You are here looking for a woman? I thought you had come to pick up, shall we say, an honorarium."

Anderson was overcome with anger at this insult. He fought hard to maintain his composure. It was important that he deny Van Tat the satisfaction of knowing he had touched a nerve. Finally, he answered, "An honorarium? For what?"

Van Tat began fingering his Fu Manchu mustache between his left thumb and index finger. "In appreciation of our fine police officers who protect humble businesses such as mine."

"From what?" Anderson asked.

"Undesirables and troublemakers. The streets are mean, are they not, Inspector?"

"Oh, I see. And how many of these dedicated police officers receive your honorariums, Mr. Van Tat?" he pressed.

Van Tat shifted his weight in the chair. "I would rather not divulge that, if you do not mind." Realizing that Anderson was not the kind of officer to accept a bribe, he carefully watched his words.

Anderson smirked. "Getting back to the young woman. You say you do not know who she is?" Van Tat shook his head.

"That is strange. I have several witnesses who told me she used to work here."

Van Tat's stunned expression betrayed his usually stoic face. "May I see the photograph again?" He pretended to study the picture harder. "Oh, yes. I did not get a good look at it before. I believe she did work here briefly."

Relying on gut instinct, Anderson decided to play a hunch. He stood up and took four photographs from the envelope and threw them on the desk where Van Tat was sitting. "These women also worked here," his stern voice raised slightly.

He pushed his chair away from the desk. "I cannot keep up with all the people in my employ. Many of these women have outside vocations. They make contact here and then leave to pursue their own goals. Most are young and impulsive. What they do outside this club is not my concern, Inspector."

Anderson's bluff worked. Now he had a common link among all five of the young women. "I want you to find out when these women worked here and when they left your employ." He tossed his card on the desk. "And I want this information on my desk before six p.m. tomorrow. You understand?" Van Tat bowed slightly.

Anderson turned around as he reached the door. "I don't take bribes," he said in a firm voice that matched the look in his eyes. Walking through the club, Anderson felt elated. Experience told him he was about to break this case—finally.

His driver was standing by the car when he came out. He opened the car door for his boss, then climbed behind the wheel. "Where to, Inspector?"

"Just pull over to the side. I want to talk to some of the women in there as they come out. It is too dangerous for them to be seen talking with me inside the club. Tonight, my young apprentice, you are going to learn how to solve crime.

Chapter 32

Townsend walked over to where Broussard was sitting and smoking a cigarette. "Hey Paul. You look deep in thought."

"Oh, hey, Brad. I'm just going over everything to make sure I have all bases covered."

"Great. You've got the tear gas and smoke grenades?"

"Yes."

"And everything is okay with your exploding belt?" Townsend asked, referring to the belt of C-4 to be used to break the mortar away from the stone bulb of the spire.

"Uh, huh. At first, I made it sixty inches. But I increased it to seventy-two inches just to be safe."

"Well, if that piece is bigger than six feet in circumference, then we are in trouble anyway. The chopper will not be able to lift it. I feel sure it is less than sixty inches. But I do appreciate your extra efforts. We can't be too careful. Anything else?"

"Uh, yes." He paused as he took a drag from his cigarette. "I know about you and Glory."

Townsend's heart beat faster and harder. He tried to find an appropriate response.

Broussard played with his cigarette. "And I want you to know that I am ok with it. I love her, but in a different way. I always will. I have looked after her and she has looked after me." He took another drag and slowly blew out the smoke. "But she needs a man that she can love and love her in a romantic way...and I can't think of a better guy than you, Brad. She does really love you, man. And I think you've got a thing for her. All I ask is that you never hurt her. She has had enough pain...some of it from me."

After a few awkward moments, Townsend put his hand on Broussard's shoulder. "I would never hurt her...at least not intentionally. She is a remarkable woman, and I do have strong feelings for her. I also know that the two of you have a special bond, and I would never try to change that."

"Like I said, I'm all right."

"Paul, I really appreciate what you have said. You know she loves you too."

Broussard looked up and smiled. He understood what Townsend meant. "I know."

"It's almost dark. I guess we better get ready." Townsend walked over and began talking with Jim Lee. Their conversation was interrupted a few minutes later by Taylor.

"Hey Brad. Check out our friends." Townsend looked over. The two Asians appeared to be trying to sneak into the helicopter. "Watch this." He pulled back the slide on his forty-five and let go. The Asians popped their heads in the direction of the loud click. They quickly stepped away from the chopper and began securing the fuel hose. "I guess they were looking for their candy," Taylor joked.

Townsend laughed. "There is certainly nothing wrong with their hearing, is it?" The Asians looked their way and started talking fast. "I wonder what they are saying?"

"I don't know. Sounds like gibberish to me," Taylor answered. "Let's ask Jimmy." He called Jim Lee over. "What are those two guys saying?"

He listened for a moment. "Sound like gibberish!" Townsend and Taylor cracked up with laughter at his response.

"Jimmy, you are going to have to be very careful with them," Townsend warned.

"Don't worry. Me and Mr. Henry will take care of them. And Miss Gloria too," he added.

As Townsend walked away, he saw Gloria. He motioned with his head to meet him by the truck. She came over. "Paul and I just had a little talk," he informed her.

"About us?" she guessed.

"Yes. He says he is ok with everything."

She nodded. "If he told you that, then he is."

"You don't act surprised."

"Not really. As you probably know, Paul is an unusual man. He doesn't think like most people, but I understand his logic. He wants me to be happy, even if that means me being with someone else. But he knows that we will always be there for one another if we ever needed anything. I hope you understand that."

"I think I do," he answered. He pulled her closer. "How about a good-bye kiss?

She looked up at him. "No, I will not give you a good-bye kiss...but I will give you a good luck kiss."

"I'll take it." After the kiss, he headed straight to the chopper and climbed in. Taylor was in the co-pilot's seat. "Are you ready?"

"I've been ready," he answered. They began an abbreviated pre-flight check. By the time they finished, Broussard had taken his place in the cabin.

"Ready, Paul?" Townsend asked.

"Yep. Let's do it."

As Townsend was about to hit the switch, he saw Gloria come running toward the aircraft. She jumped in the back with Broussard. "Hey, where's my good luck kiss?" She leaned over and kissed him on the lips. She saw Taylor looking back so she crawled to the cockpit and gave him one too.

Townsend grinned, "Hey, how about me?"

She looked over at Taylor. "Think he needs another?"

Taylor nodded.

Gloria gave him a quick smack on the lips. "You boys be careful." She jumped out and joined Jim Lee and Salazar as they watched the *Suzy Q* spin her blades for a couple of minutes before disappearing into the night.

The chopper glided effortlessly through the clear, starlit sky, the cadence of her blades providing a calming effect on Taylor. He looked at the string of lights that snaked through the darkness below.

"That's the shoreline," Townsend informed him. "We are about to cross the Gulf of Marturban. For the next forty minutes or so we will be over water." He looked over at his friend. "Nervous?"

"A little," he answered.

"Me, too," he smiled. "How about you, Paul?"

"I'm fine, Brad," Broussard answered.

Gloria sat across the lantern from the two Asians. She cut her eyes at Salazar as the men began having difficulty pinching their egg noodles with the chopsticks. Their eyelids continued to grow heavy until one dropped his plate and fell forward. Realizing something was happening, the other man reached for a knife concealed under his shirt. As he tried to rise, his knees gave out and he fell beside his partner. Jim Lee, who was watching from a distance, rushed over. "We tie them up and put in truck with other man." He handed Salazar some duct tape and they secured their hands and feet. As he was preparing to place tape over their mouths, Gloria stopped him.

"No Jim. Let them breath. They will not be making any noise."

"Ok," he responded.

Salazar helped him place the two men in the back of the covered truck with Deng. "We go now," Jim Lee insisted. "You drive this truck and I drive tank truck. Miss Gloria, you ride in back of truck and keep eye on men." He took the pistol from her holster, chambered a round, and released the safety. "All you have to do is pull trigger."

Gloria was shocked as he handed her the readied weapon. "Jimmy..."

"Captain Brad's orders," he reminded her.

Salazar walked over. "He's right, Gloria. It's just in case. But don't worry, they will not be waking up for a while." He helped her in the back of the truck. "How long to the next stop, Jim?"

"About half hour. We go now." He got in the tank truck and pulled out. Salazar followed.

Chapter 33

Anderson noticed Pryang check his watch again. "It is ten minutes later than when you last looked, and almost two hours since we arrived. This is the routine, boring part of being a detective, but it is still an essential part, my young friend."

Soon after delivering his lecture to Pryang, a woman came out of the Mekong Club. Anderson studied her face. "She is the young woman I was talking to inside. Follow her down to the corner, out of sight from the doorman."

Pryang started the car and eased ahead of the woman. He turned onto a side street and pulled over to the curb. As the woman reached the corner, Anderson approached her. "Can we finish our conversation?" Without waiting for a reply, he gently took her arm and guided her to the car.

Chapter 34

"Lights of Rangoon dead ahead," Townsend announced. "ETA...twelve minutes."

Taylor's earlier calmness was shattered by the pounding of his heart. He felt the same sensations years before when entering a hot zone. A couple of deep breaths eased the palpations, but his chest was still tight with anxiety.

Townsend sensed his co-pilot's apprehension. "Okay, guys. Everyone knows what to do. We have gone over it many times. Just do what we practiced and things will be fine." He looked back at Broussard. "Ready?" Broussard gave him a thumbs up.

Townsend returned it. "I don't want to stay over the target any longer than ten minutes." He looked at Taylor. "Jeff, you better get ready."

Taylor climbed out of his seat and joined Broussard in the cabin. He felt a slight change of direction as Townsend began the final approach.

"There it is," Townsend called out. Taylor and Broussard looked out the window. Two miles away the golden spire reached up in the dark sky like a giant yellow light bulb.

"Damn," Broussard whispered in awe of the shrine. Less than a mile away from target, he opened the cabin door and readied his equipment.

Townsend circled the site to determine the status of security below. He saw only two men who appeared to be unarmed. Satisfied with the situation, he maneuvered the Suzy Q to less than twenty feet above the top of the spire. "Ok, drop the smoke," he ordered.

Taylor pulled the pins on two smoke grenades and tossed them out. "Smoke dropped," he informed Townsend.

Broussard snapped the hook of the winch line to his harness and grabbed the web netting. "Ok, Brad, we're ready."

Townsend positioned the chopper fifteen feet directly above the spire vane. The absence of significant wind made it easier for Townsend to hover in place. "I'm set...go!"

Broussard slipped out of the aircraft. Taylor slowly let out on the winch line. "Lower...lower...lower...ok," Broussard guided him. "Brad, give me three feet port." Townsend eased his foot on the left pedal. "Just a hair. I'm almost there." Townsend pushed lightly. "Ok. I'm on it. Hold what you got. Jeff, give me a couple of feet of slack...that's it. Stop!" Broussard wasted no time in tying the C4 belt around the base of the bud. After securing it, he placed a canvas cover over the bud, secured the fabricated web harness over it, and attached the harness cable to his belt. He gave it a quick double check. "Ok, bring me up."

Taylor reversed the winch. Back on board, Broussard secured the winch hook to the cable connected to the harness. "Go up about forty feet, Brad. That should be enough." He directed Townsend as the chopper lifted to ensure there was plenty of slack in the cable. "That's good. I'm going to fire now." He waited a couple of seconds, then he flipped the switch. The C4 fired with a muffled explosion. Broussard knew his job. Not a piece of debris hit the chopper. "Ok. Get me back down there."

Townsend lowered the aircraft. One of his fears was now realized: the absence of ground wind caused the smoke to rise higher than he had hoped. The blades of the chopper were swirling it around hampering his vision. "The smoke is too bad. You guys are going to have to guide me by the marks on the cable."

"Will do," Taylor answered. He carefully reeled in the cable slack. "We are about twenty feet above, ten feet aft. Townsend maneuvered the bird according to his directions. "Hold it there."

"See if you can winch it up," Townsend suggested.

Taylor eased the cable taut. "The winch is as far as it will go. It's still attached."

Townsend looked at his watch. Nine minutes had passed. He checked the fuel gauge: it was approaching half a tank. He tried to lift the chopper but soon let off out of fear of snapping the cable. "We're running out of time, guys. Any ideas?"

Broussard put his gloves back on and slid down the cable to the spire.

"Paul just went down the cable," Taylor reported.

"Oh, shit!" Townsend spewed. "Paul...Paul. Answer me. What are you doing?"

A minute later Broussard responded. "It is stuck at one spot. I think I can break it loose with the gun."

"Ok. But hurry. The gauge is almost at half a tank. You got

one minute. If you don't have it by then, disconnect the harness and get your ass back up here."

Broussard fired five quick shots at the snag. He then gave it a bump with all of his weight and it broke loose. "She's free! She's free! Take her up!"

As Taylor raised the winch, he heard an occasional metallic sound. A hole appeared near the door. "Damn, Brad. They're shooting at us."

Townsend saw a hole appear in the green house window above his head. "Drop more smoke...and some tear gas," he yelled.

Taylor followed his orders and returned to the winch. He felt the bud separate from the spire. The winch struggled, but after a long minute, the jewel-encrusted stone appeared in the doorway. He wrestled with the four-hundred-pound prize to swivel it inside the chopper.

"How are you coming?" Townsend asked.

"I just got it in. I'm about to unhook the cable and send it back to Paul," he answered in between breaths.

"Ok. Hurry."

"Don't worry about me," Broussard piped in. Just go on. You're low on fuel. If you don't leave now, you won't make it...besides, I'm hit," he moaned.

"We're not leaving without you. Now grab that damn cable and let's get the hell out of here!" Townsend ordered.

"Go on, I said," Broussard repeated.

"Jeff, come take the stick." Taylor climbed forward and took the controls.

Townsend passed the winch remote to Taylor, then quickly put on a headset and pair of gloves. He wrapped his arm and leg around the cable and slid down until his foot touched the hook. "Jeff, move starboard four feet and ease the winch up. I'll tell you when to stop."

"Ok."

The chopper jerked, slamming Townsend against the spire with a hard thud. "Ooh. Easy, Jeff."

"Sorry, Brad. Are you all right?"

"Yeah. Now pull me up...a little more...a little more...stop! Now hold what you got." Broussard was on his stomach, balanced across a circular perch eighteen inches in diameter

146

where the bud had been attached. Townsend grabbed on to him. "Paul...Paul...can you hear me?" Broussard tried to lift his head. Townsend knew he was in pain and going into shock. Without hesitation, he attached the cable hook to Broussard's harness and wrapped his arms around his wounded comrade. A bullet zipped by his ear. "Get us out of her, Jeff. They're still shooting!"

Taylor manipulated the winch remote with his left hand while operating the collective. He bumped the cyclic, moving the chopper aport slightly, dangling Townsend and Broussard in the cloud of smoke.

Townsend steadily called out the distance to the chopper. "Stop!" he yelled out upon reaching the winch. Broussard had passed out. It took all of Townsend's strength to wrestle him inside the aircraft. Adrenalin was the only thing keeping his fatigued body from stretching out next to Broussard. "We're in. Let's get out of here. Stay on the course we came in on." He glanced at his watch. They were over target seven minutes longer than scheduled. No time to worry about that now, he thought. He had more pressing business at hand.

Taylor turned the bird around and headed toward the gulf. His focus on flying the aircraft caused him to forget about the anxiety he was experiencing just minutes before.

Once Townsend got Broussard lying on is back on the floor, his combat experience took over. He placed a seat cushion under Broussard's head and instinctively reached for the first aid kit. Holding the flashlight with his teeth, he wrapped his belt around Broussard's upper right arm and swabbed the distended antecubital vein with alcohol.

Taylor looked back, but remained silent. He knew his pilot was trying to save a life and he did not want to interrupt his work.

Townsend hung the IV bag from the ceiling and inserted the needle. He taped the hose to keep it in place and removed the tourniquet. Once the drip started, he opened Broussard's shirt. Blood covered his chest. "Keep flying level, Jeff. The bud is not secured. We don't want it rolling around in here."

"Will do. How's Paul?"

"He's unconscious. I started an IV. I'm about to check his wound. He's pretty bloody." Townsend went back to work, cleaning the wound with alcohol and applying antibacterial cream. He then wrapped a bandage around Broussard's waist. "Ok, Jeff. Here's what we've got. A bullet pierced his left side and exited. I'm not sure what it hit inside, but the bleeding has almost stopped. My guess is he has not lost too much blood."

"Thank God. You want to take the stick now?"

"Yeah. I feel better playing pilot than doctor," he sighed.

Chapter 35

Jim Lee pulled the tank truck up to the front of the rusting corrugated metal building. He got out and scanned his surroundings before unlocking the two large doors. After making a quick check inside with his flashlight, he swung the doors open and motioned for Salazar to move his truck in. He then pulled in the tanker and closed the doors.

Gloria checked on her three wards. Satisfied they were still out, she climbed out of the truck and joined Salazar and Jim Lee in the middle of the building. In the dim light she noticed two cars off to the side. "Whose are those?" she asked Jim Lee.

"For us if we need them. Captain Brad call them insurance."

"Gloria, how about those *hombres* in the back? Are they still out?" Salazar asked.

"Yes. They will be ok for a while." She turned to Jim Lee. "When is the helicopter due?"

He shrugged his shoulders. Sensing that she needed something more tangible, he said, "Maybe one hour."

"Is there something we could be doing?" she asked.

"One moment please." He walked over and took some keys hidden under a worktable. He handed them to her. "You can make sure cars start." She looked at him with a puzzled expression. He saw that she did not understand the purpose of the assignment. "Very important to know cars available in case we need them. Check gas level too, please."

Gloria suddenly realized he was trying to keep her busy so she would not have time to worry about the helicopter crew. "Thanks, Jimmy." She reached over and hugged him.

His face turned red. "You are welcome."

"What can I do?" asked Salazar.

"Come with me." Jim Lee led him to an old wooden ammo box. He took out a string of lights. "Take the battery out of that truck and bring outside." He then went out and began arranging the lights as a landing beacon for the chopper.

Chapter 36

Townsend looked back into the dark cabin. "How's Broussard doing?"

"He's still out, but he's not bleeding," Taylor reported with the sound of relief in his voice.

"Good. Is the bud secured?"

"Yes. I took care of that a few minutes ago."

"Why don't you grab a knife or screwdriver and see if you start taking gems from that rock. Start with the big diamonds or anything that is easy to dislodge. This will save us some time on the other end."

"Ok. How's the fuel?"

"Less than half a tank. "We used a lot more than planned over the spire. Something else...we're losing oil pressure. We must have taken a bullet somewhere."

Taylor stuck his head in the cockpit and surveyed the instrument panel. "Oil temp ok...oil pressure left of center, but loss not yet significant," he confirmed. He knew from experience that a critical drop in pressure could occur any time the system was compromised. He placed his hand on Townsend's shoulder. "Keep me informed."

"Will do," Townsend assured him.

He returned to the cabin and began removing diamonds with a sawtooth knife. Like Townsend earlier, he resorted to holding the flashlight with his teeth to see what he was doing. The chopper was completely blacked out except for the dim green lights illuminating the instrument panel. The dark working conditions did not bother him. He knew they had to fly without cabin or running lights in order to minimize detection. Although it was dangerous, it wasn't the first time he had found himself in this situation. He and Townsend had done it a number of times on black ops missions in Cambodia and Laos during the war.

After ten minutes, Taylor's pockets were beginning to fill with an assortment of diamonds and emeralds. While looking for a larger container for them, he checked on Broussard. The bleeding had stopped and his pulse was strong. Pleased with his status, he returned to his assignment. He worked out a technique in which he scraped around the gem, then popped it out with the knife, using his forty-five as a fulcrum. Most of the gems took only a few seconds to dislodge. The more embedded ones were by-passed.

"Jeff. I just wanted to let you know we are past the halfway point," Townsend informed him. "How's your patient?"

"He's stable. I just checked on him a few minutes ago. How's the oil pressure?"

"It's still falling, but very slowly. I think it may be a vibration fracture in the line."

"And the fuel?"

Townsend paused before responding. "That's another story. It's going to be tight...very tight," he answered solemnly. "You can start transferring the fuel from the Jerry cans."

Taylor hooked up the pump Salazar rigged and pumped the fuel into the chopper tank. With only six cans, it took only a few minutes to suck out thirty gallons. He then went back to work, immersing himself in the job at hand. He didn't want to think about the problems with the chopper, the wounded man lying next to him, or the police dragnet that would soon be tightening around him and his accomplices.

Chapter 37

Jim Lee made a final check of the light string. Satisfied with its circular layout, he flipped the switch. The lights flashed in a ring of blue. Gloria and Salazar checked out his handiwork. "Captain Brad will be here very soon. We wait outside and listen for the helicopter." He turned off the lights. "When we hear motor, I will turn back on," he explained.

Gloria's hands began to perspire—a sign of her nervous state. She maintained her vigil of looking to the sky, waiting for the sound of the chopper, wringing her hands unaware, as if that would remove the dampness in her palms.

Salazar watched her nervous manifestations for a few minutes before deciding to intervene. "You ok, Glory?" He thought using her pet name would make her feel more at ease.

"Just a little antsy," she answered, still rubbing her hands.

"Yeah, me too. How about a cigarette?"

"Thanks, Henry. But I don't smoke."

"I know you don't. But it will calm your nerves." He pushed a cigarette to her. "Go ahead and take it."

She smiled as she reached over and collected it between her fingers. He lit it and one for himself. "Thanks, Henry."

"You're welcome."

After a few drags, she did feel a little less tense. "You are right...it helps."

Chapter 38

"Jeff, the fuel light just came on," Townsend called out.

Taylor knew that meant about twenty minutes of fuel. "How far are we from the LZ?" he asked, falling back on his military jargon.

"About forty-five to fifty clicks."

Taylor made a quick calculation in his head. "That's cutting it close."

"Yeah. How many jewels are left in that rock?"

"I got about half way. Why? You thinking about dropping it?"

"Only as a last resort. Just get as many out as you can. I'll let you know...kill the light!" he shouted suddenly. "Aircraft approaching!"

Taylor turned off the flashlight. "Where?"

Aport...eleven o'clock...about three miles out. Come up and cover the panel."

Taylor jumped in the left seat. He took off his shirt and held it over the green glow emitted by the instruments.

"They are probably choppers from that army base near Lamoing heading to Rangoon," Townsend said.

After the aircraft passed, Taylor climbed back in the cabin. He extracted only a few stones when he heard Townsend call out that the coastline was ahead. He looked out the window. The lights dotting the shore were a relief. At least we won't have to sit down in the soup, he thought.

"Jeff, the tower lights from the Three Pagodas should be coming up on the port side in a few minutes. Once we reach them, we are almost home."

Two minutes later the red tower lights appeared and Townsend turned the chopper southeast.

Gloria's heart raced at the whooping sound of the helicopter in the distance. "It's coming...it's coming!" she shouted. Jim Lee hit the switch, illuminating the landing pad.

Townsend spotted the ring of blue lights. "Ok, Jeff. There she is. I'm going to set this baby down."

Taylor quickly wedged his pistol under the stone as an added precaution against rolling. He then scooted over and braced

Broussard for the landing.

Townsend worked his magic with the collective, easing the tired war bird to earth with a soft bounce. Before killing the engine, he glanced at the gauges. He gave a big sigh of relief as he switched off the ignition, ending what was to be his last flight in the *Suzy Q*. As he opened the door, he was greeted by a big smile on Jim Lee's face. "Jimmy, go get a blanket." He climbed out of the chopper, ducking his head until he was out of the path of the blades. Gloria ran up and buried her head in his chest. He let her keep it there a few seconds before reaching down and gently lifting her chin. The look on his face told her something was wrong. "Gloria, Paul is hurt."

She released him. "What?"

"He's been shot."

She shook her head as she stepped backwards. "No...no," she screamed. She turned and ran to the helicopter, completely oblivious to the twirling blades. Her knees buckled as she looked in and saw Broussard stretched out on the floor. Taylor flipped the cabin light off, but it was too late to hide the blood-soaked clothes and red splotches on the metal floor. She had seen many gunshots wounds in her tenure in the emergency room at New Orleans Charity Hospital. But this time it was different: the patient was one of the few men in the world she truly cared about. She held on to the door to steady herself as she began to gag.

The four men carefully lifted Broussard onto the blanket and carried him inside the building. Gloria walked beside them carrying the IV. "Put him on the table," Townsend directed them. He looked at Gloria. She was trying hard not to cry, but tears dripped from her chin. "Gloria, take care of him." He turned to Taylor. "Let's get the bud in. There's a cart over there." He looked back at Gloria as he followed the others outside.

She wiped at her tears. "Is that all you can think about...those damn jewels? What about Paul?"

Taylor motioned to Salazar and Jim Lee with his head for the three of them to keep walking. He knew Townsend needed some time alone with her.

"I am concerned about him," he said walking to her. "But we still have a job to do...and each of us must do ours. Now stop the bitching and tend to him!" He turned and walked outside.

His words and tone surprised her, but she got the message. She fashioned an IV holder out of a board with a protruding nail and began cleaning his wound.

Salazar and Jim Lee wheeled in the bud. Everyone gathered around the object of their efforts. Jewels sparkled in the dim light. Most were uncut, hiding their luster within the rough surfaces. Salazar held one of the uncut diamonds to the light. "Damn, this thing is as big as a grape!"

Taylor tossed him a canvas bag. "Check these out."

A big grin appeared on Salazar's face as he fondled the bag. He reached in and pulled out a handful of gems in varying sizes. "There's got to be four or five pounds of these," he announced.

"Pour them on the table so everyone can see what all this is about," Townsend directed. Salazar eagerly followed his orders.

Gloria's eyes grew. "Wow! Looks like Mardi Gras beads."

She picked up a green stone and rubbed it between her fingers. Emeralds had always been her favorite gems. Her father used to buy them for her, telling her she loved them because of the Irish blood in her.

"Matches your eyes," Townsend complimented her.

"That's what daddy used to say. She found two smaller ones and held them to her ears. "So, what do you think?"

"Nice," Townsend answered. The other men agreed.

She separated a handful of emeralds from the other stones and rubbed them with her fingertips. They appeared to intoxicate her.

"You know what you are holding?" Townsend asked.

"What?" she answered without taking her eyes off the gems.

"The tears of a princess."

"Huh?"

"I will tell you the story later. I want everyone to pick out two stones for your self. I suggest cut ones." They gathered around and made their selections. "Gloria, pick out two for Paul." She selected two diamonds, knowing he would select the more expensive stones.

"Now take a good look at them and remember what you got. I'm going to collect them. I'll carry them. Better to have one person holding them than everyone...unless you want to swallow them, then retrieve them later." He saw the surprised

155

look on their faces. "It's a shitty job...but very effective!" They all laughed. "Seriously, that is how a lot of diamonds are smuggled. Any takers?" There were none. They realized he wanted to be the one to take the risk in the event they were searched, so they handed him their choices. "Ok, Jeff. Get back to work. Gloria, help him. Henry, you and Jimmy come with me.

Taylor and Gloria had removed a handful of gems when they heard a truck start. They looked at each other, but kept on working. Forty minutes passed before Townsend returned.

"What's going on?" Taylor asked.

Townsend walked over to him. "We sank the *Suzy Q* out there in the reservoir."

Taylor looked stunned. "Why?"

"The authorities are going to be looking for a chopper all over Southeast Asia. We can't risk taking her back up. We came in on fumes and ten pounds of oil pressure. We don't have the oil or parts for repair. I couldn't stand the idea of her falling into anyone's hands and I don't have the stomach to blow her up. Besides, the explosion and flames would draw attention. That's why this spot was picked as a backup. It is secluded and the lake is less than a hundred yards away. There is a deep drop-off by the levee. We laid her to rest in thirty-five feet of water. I don't think she will be found." His eyes appeared to tear up.

Taylor understood his rationale. He knew it was hard for him to ditch the *Suzy Q*. Townsend loved the aircraft even more than he did. That is why they went to all the trouble of hiding her fifteen years ago when they could have easily destroyed her. "How are we going to get out of here?"

"That's what the cars are for. We are going to drive to Bangkok."

Taylor looked over at the cars. "What about Deng and those two stooges?"

First, we drop the stone in the lake. Then, we take Deng and his boys in the trucks up about ten clicks between Three Pagodas Pass and Sangkhla and hide them off the road. We'll disable the vehicles to make it look like they broke down. Any more of that sleep medicine left, Gloria?"

"Just a little."

"We will give them some more. If they wake up before being found, they will have the option of hightailing it, or explaining to Van Tat what happened to them. And I don't think they want to face the Chinaman. In any case, it should buy us some time."

Taylor laughed. "Boy, you did think of everything."

"Gloria, how is Paul?" Townsend asked.

"He's better. He opened his eyes a few minutes ago. Brad, I'm sorry about going off on you earlier. Jeff told me what you did for Paul."

"It's ok. I know you were upset. We are all wound kind of tight right now. Will he be able to travel?"

"The bleeding could start again. He really should be treated by a doctor."

Townsend hung his head. "That's the one thing I did not plan for."

Gloria walked over to hug him. As she squeezed her arms around him, he flinched, favoring his left arm. His response surprised her. At first, she thought he might be angry at her about what she had said earlier. But she soon realized that was not the reason for his reaction. "What's wrong, Brad? Are you hurt?"

"I'm all right. I just banged my arm a little."

"Let me see."

"It's nothing."

"I said let me see," she persisted." Take off your shirt."

He removed his shirt to appease her. She rolled up his tee shirt sleeve. He had a large red area on the upper humerus. "Oh, Brad. You are going to have a big bruise there. Does it hurt?"

"A little when I move it a certain way."

She poked the redness with her fingers, causing him to tense up." You may have a hairline fracture there."

"Well, there's not much I can do about it now. I'll have it looked at when we get back to the States."

"I'm finished here," Taylor announced, after the last jewel was removed. "Brad, you stay here and I'll go drop off the trucks. Come on, guys. Help me get this rock out of here."

"You better take care of the three passengers," Townsend advised Gloria. As she headed out of the building, he called to her. "Save a little for Paul in case he needs it." She nodded.

157

Townsend enjoyed having a few moments to quietly sit and think about his next step. Things thus far had not worked out exactly as planned. He did have the jewels, but he also had a wounded man whose ability to travel was doubtful. He felt bad about Broussard getting shot. But he wondered if the firing from the ground was in response to his using the forty-five to dislodge the bud. The soldiers on the ground may have thought he was shooting at them. It no longer mattered, he thought. They were here and they had what they came for. He sat down and closed his eyes. In less than a minute he was asleep.

Gloria came back in and saw him in the chair, his chin touching his chest. She knew he had to be exhausted, so she remained quiet and let him sleep.

Chapter 39

"Brad, we're ready to go," Taylor said softly as he gently shook Townsend's right shoulder.

He popped his head up and looked around. "Huh?"

"It's time to get out of this place."

Townsend moved his head back and forth and in a circular motion in an effort to work the soreness from his neck. "What about the gems?"

"They are in the spare tire. This place has been swept twice to make sure nothing to link us is left behind, and Paul is conscious. Everything has been done. We are ready to leave."

He looked at Gloria. "Damn. How long was I asleep?"

"Not long. We thought you needed the rest, so we took care of everything." She handed him a cup of coffee.

"Where did this come from?"

"Jimmy had a pot and some coffee stashed. He knows how much you love coffee."

"Thanks...to both of you."

"Paul says he can travel," she informed him.

He would not have expected Broussard to say otherwise, no matter how bad he was wounded. "What do you think?"

"I wish he did not have to be moved. But there is no choice," she replied.

"What about Deng and the other men?" Townsend asked.

"We dropped them and the trucks off where you said. Gloria followed us in the car and brought us back," Taylor reported.

"Ok. Then let's get rolling. Jimmy, you drive the lead car with Jeff and Henry. Gloria and I will follow with Paul in the back seat. Be sure you have your pistols...but keep them out of sight." He looked at his watch. "It's been almost three hours since we left Rangoon. The police will be looking for a chopper, so I don't think there will be any roadblocks for a few hours, that is, if we landed undetected. We should make Bangkok before dawn. Let's hit the road."

As the cars were being loaded, Townsend motioned Jim Lee over. They had a brief chat before getting into their designated vehicles for the three hundred fifty-kilometer drive.

Two hours had passed since Townsend climbed behind the

wheel. Traffic on highway 323 was light, allowing them to make good time. Other than an occasional remark, he and Gloria did not talk much. It was difficult for them, but they contained their desires to touch and share verbal intimacies.

Broussard sat up and massaged his brows in an attempt to rub away the groggy feeling in his head. "Where are we?"

Gloria looked back, surprised to see him up and alert. "About three hours from Bangkok," Townsend answered.

"Last thing I remember I was hanging on to the rock with bullets whizzing by my head."

Gloria reached back and touched his hand. "How are you feeling?"

"Like I've been shot." He squeezed her hand gently and smiled. "I'm ok. My side hurts though."

She handed him a pill and canteen. "Take this. It will help with the pain."

He washed the pill down and sat back. "This water sure tastes good. My mouth is so dry," he said, before taking another swig from the canteen.

Gloria leaned over the seat. "Let me check your bandage." He lifted his shirt. She examined the wrapping with a flashlight. "Small splotches of dried blood...no sign of fresh bleeding...looks good. Now lay back down. The more rest you get, the better." He did not protest her order.

The long drive gave Townsend time to think and rethink his next moves. Suddenly, an idea flashed in his head. He blinked the headlights on and off until Jim Lee pulled the lead car to a side road.

"Do you want to stretch your legs?" he asked Gloria. She got out and waited by the car while Townsend joined the other men.

"What's up?" Taylor asked.

"I think we need to make a little detour ahead." He shined the flashlight on the map spread out on the hood. "We are supposed to travel this route, which will bring us about twenty clicks south of Bangkok," he pointed to a spot on the map. "Instead of using highway 323, let's cut up to highway 338 here on the other side of Tha Muang and come into the city from the north." They followed his finger as he traced the route.

Salazar looked puzzled. "But that's a longer way."

160

Townsend nodded. "It will add nearly an hour to the trip, but I think it is time well spent."

"It's the Chinaman, isn't it?" Taylor cut in. "You think he may be arranging some surprises for us along the way? Good thinking, Brad. He is a sly son-of-a-bitch and an ambush is just his style. Why split when he can take it all? What are a few lives to him?"

"Maybe I'm getting a little paranoid carrying millions of dollars in diamonds and emeralds, but I'll feel better," Townsend confessed.

"You not paranoid, Captain Brad," Jim Lee assured him. "Vat Tat is dangerous man and I bet you right about ambush."

Townsend placed his hand on Jim Lee's shoulder. "Agreed? Let's go."

"Brad, how is Paul?" Taylor inquired.

"He seems to be doing better. He sat up for a while and drank a little water. Once we get into Bangkok, we are going to take him to a doctor that Jimmy knows...one who knows how to keep his mouth shut."

While the other men got back into their car, he walked over to Gloria and gave her a hug. She squeezed him tight. "Thanks, I needed that," she sighed.

He patted her on the butt. "There's plenty more where that came from."

"I'm counting on it," she smiled.

They got into the car and fell in behind Jim Lee. At the designated turn, the cars left highway 323 and took the road that connected to highway 338.

Broussard, nodding since receiving the painkiller from Gloria, stretched out in the back seat. As he dropped off, his thoughts were of the French Quarter. He loved New Orleans. The only other time he spent away from the Crescent City was his three years in the army. Even his occasional incarcerations were spent in the Orleans Parish lockup. He promised himself that if he ever got out of Nam alive, he would never again leave the city. This time was an exception. But it wasn't the promise of a big paycheck that lured him. His parents left him property and a bank account in excess of a quarter-million dollars—which he had more than doubled over the last ten years through his many shady dealings. What got to him was the lure of

161

excitement, like nothing he had experienced since his release from active duty. In Townsend and his plan, he saw a way to break out of the alcohol-dominated rut into which he had fallen. He would gladly take another bullet and its pain for the rush he got working his juice. So close to death, but so damn alive, he thought.

Chapter 40

Dawn was breaking as the two cars entered the northern outskirts of Bangkok. A haze of smog hung over the streets, already beginning to fill with bicycles weaving in and out of the slow stream of motor vehicles of every description. "Good thing we are not in New Orleans," Gloria remarked, as she watched the dangerous game of two-wheel dodge. "Half of the bike riders would be dead," she joked.

Townsend looked over at her. "I didn't think the traffic there was that bad."

"I'm talking about the temper of the drivers at rush hour in the Quarter."

Townsend laughed. "I'll have to remember that when we get back." She placed her hand on his knee, a reaction that she liked his reference to being in New Orleans together.

Following Jim Lee's lead, Townsend turned onto a side street and brought the car to a stop in front of a two-story building. Jim Lee walked up to his window. "We'll wait here while you go in and check things out." Jim Lee nodded. He then disappeared into the building.

"Where is he going?" Gloria asked.

"To get a doctor for Paul."

"Really?" she said in a surprised voice. She thought for a moment. "Is it safe?"

Townsend smiled at her. "I think so. Dr. Nguyen is Jimmy's cousin. Jimmy helped him escape the communists after the fall of Saigon. He also helped him set up his practice in Bangkok."

"Jimmy is very resourceful, isn't he?"

"Very."

"Then I say Paul will be in good hands," she smiled.

Townsend touched her face softly, letting her know he was ok with her concern for Broussard. She rewarded him with a tender kiss.

Jim Lee came out of the building and signaled the others to come inside. Gloria gently roused Broussard while Taylor and Salazar stood by to help him inside. Still groggy, he insisted on getting out of the vehicle by himself. He was unsteady as he got to his feet, so he relented and allowed the two men to place his arms on their shoulders for support. Gloria scanned the area.

163

She was relieved to find very few people on the street.

While Broussard was being helped, Townsend was under the hood removing the rotor from the distributor as a precaution against any thieves hot wiring the car and making off with the goods in the trunk.

Chapter 41

Anderson kissed his wife and walked out of his house. His driver was standing by his vehicle. He timed the steps of his boss, flinging open the door at the last moment to keep Anderson from breaking stride. It was a little game he liked to play in order to impress his mentor. Anderson's wife, watching from the door, seemed to enjoy the little display more than her husband.

Anderson dozed off during his ride to the office. The activity at the Mekong Club the evening before caused him to get in late. He followed the owner to a warehouse. After several hours of stakeout, the owner returned to the club. Still, he had the feeling in his gut that something big was about to go down.

Chapter 42

The doctor exited the examination room and walked over to where Townsend and his team were waiting. "How is he, Doctor?" Townsend asked.

The doctor smiled and nodded. "He will be all right. The bullet grazed his kidney and exited. There appears to be no serious damage," he stated in his broken English.

"That's great news, Doctor. Thanks," Townsend offered as he pumped his hand in gratitude. "How long before he is able to travel?"

"He needs rest and to rebuild his strength. I would say a couple of weeks at least."

Townsend looked at the others. "But we are scheduled to fly back to the States tomorrow."

The doctor shook his head. "That is out of the question," he said firmly. "He is too weak and has a fever. The bleeding would start again."

Townsend absorbed this news for a moment. "You're right. Thanks for treating him."

The doctor acknowledged with a nod. "You and your friends look tired. My nurse has set up my quarters for you. Go and rest. We will talk later."

"Oh, Doctor. Can you look at Brad's arm?" Gloria asked.

"I'm okay," Townsend said with a frown.

The doctor walked over to Townsend. "Remove your shirt, please." He complied with the order and allowed the doctor to examine his arm. "That's going to make an ugly bruise." He touched it lightly causing Townsend to grimace. "You could have a fracture. Let me x-ray it."

"Please do," Gloria interjected before Townsend could say no.

While waiting for the results, he began thinking about how they would proceed with Broussard unable to travel.

The x-ray revealed no fracture. The doctor gave Gloria some salve for it.

"Thanks, again," Townsend offered the doctor.

Townsend was exhausted and still feeling the effects of his slam into the spire. He had to come up with a solution to this unexpected twist, but he was too tired to focus his thoughts.

Jim Lee sensed his weariness. "Come, Captain Brad. Let us get some rest," he suggested as he motioned to the makeshift quarters.

"But we've got to come up with a new plan."

"You will think better after a little rest," Jim Lee insisted.

Gloria stepped in to end his resistance. "Jimmy is right, Brad. We all need some rest. Then we can come up with a new plan." She put her arm around him and led him to the cot. He stretched out and gently grasped her hand in appreciation. By the time she finished unlacing his boots, he was asleep.

Taylor turned to Jim Lee. "You and Henry need to get some sleep. I'll keep watch."

"No, thank you, Captain Taylor. You and Mr. Henry rest. I will watch. Besides, I am not sleepy."

Taylor cracked a smile. He knew he was as tired as the rest, but realized he could not change his mind. "Ok, my friend. Watch over us."

Jim Lee nodded. "It is safe here. You get sleep." He found a spot at the window so he could keep an eye on the car. Their trust in him made him proud and he would lay down his life, if necessary, before compromising it.

After a couple of hours of tossing and turning, Townsend sat up on the cot. He looked around. Jim Lee was sitting guard at the window while the others slept. He walked over to his vigilant friend. "Jim, get some rest." Jim Lee remained seated. "It's all right...go ahead. I'm going to need you rested up for later."

His weary friend got up and slid onto a cot.

Once the rest of his team was up, Townsend called them together. "I've decided to stay behind with Paul until he gets well enough to travel. The rest of you will catch the flight tomorrow as planned."

Taylor and Gloria looked at one another with jaws gaped. "You can't, Brad," Taylor insisted. "You are the glue that holds everything together. Let me stay."

Townsend glared at him using the look in his eyes to remind him of his promise to Suzy. "No."

"But we need you to get everyone back and get our jewels to the buyers. You're the only one who can do that."

"I said no," Townsend repeated tersely. An awkward quiet fell on the group.

After a couple of minutes, Gloria broke the silence. "I'll stay with Paul. You know how he is. He would not want anyone but me with him."

"Glory's right, Brad," said Taylor. "She's the only one who can handle him...and she damn sure can't sell our goods."

Salazar nodded in agreement.

Townsend knew they were right. After assessing the options, he relented. "Ok. I don't like leaving you behind, but I guess it's the best plan under the circumstances."

"I'll be fine, Brad."

"We will need to get your tickets changed." He got up and walked toward the door.

"Where are you going?" Taylor asked.

"To find a pay phone and call the Chinaman. I want to arrange for a meet tonight to get rid of these damned rocks."

"I have a bad feeling about this," Taylor informed him.

"So do I. But if we don't go through with the deal, he won't let us leave the country."

Taylor nodded. "Yeah. I just wish there was some way we could take all the jewels and leave that bastard nothing."

"Me, too. But a deal is a deal, even if it's with a snake."

Gloria got up. "Hold on. Let me go with you and we can change the flight reservations. I'm sure you don't want me to call from here."

"Ok. You guys stay here and keep an eye on the car. We'll walk."

Chapter 43

Anderson was nodding off at his desk when the phone awakened him. It was the supervisor of the forensics team he had dispatched to examine the warehouse he staked out the evening before. Between the pallets of rice, several dried bloodstains were found on the floor. Attempts to wipe them up had been made, but there was enough residue for tests to indicate the blood was from more than one person. The freshest was several days old. Anderson leaned back in his chair and analyzed this information. He called his wife to let her know he would be working late again.

Chapter 44

Gloria slipped her hand in Townsend's as they walked down the street. "This feels good," she said.

"What?"

"Walking hand in hand with you. This is the first time we have been alone in an exotic place, and I like the feeling."

He kissed her on the top of the head. "So do I."

After a couple of blocks, Townsend spotted a phone. He made the reservation changes and then called Van Tat. The original plan was to make the exchange a few hours before the flight on the next day. Townsend insisted that the deal had to be moved up to that evening. The Chinaman did not like changing plans, but he reluctantly agreed to it.

It was beginning to turn dark when they returned to the doctor's office. Once inside the door, Townsend pulled Gloria close and kissed her passionately. Her whole body responded. "Just a little something to hold you over."

"Mmm," was her only response.

Taylor was waiting for them at the top of the stairs. "How'd it go?"

"No problems. Paul and Gloria leave in fifteen days...and we meet Van Tat in about three hours. We need to go over some last-minute details. Is Jimmy still asleep?"

"No. He only slept for an hour."

Chapter 45

According to plan, Townsend and Gloria got in the first car with the jewels and headed to the rendezvous. Taylor and Salazar followed. Jim Lee left a couple of hours earlier in a car he borrowed from his cousin.

Townsend was apprehensive as he cleared the city traffic and headed down the dark road to the exchange point. After all they had been through, this should be a piece of cake, he thought. But there was something in the air that kept gnawing at him. To make matters worse, Gloria was right beside him. He rationalized she was needed to take Broussard's place. Still, it did not sit well with him. After a forty-minute drive, he pulled the car to a stop in the middle of the unlit road and checked the directions he received. "That should be it just ahead...the place on the right," he said to Gloria. He got out and walked back to the other car. "Ok, guys. This is it. Jeff, you get in the car with us. Henry, hide the car about a hundred yards away. It will be our back up...just in case. Be sure to wipe it down. We don't want any prints on it. Also, find a good place to stake things out to cover our backs in the event we get some uninvited guests. You got your pistol?"

"*Si*," he answered as he patted the forty-five on his hip.

As they walked to the lead vehicle, Townsend turned to Taylor. "Are you ready, Jeff?"

"Yes, I am," he answered quickly. "How about you?"

Townsend stopped. "I don't know, Jeff. I just have a feeling...I can't really explain it."

"Like get ready to expect the unexpected? Brad, that is the way I am approaching the whole thing because of who we are dealing with. I know that bastard is going to try and pull some shit. I am not about to let my guard down. Just be cool, brother. I got your six."

He slapped his buddy on the back. "Thanks for reminding me. I guess I just needed a little reassurance."

They got in the car and eased down the last quarter mile to the warehouse. Townsend pulled the car near the front entrance of the metal building. He parked it headed out toward the road. "Gloria, slide over behind the wheel. I want you to keep your eyes open and your hand on that pistol. Be ready.

We may have to get out of here in a hurry."

He turned to walk toward the entrance, but spun around and leaned down to Gloria. He gave her a quick peck on the lips. "For luck. And keep the doors locked."

Gloria tried to will away her anxiety as she watched him walk to the door. She would give it all up just to be back in New Orleans with him. After saying a silent prayer, she locked the doors and placed the forty-five in her lap with the safety off.

Townsend stood under the single bulb illuminating the doorway. He paused a moment before slowly turning the knob. "I'll go in first," he told Taylor.

"No, let me." Taylor whispered. "You are the key to everything. We can't take a chance on something happening to you."

Townsend shook his head. What he said might have been true, but in his way of thinking, what his best friend had waiting on him back home was a lot more valuable than the jewels in their possession. He also planned on keeping his word to Suzy. "Just cover me until I check things out." He pushed the door open and waited a few seconds before entering. Convinced there was not a booby trap, he stepped inside. A musky smell greeted his nostrils. He took a couple of steps and surveyed his dimly lit surroundings. Neatly stacked rows of burlap bags rose almost to the twenty-foot ceiling.

"Good evening, Captain Townsend."

Townsend immediately recognized the distinctive voice. It was Van Tat. He watched cautiously as he and an Asian man appeared from behind a forklift.

"Good evening to you too, Captain Taylor. It is good to see both of you. I must say that your work has all of Southeast Asia buzzing."

"I'll take that as a compliment," Townsend answered. "Let's forget the small talk and get down to business. But before we do, I just want you to know I didn't appreciate those lackeys you sent to spy on us. You know my word is good."

Van Tat stepped forward and bowed his head slightly. "Please do not be offended, Captain Townsend. My associates were sent merely to protect you...and our investment. And I must say you did not treat them too well. Mr. Deng was incoherent. Mr. Chang was forced to quieten him."

"Bullshit," Taylor blurted out, his face red with anger. "They were spies and thieves who would have taken all the stuff and left us with nothing if we had let them. They are lucky we left them with their slimy lives."

Townsend did not attempt to control his friend. He wanted to see Van Tat's reaction. But the Chinaman just smiled and maintained his cool appearance. He was not easily flustered—the only trait about him that Townsend respected.

"I am sorry you feel that way. But shall we, as you say, get down to business? Where is my merchandise?"

"We've got it. Where is what I asked for?"

Van Tat motioned to the other man who produced an attaché case. "You remember Mr. Chang. He has what you seek."

Townsend took the case and opened it. There were ten stacks of hundred-dollar bills and an envelope. He handed the cash to Taylor. "Check it out." Inside the envelope was a Swiss bank account number with verification of a $900,000 deposit and a password to access it. "Is this the only copy of this number?"

Van Tat nodded. "I have held up my end. Now where are my jewels?"

Townsend put the envelope in his pants pocket and turned to Taylor. "Go bring it in. I'll hold on to this," he said as he took the case. While Taylor was gone, he scanned the place trying to get a good lay of it. Knowing that Van Tat was a very cautions man, he figured he had some of his goons hidden in the stack of brown bags that surrounded him.

"Here it is," Taylor announced as he rolled the tire in.

The surprised look on the Van Tat's face was replaced with a grin as he realized his fortune was in a twenty-dollar tire. "Very clever. I must commend you, gentlemen. Can we see them?"

Taylor got his cue from Townsend. He produced a knife and cut the valve stem. After the air escaped, he took two tire tools and separated the tire from the rim. He retrieved three cloth bags and tossed them one by one to Chang. The Asian opened the bags and placed the contents in a teak carrying case. For once, Van Tat's face betrayed him. He was awed at the sight of the diamonds and emeralds. He ran his hand through the multicolored gems, continuing to pick them up and drop them back in the wood box like a child mesmerized by some new toy.

When he noticed that everyone was watching him paying homage to his new wealth, he regained his stone face and closed the case. He handed it to his associate.

"Well, the deal is completed," Townsend announced. "We've got to go now." He and Taylor started toward the door.

"Gentlemen," Van Tat called out. Townsend and Taylor stopped and turned. "You know I cannot allow you to leave."

"I told you he was going to pull some shit, Brad."

Townsend slipped his pistol from under his shirt hidden by the attaché case. "Look, Van Tat, we had a deal. I held up my end. What's the problem?"

"The problem, gentlemen, is you have my money and you cost me a lot of money years ago when you flew away in your helicopter and took my narcotics with you. So, you see, you already owe me a lot of money. And please do not get any ideas about using those firearms. You see I have had weapons trained on both of you since you arrived." He was interrupted by another associate who walked up and whispered in his ear. Van Tat said something to the man and he left.

Townsend read Taylor's eyes. They were about to chance it when two of Van Tat's associates brought in Gloria and Salazar at gunpoint.

Gloria ran up to Townsend and hugged him. "Are you ok?" he asked.

She nodded with her head buried in his chest. "I'm sorry, Brad. They snuck up on me and stuck guns in my face. I didn't have time to do anything."

"Surrender your weapons, gentlemen. I don't want this lovely lady to be harmed," Vat Tat demanded. He then barked Chinese to his two gunmen who collected Townsend and Taylor's pistols. Two more gunmen climbed down from the stack of bags.

Taylor leaned over to Townsend. "Well, I'll be damned. For the first time in his life the old bastard was telling the truth. He did have a couple of bushwackers covering us."

Townsend did not answer. Every time he looked over at Chang, he noticed that his eyes were fixed on Gloria with an evil grin on his face. "So, what's next, Van Tat? Are you going to kill us now?"

He stroked his beard and smiled. "No, I am not going to kill you. That is Mr. Chang's job. And Mr. Chang is a man who takes great satisfaction in his profession. You may have read about some of his work in the newspapers. He is getting quite a reputation here in Bangkok, especially with women."

"You mean that cold blooded woman killer that has been terrorizing the city?" Townsend remarked.

Van Tat and Chang walked over to him. "No need for name calling. You don't want to upset Mr. Chang, do you?"

Chang moved over to Gloria. Leering at her, he reached out and touched her hair. She jerked away and buried her head in Townsend's chest. As he leaned his head down to comfort her, she whispered in his ear. "My gun is in my pants."

Townsend tightened his grip on her as a reflex to her revelation. "Is it cocked?" She nodded. "When I take the gun, drop to the floor," he whispered. He reached down and slipped out the automatic. As Gloria fell, he quickly grabbed Van Tat around the neck and placed the pistol to his head. "Tell your goons to drop their guns or I will blow your brains all over this place."

Van Tat's eyes grew big in fear. "But, Captain Townsend, if you shoot me, my men will shoot you and your friends."

"That may be. But you won't be around to see it. Besides, you were going to kill us anyway. So, are you going to tell them to drop their weapons, or are you ready to meet your ancestors?" Townsend pressed the barrel harder against his head to emphasize his impatience.

"Do as he said," he commanded his men.

As Van Tat's men laid down their weapons, two men suddenly appeared with guns drawn. "Police! Stay where you are. You are surrounded and there is no escape," the officer called out. He scanned the room. His eyes stopped at Townsend. "You sir, drop your weapon, please." Townsend complied with his order.

"I am Inspector Anderson. This is Officer Pryang. The building is surrounded by police. We have been observing your transaction and have learned a great deal of interesting information." He turned to his subordinate. "Pryang, radio the men to come on in." His orders seemed to fall on deaf ears. "Pryang, I said radio the others...now!" he repeated, incensed that his orders were not followed immediately.

Pryang turned his pistol on Anderson. "There are no men. I never called headquarters. It is just you and I."

Anderson looked at his subordinate in disbelief. "What are you doing, Pryang?"

"I am doing what I am paid to do."

Van Tat's face beamed with his familiar obnoxious grin. "A pleasure to see you again, Inspector. As you can see, Officer Pryang is also in my employ. Now please hand over your weapon to Mr. Pryang."

Anderson surrendered his revolver. "Pryang, you disappoint me. You could have had a great career in law enforcement."

"Perhaps. But Mr. Van Tat is very generous to me."

"I could be very generous to you also, Inspector. My offer of an honorarium to you still applies. I could use a man in your position," Van Tat offered.

"I told you before, I don't take bribes. Do with me what you will, but I will not change my mind." Out of the corner of his eye, he noticed the long nail on the left little finger of Chang. He is the serial killer he had been looking for, he thought.

Chang took out a knife and stepped toward Gloria. A shot rang out sending him to the floor. With the distraction, Anderson grabbed for Pryang's gun. In the struggle the pistol fired, striking Anderson. Pryang was about to shoot him again when another shot rang out, exploding his skull. There was a scramble for weapons followed by a hail of bullets. Townsend covered Gloria with his body and began firing. Holding his side, Anderson retrieved his service revolver from the floor and fired twice, dropping two of Van Tat's men. The other two men tried to make it to the door but were stopped in their tracks by the sniper. The shooting lasted less than a minute.

Townsend rolled off of Gloria. "Are you all right?" She was shaking, but managed a nod. "Jeff...Henry, you guys all right?"

"I'm okay," Taylor responded.

"*Si,*" Salazar confirmed.

Townsend got up and surveyed the battle scene. The smell of gun smoke hung heavy in the air. Eight bodies lay on the floor. Only one showed any sign of life. It was Anderson. "Gloria, take a look at him." She went over and assessed his wounds.

"Jeff, you and Henry check those other guys. Make sure they are no longer threats," he cautioned.

176

"This one is still breathing," Salazar called out.

Townsend walked over and turned the man on his back. It was Van Tat. He had been shot in the back, apparently from one of his own men firing at Townsend.

"That's too easy a death for him," Taylor remarked. "He deserves something a lot worse for all the pain, suffering, and death he has caused. Maybe he can think about that as he lays there with his life oozing out of him."

Townsend went over to where Gloria was treating Anderson and handed her a handkerchief for the blood on her hands. "How is he?"

"He has not lost too much blood. I think he will be ok if we can get him to a doctor soon." She dabbed at the blood on her hands. "Brad, where did those first shots come from?"

He took her in his arms. "From our sniper we had concealed," he grinned.

"What sniper?"

"Look for yourself. He's right behind you."

She turned her head. Jim Lee was holding an M-16. She eased out of Townsend's arms and gave him a big hug. "Oh, Jimmy. You saved our lives!"

Jim Lee blushed. "Our people ok?" he asked Townsend.

"Yes, Jimmy. Thanks to you. All that range time I had you do sure came in handy, didn't it?"

He nodded. "Chang is the man who killed my sister. All these men responsible too. That is why I do not feel bad about killing them." He walked over to Anderson. "This man work hard to find her killer. I make sure he is taken care of."

Vat Tat moaned. Gloria walked over to him. "Let me check him," she said, looking to Townsend for permission. Townsend turned to Taylor.

Taylor nodded his approval. "I wouldn't even let a dog just lay there and bleed to death."

Gloria surveyed the wound. "It doesn't look that bad. With medical attention he will probably live. What should I do?"

"Just try to stop the bleeding and patch him up as best you can for right now," Townsend instructed her.

Taylor walked over with a pistol in his hand. Realizing that the Chinaman could recover changed his earlier feelings about tending to him. "I can put him out of his misery," he volunteered. "It's a lot better than he would have given us, especially Gloria."

That statement hit a nerve with Townsend. He knew his friend was right. Van Tat would have had the men killed and let Chang turn his knife on Gloria for his perverted pleasure. Still, he could not condone cold-blooded murder, and he would not let Taylor do something in a moment of anger that would haunt him later. His friend was not that kind of man. "It's a tempting offer, Jeff. But let's leave him here. We will call the police once we are back in the city."

"But, Brad. If we don't finish him now, we will never be able to enjoy what we have worked hard for. He will spill his guts to the cops just to spite us. Or worse, send some goons to the U.S. to bump us off...our families too!"

Townsend was bothered by Taylor's reference to Suzy and Scotty. The Chinaman was the kind of beast to go after an adversary's family in retribution. If he was in Taylor's place, he would not want that uncertainty hanging over his head either. For a few moments he reasoned that killing Van Tat was the only solution. After all, it would not be the first time that he had faced a life taking decision, he thought. During his time in country, he was responsible for the deaths of many men directly or indirectly. But they were the enemy. This was different. He was not serving his country. He was serving himself. His conscience prevailed. "We will just have to take our chances. Killing a helpless wounded man is bad *karma*."

Jim Lee walked over and put the rifle to the Chinaman's head. "I will do it."

"No, Jimmy. Not like this. The other guys were different. They were going to kill us. But I do appreciate your offer," Townsend said.

"What about the Inspector?" Gloria asked.

Townsend looked at Jim Lee. They all knew that he had thrown a twist to the plan. As long as he was alive, he could identify them and put out an alert that would prevent them from leaving the country. But they could not leave him to die. "We will take him with us and drop him off at a hospital."

"Then we better get going," Salazar advised.

"That's a good idea, Henry. Jimmy, get any weapons we may have touched. We don't want to leave any fingerprints. Jeff,

178

you and Henry help the cop to the car," Townsend directed. He walked over to Van Tat and placed the remaining bag of heroin in the pocket of his white jacket.

"What are you doing?" Taylor asked.

"I've changed my mind. I am giving back the Chinaman's dope. It may help the cop when his buddies arrive."

Anderson opened his eyes as he was being lifted. He had heard the conversation. "No. Leave me here. After you get back to Bangkok, call the police and they will come for me. I will not interfere with your escape." His request surprised Townsend and the others. "You can take the jewels. I have solved my case. Just leave my pistol please."

"Will he be ok for about an hour?" Townsend asked Gloria.

"I think so."

"Then let's get out of her," Taylor suggested.

Townsend placed the pistol in Anderson's hand. Looking down at the wounded policeman, the two men sealed their deal with their eyes. Townsend picked up the case and led his team out. As they walked to the car, a single shot rang out. Everyone stopped and turned. "Just keep walking," Townsend ordered.

Gloria walked over to Jim Lee. "Jimmy, I am sorry to hear about your sister."

He appreciated her condolence. With her words of concern, she had converted yet another admirer. "Thank you, Miss Gloria." She gave him a hug and peck on the cheek, then got into the car.

Townsend dropped Taylor and Salazar off at their car and headed back to Bangkok. Gloria was quiet. Townsend sensed something was on her mind. "What's wrong?" he asked.

"Nothing."

He put his hand on her leg. "Come on, now. Something's bothering you. Was it all the shooting?"

She had a concerned look on her face. "Well, that too."

"What else?"

"Brad, did you kill any of those men?"

He thought about her question. "I don't think so. I believe I hit one of the men in the leg. I fired and saw him grab his leg before one of the cop's bullets took him out. Why did you ask me that? You know it was us or them."

She put her hand on his. "I know, it's just I don't want to think that you killed someone for those jewels."

He thought about her answer. "Well, you know I killed a lot of people in the war. I don't even know how many," he informed her.

"Yes, but that was different. That was war. You were just doing..." she stopped in mid sentence, rubbing her fingers. There was blood on them. "Brad, you're bleeding...it's your shoulder. Let me see." She turned on the interior light and inspected the suspected area. "A bullet must have grazed you." She ripped a sleeve from her blouse and dabbed at the superficial wound. "You will live," she said with a kiss on the cheek.

"I must be a magnet for bullets."

"You must. But..." she suddenly became silent.

"But what?"

She gasped for breath. "If you had not laid on top of me, that bullet would have hit me in the head." Her eyes teared.

He pulled her over to him. "Maybe. Hey, it's almost over," he tried to comfort her. But she knew that New Orleans was still a long way off, and she would be staying behind in a strange country without him. She snuggled closer, wanting to savor every second with him.

Anderson took a deep breath and placed the revolver on the floor next to him. He checked his side: the rag that Gloria placed over the wound was wet, but the bleeding appeared to be minimal. He thought about how nice a cup of tea would be. Ten feet away, blood from Van Tat's head wound oozed in the dead eyes that stared at him. In his right hand was the pistol he had concealed. Justice had finally been served in the death of his daughter two years before at the Mekong Club. The official cause of her death was accidental overdose. But he knew it was Van Tat or one of his confederates that put that fatal dose of heroine into his beloved Achara's arm. One small bullet brought him so much relief. He no longer felt the pain in his side.

Jim Lee knelt down and gently helped Anderson lie back on the concrete. He changed the rag on his wound and placed an empty rice bag under his head to comfort him. Anderson grasped his wrist. "Now, our girls can rest," he said in a weak voice.

Jim Lee nodded slowly. He knew what he meant.

When Townsend and Gloria arrived back at Dr. Nguyen's office, they were surprised to see Broussard sitting up smoking a cigarette. "So, how did it go?"

Gloria could not believe her eyes. She rushed over and hugged his neck. "What are you doing up?"

"A guy can only sleep so long...especially when he is missing out on the action," he quipped.

"Well, you are right about that. There was a lot of action...bullets flying all over the place!" Gloria related in an excited voice.

"She was a real trooper," Townsend added.

"No, I wasn't. I was so scared I almost peed on myself," she laughed.

The smile disappeared from Broussard's face. "Where are Jeff and Henry...and Jimmy?"

His concern pleased Townsend. He noticed that over the last few days that cold facade of Broussard's was thawing. "They are right behind us," Townsend informed him.

Gloria used her fingers to comb Broussard's mussed hair. "So, how are you feeling?"

He pulled his head away. "The wound hurts a little and I'm sore all over, but I will live," he confidently informed her as he took a drag from his cigarette.

"Paul!" Salazar called out as he entered the room.

Broussard smiled. "Hey, *amigo*. I see you still got your scalp."

"*Si*, but just barely. I have not seen that kind of action since Nam."

"Here, have a smoke and tell me all about it," he motioned to him.

While the others were relating the events that went down at the warehouse to Broussard, Townsend's mind was on the next step.

"Brad, you've been awful quiet over there," Taylor said to his friend.

"Yeah, what's going on in that little head of yours?" Gloria

181

added.

"I've been thinking about what to do. You know we have less than ten hours before our flight leaves."

"What have you come up with," Taylor asked.

"We don't know if the Chinaman put that $900,000 in the Swiss bank account. But we do know that we have $100,000 in cash, and anywhere from two to five million dollars in jewels, but that ain't money in the hand. I propose that we split up the cash now, six ways instead of five. I think Gloria deserves a full share. Any objections?

"I agree," Taylor seconded. "She has been a tremendous help to us."

"Yes. She has rated it," Salazar added.

Gloria smiled in gratitude. "But I am ok with the original..."

"Then it is settled," Townsend cut her off. "Next, I am going to give you back the stones you picked out. We will sew them into the linings of the clothes we are wearing, along with any additional ones we can carry without becoming obvious or giving ourselves away. The rest of the jewels we will leave with Jimmy. He can take care of them until we can arrange to get them later. As for the money in the bank account, if there is any, we will split six ways. That will be $150,000 each. The same goes for the gems once they are sold. Paul, by the time you and Gloria get back to New Orleans, I should have the cash from the Swiss bank waiting for you.

"What are you talking about? I'm leaving in the morning with the rest of you," Broussard informed him.

Townsend was surprised at his announcement. "Paul, you are in no shape to travel. Dr. Nguyen said you need at least two weeks to heal. Gloria is going to stay and look after you until you can travel. We have already changed the reservations."

Broussard lit another cigarette and took a big drag, exhaling the smoke through his nostrils. "Look, I appreciate your concern for my health, but ain't no damn way I am staying here. I can rest on the plane."

Gloria walked over to him. "Brad is right, Paul. You are too weak. Walking may start your bleeding again. I will be here with you. It will be all right."

"I'm going. So, you better start sewing those rocks in my clothes and figure out a way to get me back on my flight."

"Now just how the hell are we going to do that at the last minute?" Townsend asked him.

Taylor saw Townsend's face turning red. He knew he was extremely pissed. "Wait...I have an idea. Let's get the doc to put a cast on Paul's leg...or both legs. We can put the jewels in them. Then we wheel him up to the reservations desk and tell them that it is a medical emergency and that he has to return to the States immediately with his nurse for further medical attention."

"And the cast will keep Paul from moving around so much, minimizing his chances of causing the wound to bleed," Gloria added.

"*Si!* Great idea!" Salazar concurred.

Townsend read their faces: they liked the idea. "You know, this just might work. And with two full leg casts, we could take almost all the jewels. I would still like to leave some with Jimmy, just in case." His eyes twinkled with excitement. "What do you think, Paul?"

"I'm in," he responded calmly.

"Then let's call the doctor and get busy. I will carry the stones that we picked out for ourselves. That way, only two of us will be carrying contraband. As for the stones..."

"Brad," Broussard interrupted. "There is no point in you sticking your neck out. Let me take all the stones."

Townsend walked over and put his hand on Broussard's shoulder. "I appreciate the offer, Paul. But this way, if one of us gets caught, there will still be some stones left."

"Hey, knock off all this talk about getting caught. We are all going back to the States as one group. We are going to clear customs and we are all going to be rich!" Taylor encouraged them. "So, let's get ready."

"You heard the man," Townsend said. "I'll carry the small stash. Let's split up the cash now. Each of you can carry your share." He opened the leather case and took out the money.

"Aren't we going to wait for Jimmy?" Gloria asked.

"Jimmy is outside keeping watch. I'll take care of his share." He laid the money on the table. I suggest that we take six thousand off the top, a thousand each, for Doctor Nguyen's help." He looked around for confirmation of his proposal. Everyone nodded in approval.

183

After splitting the money, Taylor and Salazar put Broussard in a wheelchair and took him into the clinic where the doctor was waiting for him.

Townsend sat on the sofa and rubbed his forehead. "What's wrong? Got a headache?" Gloria asked. She moved behind him and began massaging his neck and shoulders. "There is a lot of tension there. Try to relax."

He put his hands on hers. "Thanks. Maybe I can when all this is over and we are safe back home safe.

"I know I will." She hugged him. "You look so tired."

"I feel like I could sleep for days, but not until I get out of Thailand."

Three hours passed before Broussard was able to be moved. The doctor gave Gloria antibiotics and bandages for the trip. He made one final plea not to move his patient, knowing it would be in vain. Satisfied he had done everything he could, he offered them a prayer for their trip and shook the hand of each of his new friends. When Townsend handed him the money, he politely refused. It was only after Townsend informed him that his guests would be offended if he did not take it, that he reluctantly accepted their gift in appreciation for all his help.

Gloria left the room for a few minutes. When she returned, she was wearing the nurse uniform given to her by the doctor. "Tada," she said as she imitated a model showing off a new fashion.

"You look just like a nurse," Townsend joked.

"Yeah, but I never had a nurse that looked like that," Salazar complimented her.

Gloria smiled. "Thank you, Henry."

Jim Lee entered the room. When he saw Gloria, he gave her a smile of approval.

"It's time to go," Townsend instructed the others. They said their good-byes to the doctor and quietly departed.

Broussard was carefully placed in the car. He had to lie in the seat to accommodate his cast. Gloria put her medical bag in the trunk and got in the front seat with Jim Lee.

Townsend's car followed them to the hotel. Once they arrived, Jim Lee pulled up to the front door and summoned the chief valet to bring a wheelchair. Gloria went inside and made an appointment for the concierge to schedule an ambulance transport to the airport.

Townsend parked on a side street so it would not appear they arrived together. Salazar got out first and went into the hotel. A minute later, Taylor went in. Townsend wiped the fingerprints from the car before making his exit.

Townsend saw Jim Lee in the lobby and asked him to meet him in his room. A few minutes later, Jim Lee knocked on the door. "Come on in, Jimmy." Townsend handed him a small leather bag. "Here are the rest of the jewels. I want you to hold on to them. I will contact you later about them." He nodded. "Also, this is for your friend for making our rooms look like they have been stayed in."

He held up his hands. "That is not necessary, Captain Brad. My cousin was glad to help out. I will reward him for his efforts."

Townsend knew better than to argue with his friend. "Jimmy, I don't know what we would have done without your cousins. But most of all, we could not have done this without you. And I am very sorry about your sister. What is her name?"

"Mai."

"Mai? That is a beautiful name. It means flower, doesn't it?" Jim Lee nodded. "And how is your mother?"

Jim Lee really appreciated Townsend's concern. He knew it was from the heart. His mother never met Townsend, but she was fond of him for watching after her son and for the money he sent them on several occasions, which allowed them to eat and stay together during their escape to Thailand after the fall of South Vietnam. "She is very sad, but when I tell her that Mai has been avenged, she will receive a little relief from her grief."

"Thanks, my friend, for everything. I put your share of the money in the bag with the jewels. I know you have a safe place for them."

"Yes. Thank you for all you have done for me and my family, Captain Brad."

"You're welcome. And you will take care of the cars?"

"Yes."

"I have one last thing to ask of you, Jimmy."

"Anything."

"I want to hear you call me Brad."

Jim Lee looked a little surprised at his request. After

185

hesitating a moment, he smiled and said, "Brad."

Townsend hugged his friend. Tears filled the eyes of the two men as they parted company.

Chapter 46

Anderson struggled to open his eyes in response to the rubbing on his forearm. Finally, Han's face appeared. They exchanged smiles. He scanned the hospital room, recognizing a police inspector and another officer sitting in the corner. He was not up to answering any questions, so he squeezed his wife's hand and went back to sleep.

Although he was an honest cop and loyal to the force, he felt no guilt in keeping what happened at the warehouse to himself. The robbery was not committed in his country, he reasoned. He felt he owed the unknown perpetrators his silence as they saved his life, revealed a traitor within his department, and put a major drug trafficker out of business for good. But most of all, they unknowingly helped him solve the case of the serial killer who had terrorized the young women of his city for years, including his own daughter. He was comforted knowing that justice had finally been served in the death of his beloved Achara.

Chapter 47

After a couple of hours rest, Townsend watched as the ambulance carrying Broussard and Gloria pulled out of the hotel driveway and headed for the airport. He felt a little apprehensive, not about the money, but for the well being of the woman he was falling in love with. If something happened and he did not get a cent from this whole crazy escapade, he would be happy as long as he could be with her. She made him feel things inside that he had not felt since he and Suzy were together, and that seemed so long ago. He tried to think of other things, like fencing the jewels or what he would do with his share, but she kept popping back in his mind.

His thoughts were interrupted when he saw Salazar go to the front desk and check out. A few minutes later, Taylor came down. They waited in the lobby for the airport shuttle. Occasionally, they would glance at one another and exchange eye language, but there was no conversation. They continued to maintain the pretense they were strangers to one another.

The ride to the airport allowed Gloria the opportunity to reflect on the events that had transpired over the last week, and wonder how things would work out with Townsend. She wanted to be with him, whatever that meant. But Broussard would need someone to stay with him until he recovered. No matter how much she cared for Townsend, her sense of loyalty would not allow her to walk away from the man who rescued her from the streets during his time of need. She felt confident that he would understand—at least she hoped.

As the shuttle arrived at the airport loading-zone, Townsend noticed that security appeared to be heavier than normal. He watched as Broussard was being helped from the ambulance into the wheelchair. As a porter pushed the wheelchair, Gloria followed behind him with a small black bag containing medical supplies. Townsend was impressed at how convincing they looked in their roles. The guards gave them a quick once over before moving aside to let them pass.

The agent checked, but could not find their names on the flight roster. Gloria tried to hide her nervousness. She expected Broussard to explode at any minute, but he kept quiet.

"We have our tickets to show that we are supposed to be on

this flight," she informed him.

"Yes, ma'am. My records show that you were on this flight, but your reservations were changed for a later date."

"That's because Mr. Brewton was injured in an automobile accident. But the doctor said he needed to get back to the United States for surgery as soon as possible, so we called a few hours ago and the airline approved an emergency change." Gloria started to get rattled.

Sensing her anxiety, Broussard placed his hand on her forearm to calm her. "Sir, can you check your list?"

"I have checked it twice already, Mr. Brewton," the agent politely informed him.

Broussard smiled. "Would you mind calling your supervisor? I'm sure we can work this out."

The agent left the desk and returned a minute later with another employee. "Yes, may I help you?" the supervisor asked.

"I am trying to get back to America for surgery. We called the airline earlier and were told that we have a place on this flight."

The supervisor turned to the agent. "Are their names on the list?"

"No, sir."

The supervisor opened the notebook he was carrying. "Oh, here it is. The change was made before I came on duty, but was not posted on the flight. You and your nurse are free to board, Mr. Brewton."

"Thank you," Broussard said.

Gloria took a deep breath. As they continued to the boarding area, she noticed Townsend in line. He made brief eye contact with her, which made her feel better.

Armed soldiers stood guard at the gate searching all carry-on luggage and purses. Gloria handed over the bag. Seeing that it contained medical supplies, the soldier handed it back to her and motioned for her to proceed.

A second porter helped wheel Broussard onto the aircraft and assisted him to a reclining seat in first class. Gloria took the seat next to him. "Are you comfortable?" she asked.

"Yes. This is not as bad as I thought it would be." He leaned over. "What did you do with the cash?"

She grinned. "It's in my panties," she whispered.

189

His eyebrows raised. "Damn. That is some expensive stuff you got there!"

She contained her laughter. "Hush. You are supposed to be in pain."

Fifteen minutes passed before Townsend and the others boarded. He winked at Gloria as he made his way down the aisle. At mid ship, he stowed his bag in the overhead compartment and eased into his seat. Clasping his seat belt, he felt anxious. The end of the journey was in sight, but for the next seventeen hours someone else would be in control of his body. Many pilots felt that way. They were used to being in charge of the aircraft and making the decisions. Now, he had to rely on some stranger to safely transport him, his friends, and a couple of million dollars of stolen jewels. He laid his head back on the seat and closed his eyes. If he could just take a long nap and wake up in L.A., he thought.

The door of the aircraft closed and a voice over the intercom announced their impending departure. Just the idea of getting in the air was a relief to Townsend.

Suddenly, there was a banging on the door. The flight engineer left his seat and opened the door. Five armed soldiers entered and posted on the landing. The officer in charge exchanged words with the crewman. A few seconds later, the pilot announced that the soldiers were onboard to check the papers of passengers.

Townsend's heart began to pound. His mind was bombarded with thoughts: maybe the Inspector changed his mind and talked, or one of Van Tat's men fingered them, or their fake passports had been discovered. He felt trapped. After a minute, he recognized this counterproductive game playing in his head. He told himself to try and be cool. A couple of deep breaths helped.

The soldiers began their sweep row by row, inspecting passports and visually checking the passengers. Gloria and Broussard quickly passed scrutiny. Townsend's anxiety increased the closer they got. Finally, he was next. He offered his passport. The officer looked it over, glanced at him with an expressionless face, then handed it back to him. He concealed his sigh of relief. Now, if Jeff and Henry can just pass inspection, he thought.

A disturbance broke out a few rows behind Townsend. The two soldiers in the front of the plane rushed back. There was shouting in Thai. Townsend could not make it out, but knew they had found what they were looking for. Women began screaming. He leaned over and looked back from his aisle seat. All he could see was a sea of green from the uniforms of the soldiers. He winced at the unmistakable sound of blows to the body. Then, things became quiet, except for the low sobs of female passengers who had been unfortunate enough to witness the arrest. The soldiers turned and headed toward the front of the aircraft carrying the unconscious object of their search. As they passed, Townsend noticed the man was Asian. He felt bad for the bloody man, but was relieved to see it was not one of his friends.

After the soldiers exited the aircraft, the voice on the intercom made an apology for the delay, and announced the flight was ready to depart. Within minutes the plane was airborne.

Chapter 48

Anderson opened his eyes and saw the face of his wife smiling at him. "How do you feel?" she asked.

"Much better," he whispered. "How are you, my wife?"

"I am fine. You look much better. Your color is coming back. Are you in pain?"

"No." He looked around the room. "Where are the men who were here earlier?"

"They left after you fell asleep a few hours ago. The inspector said he would be back later. But he left a man outside the door."

"If he comes in, I am going back to sleep. I am not ready to talk to them." He looked up at his wife and stared deep into her eyes. "I love you, Han," he said. Tears formed in his eyes, something rare for him.

She squeezed his hand. "I love you too, Sarath."

"I want you to know that when I get out of the hospital, I am going to put my papers in for retirement. We can finally travel like you want."

His declaration caused her grin to grow wider. She placed her head lightly on his chest. Finally, she would have him all to herself, she thought. She only wished their daughter was still alive to travel with them.

Chapter 49

Halfway into the flight, Gloria was starting to get antsy. It bothered her that the man she loved and wanted to be with was only thirty feet away and she could not even talk to him. She tried to sleep in order to deal with her urge to walk past Townsend just to look at him. But when she closed her eyes, she kept seeing his face. If she could only get a kiss, even a hug, to get her through the flight, she thought.

After an hour of fidgeting in her seat, she came up with an idea. She waited until the first-class lavatory was occupied, then she got up and headed to the one in the rear of the aircraft. As she approached Townsend, she noticed that his eyes were closed. She bumped his arm as she passed. He looked up at her with sleepy eyes. "Pardon me," she said with an impish grin. She dropped a note in his lap telling him to meet her in the lavatory.

He wondered if something was wrong with Broussard. Maybe he started bleeding again. He waited a couple of minutes before getting up. The lights in the cabin were low. Most of the passengers appeared to be asleep as he made his way down the aisle. When he reached the lavatory, Gloria opened the door and pulled him inside. She secured the latch and pressed her lips against his before he could say anything. It was a long, hot kiss. "Now show me how this mile-high club thing works," she whispered in his ear.

He jerked his head back. "What?"

"Well, the pilot said we were cruising at 30,000 feet...and if my math is correct, that would make it the five-mile-high club."

"Is that why you got me back here? I thought something was wrong with Paul," he said with a touch of anger in his voice.

"No. Paul's all right. I just thought..."

"Gloria," he cut her off. "This is not the time or place." He felt bad that his tone caused her to frown like a little girl being scolded. But he was also pissed that she would risk their carefully developed cover. Perhaps he was being overcautious, he thought, but he did not want the passengers to know of any association between his team members other than the one with Gloria and Broussard. He pulled her closer. "I'll tell you what. Wait until all this is over and we will visit the mile-high club."

"Promise?"

"I promise."

Her beautiful smile came back to her face. "Ok. How about another kiss to last me until we land?" He leaned down and obliged her. As they kissed, he gently fondled her breasts, sending her a signal that he had not lost interest.

He cracked open the door to make sure no one could see him leave the lavatory. Satisfied no one was looking, he slipped out and went back to his seat.

Chapter 50

Suzy was waiting as Taylor came through the gate. She ran up and threw her arms around him and gave him a long kiss. "Oh, I've missed you so much."

"I've missed you too, baby. Where's Scotty?"

"He's in school."

"What time is it?"

"1:20...in the afternoon."

"Baby, I don't know if it is jet lag, time zones, or all the shit that has gone on over the last few days, but right now, I can't even think straight."

"Well, I will just have to see what I can do about that when we get home," she said with a seductive grin.

"Umm. That sounds good. First, I need to get with Brad."

"I saw him pass through the gate just before you. I waved at him, but he just smiled at me and kept walking."

"He did that in case anyone was watching. He does not want to involve you."

"Oh. I knew something had to be going on." She was curious whether their trip was successful, but waited for him to tell her about it when he was ready.

"There he is...over by the phones," he said.

Townsend spotted Taylor and motioned for him to come over. When he got to the bank of phones, Townsend told him to pick up the receiver on the phone next to him and pretend he was talking on it.

"What's up, Brad?"

"I don't know. There was a guy on the plane who kept looking at me. I just want to be careful until we get out of this airport and away from all these eyes and ears."

"Why doesn't everyone come and stay at my house? Suzy won't mind," Taylor offered speaking into the receiver.

"I appreciate the offer, Jeff. But I think we need to stay separated. We will meet at my hotel later this evening and finalize things. Here," he slipped him a piece of paper with the address of where he would be staying. "It's an outside room, so you won't have to go through the lobby. I will call later and give you the room number. If you need me, you can reach me there. I got adjoining rooms in Broussard's alias...Brewton."

"What time?"

"Let's make it eight o'clock."

"Sounds good," Taylor answered.

"See you then. And give Suzy a hug for me."

Taylor smiled. "Will do."

Townsend covertly made contact with Henry and Gloria. The plan was for Gloria and Broussard to check into the hotel. He and Salazar would arrive later.

As soon as Suzy and Jeff arrived home, they headed immediately for the bedroom. Taylor felt a little disoriented. Just twenty-four hours before he was facing death. Now, here he was lying in bed next to his beautiful wife. Suzy pressed her bare breasts against his body and, for the moment, he quickly forgot the events of the last few days.

Chapter 51

When Townsend got to the hotel, he stashed the ten smuggled gems under the mattress and fell on top of it. He had just dozed off when he felt the bed move. It was Gloria. She slipped off her clothes and snuggled next to him. "I've finally got you to myself," she beamed.

"Where are Paul and Henry?"

"Paul is in the bed asleep and Henry is sacked out on the sofa. It seems like I am the only one who is not sleepy."

"I could use a little shut eye...but that can wait."

"Oh. See something you like?" she asked.

"Uh huh." He quickly stripped and they satisfied the passion that had been building since their night together in Bangkok.

Chapter 52

Taylor arrived at the hotel a few minutes early. He took two revolvers out of his belt and placed them on the table. "Here are the guns you wanted."

Townsend picked up the .357 magnum and examined it. "This is nice," he said as he balanced it in his hands. "That .38 with the three-inch barrel is a good weapon. I used to have one just like it. I see you are partial to Smith and Wesson."

"Yep. They can't be beat. I use them with my part-time job," he explained.

"What are those for?" Gloria asked.

"Insurance," Taylor answered. "With the amount of money that we are talking about, we still need to be on guard until this deal is done and we are home free."

"Speaking of money, let's open up Paul's cast and have a look at the take," Townsend suggested. "Did you bring those things I asked for?"

"Right here," Taylor answered.

He and Taylor took tin snips and a keyhole saw and removed the cast. The jewels were washed with detergent and spread out on the table. They sparkled even in the room's dim light. "Wow," Gloria remarked in awe. "How much do you think they are worth?"

"At least three million...probably more," Townsend answered. Of course, our take will be quite a bit less. Most of the stones will have to be cut or re-cut and the fence will take a big share. I am hoping for at least a million and a half. With the Chinaman's million dollars, that would mean about four hundred thousand bucks apiece...best case scenario."

"Damn," Salazar said.

"That is, if the Chinaman put the money in the bank," Taylor reminded him.

"He did." Townsend's announcement surprised everyone. "I called and verified the account number. The money will be wired to the account I set up at the bank in Las Vegas. We will pick it up after we meet the courier. If everything goes as planned, we will take the money and get the hell out of town."

"I can't believe this thing is finally coming to an end," Taylor remarked.

"This has been quite an adventure...but I wouldn't want to do it again," Salazar added. "How about you, Paul?"

"Hell, yeah. Count me in. Just give me a few days for this hole in my side to close." Everyone laughed.

"I think you're serious, Paul," Taylor commented.

"I am. We make a good a team," Broussard complimented the group. "Just remember, if you blow your money in Vegas, I'll be available for another job." Gloria knew he did not go along for the money—he already had more than he would ever spend. It was the action he desired, and in the process, he came to value the camaraderie. "Speaking of Vegas, Brad, what made you decide to set things up there rather than here in L.A.? Seems as large as this town is, it would be easier to be more anonymous." Broussard commented.

"Two reasons. Las Vegas is use to large cash transfers for the high rollers they see. I figured that there would be less questions asked."

"Oh, so are you going to play the role of a high roller?" Gloria teased.

"That's not a bad idea. I do plan to wear a business suit when I go in to pick up the cash...in hundred-dollar bills," he rubbed his thumb across his fingertips for emphasis.

"What's the other reason?" she asked.

"It's really just a contingency. If we are asked where we got the windfall of money, we can always say we won it in Las Vegas."

"Doesn't the casino keep records of winnings?" Taylor reminded him.

"Yes, but only if it is over a certain amount. You could win a number of one thousand dollars pots on the slots or at keno, and you would not have to complete tax forms. Table game winnings can escape notice by limiting the number of chips cashed in at one time. Of course, the IRS would want to know why the winnings were not reported. It is your money and you can do what you want with it. But don't bring suspicion on yourself by flashing large sums. Put a couple of thousand in the bank, and stash the rest in a safe deposit box. If you have bills, pay them off slowly. Remember, we are talking about four hundred thousand dollars."

"Gosh, I can't even imagine how much that is," Gloria said.

"It is so much that you will not have to worry about money for the rest of your life if you spend it wisely," Townsend informed her. "Paul, are you up for the trip?"

"Yeah. I wouldn't miss it. I've never been to Vegas."

"I thought we would rent a cargo van and put a mattress in the back so you can stretch out."

"That's not necessary. I can ride in a car."

"No, you won't," Gloria informed him. "The van is a good idea...less stress on your stomach muscles and the wound."

Broussard knew better than to argue with her. She was right. "Ok," he agreed.

"I think we should call it a night and get some rest," Townsend suggested. "Do you want to crash here tonight, Jeff?"

"No thanks. Suzy is expecting me and I sure don't want to disappoint her," he smiled. "She wants you stop by tomorrow so you can see Scotty. I think she wants to talk to you also."

"I will. See you in the morning."

"Good night, everyone," Taylor said.

"Good night," they returned as he left.

Salazar opened a bottle of tequila. Who's up for a nightcap?"

"I'll have one," Broussard said. "How about you. Glory?"

"Sure. But just one," she responded. "Have one with me, Brad."

"I am tired, but too wired to sleep. Maybe a shot will take the edge off."

The team sat around the table rehashing the events that had transpired the last forty-eight hours. Townsend and Gloria nursed their drinks, while Salazar and Broussard worked on emptying the bottle.

"Let's pull out the gems," Salazar suggested. "This may be the last time we see them all together." With Townsend nodding his approval, he spread the loot out on the table before them.

"They give me goosebumps just to look at them," Gloria giggled.

Broussard pulled out a deck of cards. "Who's for some very high stakes poker? We'll use the jewels for chips."

"Deal me in," Salazar volunteered.

"You guys go ahead. I'm going to lay down and see if I can get some shut-eye," Townsend said.

About an hour later, Gloria entered the bedroom. "Brad, are you asleep?"

"No. I've nodding on and off. What's up?"

She stretched out next to him. "Something has been bothering me over the last week."

"Do you want to talk about it?" he asked with concern in his voice.

"Well, you may think what I am about to tell you is crazy."

"No. You are beautiful, smart, and kind, but you are not crazy. Go ahead and get whatever is bothering you off your mind."

She sighed. "Ever since I saw all those poor refugees, they have been heavy on my heart. I felt helpless until an idea came to me while trying to sleep during that long flight from Bangkok." She paused before continuing. "I think we should use some of the money from the jewels to help them."

Townsend let her words soak in before responding. "That's interesting. I did a pretty good job of putting them out of my mind while we were over there, so I could stay focused on the plan. I had the responsibility of ensuring the welfare of five special friends. But now that we are back in the States, I have been giving those unfortunate souls more thought. Jeff said something similar to me, and I know that Jimmy will be using most of his take for food and medical supplies for them."

"Really!" she said excitedly as she sat up.

"The money is not mine, but I am willing to kick in from my share. We will need to get Paul and Henry's ideas."

"I already have. They said they are willing to share some of their money, if you are."

Townsend reached up and gently rubbed her back. He was touched by her compassion, and very proud of the person she was. She laid back and snuggled next to him. "I think now is the perfect time to tell you the legend of the Emerald Princess," he said. He then related the story to her.

"That's amazing. We will be helping the poor people just like she did," she beamed.

"Let's go and see what the poker boys have to say," Townsend suggested.

Broussard and Salazar were still playing cards. They had finished the tequila and were working on a bottle of Scotch.

"Well, Glory. How much money did you come up with for the refugees?" Broussard asked.

"Depends on how much you are willing to part with," Gloria answered.

"As far as I'm concerned, you can have all of mine", Broussard offered.

"That's a very generous offer, Paul," Townsend complimented. "But a man needs to be paid for hard work, and you were an integral part of this operation. In fact, this job could not have been done without you or any one of the team members. Why don't we wait until we get the final payoff before we come up with a dollar figure?"

"Ok," Broussard answered. Gloria and Salazar agreed.

"Paul, you want the honor of sleeping with the jewels since you lagged them half way around the world?" Townsend asked.

Broussard appreciated the gesture. "Sure."

Townsend held up the two pistols. "Choose your weapon."

"The .357, of course."

Townsend handed him the powerful pistol. "I am going to hit the sack." He went into the other bedroom and stretched out on the bed. A few minutes later Gloria walked in and joined him. They talked for a few minutes and he told Gloria how Jim Lee and his family were just like those refugees years ago. He saw the surprise on her face before he closed his eyes and quickly fell asleep. She made no attempt this time to deprive him of his much-needed rest.

Chapter 53

Anderson was awakened by voices in his room. He looked around to see the police chief talking to his wife. She walked over to the bed. "Sarath. Chief Kwanjai is here to see you. He struggled to sit up.

"Inspector Anderson, it is good to see you again. How are you feeling?"

"Much better, sir. Thank you for visiting me."

"No, it is I who thanks you for your service. You have solved the case of the man who was killing the young women of our city. And you killed the leader of a heroin ring. We have been after Van Tat for a long time, but could never get anything on him. Sad to say, we believe he was paying off some of our officers. Once you are recovered, I would like for you to consider a new job to investigate internal corruption. It is an assistant chief position."

The chief's offer took him by surprise. "I am honored by your confidence in me, sir."

"You have earned it. Your record is excellent. I will leave now and let you get your rest."

"Thank you again, sir."

As the chief was leaving, he stopped at the door. "Oh, when you get back to work, you will receive an award for your valor."

Anderson eased back on his pillow. He had been worried about being dismissed from the force, now he was going to get a medal. Han leaned down and kissed him. "You have always been my hero," she said.

Chapter 54

Townsend woke up, put on his clothes and followed the smell of coffee to the front room. Salazar was stretched out on the sofa snoring, and Gloria was sitting at the table eating a pastry. "Good morning," he greeted her in a tired voice.

"Good morning, sleepy head," she returned. "I've got just what you need to get you going."

"I know you do," he said with a big grin.

"I'm talking about hot coffee, silly," she smiled.

"Where did this come from?"

"I got it from the shop down in the lobby. Got some bear claws and donuts too. I was not about to face you in the morning without your coffee," she chuckled.

"Where's Paul?"

"He's in his bedroom. He and Henry stayed up late. Both were pretty smashed when they turned in," she told him.

"Where did you sleep?"

"I stayed up on the sofa until they turned in. Then, I went and got in your bed. You were so tired you didn't even know that I was there."

"Boy, I must have been wiped out. Having a beautiful woman next to me and not even realizing it," he chuckled. He took a couple of sips of coffee. "You did the right thing by not waking me."

She nodded her head acknowledging that she understood what he meant: the two of them openly going to bed together would be disrespectful to Paul. Even though he had given them his blessings, he was still the one who brought her. Once they got back to New Orleans, the new rules would go into effect.

"Brad, what is the plan for today?"

"I don't know. I thought we would just hang around and take it easy today, and we will be rested up for our trip to Vegas tomorrow."

She was not happy with his answer. "I don't look forward to staying around this hotel all day." She paused a moment. "I've got a great idea! Let's go to the beach. I have never seen the ocean and the Pacific is just a few miles away...and we could drive through Hollywood too."

Townsend sipped his coffee. She reminded him of an excited

kid, and he hated to burst her bubble. But he saw this as an extra risk that did not fit into his plan.

She stared at him with big eyes waiting for his answer. "What do you think?"

"I think you should take her, Brad," Broussard commented as he walked into the room. "She has been a real trooper and needs a little R and R."

"How did it feel to sleep with millions of dollars, Paul?"

"Pretty damn good." He was appreciative of the trust shown by Townsend in allowing him to watch the jewels. Other than his parents, he could not recall anyone ever showing so much respect and confidence in him. Townsend had made a friend for life.

All the talk roused Salazar. He sat up and shook his head. "What's going on?"

"Do you want to go to the beach, Henry?" Gloria asked enthusiastically.

"The beach? I don't like the ocean." He did not want to go into the story about the time he almost drowned in the gulf at Galveston. "You guys go ahead," he answered.

"But I want us all to go," she persisted.

"Gloria, have you forgot that Paul has a bullet hole in him and the less movement the better for him?" Townsend reminded her.

She nodded with a frown of disappointment on the face that was so happy just a couple of minutes before. "You're right, Brad. I did forget."

"You two go. Henry and I will stay here and guard the stash," Broussard stated.

Townsend admired Gloria persuasiveness. He did not have the heart to tell her no. Broussard was right. She had been a real trooper. "Ok."

She ran over and hugged his neck. "Call Jeff and get him and his family to come with us. We are going to have a great time." She then went over and gave Broussard a careful hug to thank him.

Townsend made the call to Jeff. He, Suzy, and Scotty would meet them at the Malibu Beach pier. Suzy would pack a lunch.

Chapter 55

"Stop there," Gloria said, pointing to a beach shop near their destination.

"What for?" Townsend asked.

"We need to pick up some things."

He didn't want to stymie her enthusiasm, so he pulled in the parking lot. "I'll wait for you here."

"No. You've got to go in with me. Come on." They got out of the car and she took his hand and led him into the store. Once inside, she headed directly for the line of female bathing suits on display. "I want you to help me pick one out," she explained. After considering about a half dozen suits, her choices were narrowed down to an orange bikini and a yellow two-piece. She held them up. "Which do you like?"

Townsend studied them. He knew that with her hot body she could do justice to either one. But considering she would be meeting Suzy and Scotty for the first time a more conservative look would be better. "You would be a knockout in either one, but I vote on the yellow one."

"The yellow one it is. I want to make the right impression on Jeff's wife. Let's pick you out something." She walked over to the men's trunks and held up a green and white Hawaiian print?"

"I like it," he answered.

"Now, a couple of beach towels and flip-flops and we'll be set."

He grinned at how she reminded him of a little girl excited in anticipation of swimming in the ocean for the first time. But he knew there was nothing childish about the way she could fill out a swimsuit. Yet, there was an air of innocence about her he had not seen before. "And don't forget the sun lotion. As fair as your skin is, you would sunburn in no time without it."

After paying for their items, they changed into their swimsuits. Townsend checked her out as they walked to the car. "Damn, baby. You sure look good."

She looked back at him with a slight blush on her face. "So do you."

When they arrived at Malibu, Jeff, Suzy, and Scotty had a place staked out with chairs, blanket, large basket, and an oversized umbrella. "Where's Scotty?" Townsend said, winking at Taylor.

"I'm Scotty," the boy answered.

"Oh, you can't be little Scotty. You are too big."

"Well, I am. And you are Uncle Brad."

Townsend nodded. "How about a hug for your ol' Uncle Brad?" The boy ran over and gave Townsend a big hug. "Wow, that was a very good hug," Townsend grinned.

"Mommy said I give the best hugs," he announced proudly.

"Oh, can I have one of those?" Gloria asked. He gave her one too. "Your mommy is right. You do give the best hugs," she said, as she smiled at Suzy.

Townsend turned to Gloria, who was wearing the beach towel around her waist. This is Suzy. Suzy, this is Gloria."

"Good to meet you, Gloria."

"Nice meeting you too, Suzy," she answered as she removed the towel and spread it out on the sand.

Taylor was surprised at Gloria's beautiful body. He noticed his wife checking her out on the sly. "Hey, why don't we hit the surf?" he suggested.

"Ok," Gloria answered as she clasped Townsend's hand.

Taylor extended his hand and helped Suzy from the blanket. This time he noticed it was Gloria sneaking peeks at his wife.

The five splashed around in the water for a half hour before Suzy and Scotty returned to the shade of the umbrella. She watched how Brad and Gloria interacted with one another. They looked like two people in love, she thought.

After a large wave wiped her out, Gloria headed back to the shore. Suzy watched her as she walked on the sand, admiring her cute shape. She motioned for Gloria to come over.

"Did you want me?" Gloria asked.

"Here," she patted the blanket. "Sit down and let me put some lotion on you. With your fair skin, you could get an awful sunburn."

Gloria sat down and offered her back. "Oh, that feels good."

"You have beautiful skin. You have to take care of it."

She looked back over her shoulder and smiled. "That's what my momma used to say. You are a lucky lady, Suzy. Jeff is a really great guy."

"Yes, he is. You are lucky too. Brad is also a great guy," Suzy returned.

"I know. He is the nicest, most caring, and smartest man I have ever met."

"You're in love with him, aren't you?"

Gloria acknowledged with a nod. She did not know that Suzy was Brad's first real love. "But I'm not sure he feels the same way about me."

"Well, I don't think you have anything to worry about," she assured her.

"Really?"

"Yes, really," Suzy answered.

"Thanks, Suzy. And thanks for caring about me and my white skin." They both giggled.

Gloria's reached over and touched Suzy's hand. "You know what I said about you being a lucky woman? Well, I think Jeff is a luck guy." The two women sealed their new friendship with a hug.

After the picnic, Townsend and Gloria posed for several photos on the beach with the disposable camera he purchased at the beach shop. The friends then traded hugs and said their good-byes.

Before returning to the hotel, Gloria persuaded Townsend to take a detour to Hollywood. They drove around and viewed the famous landmarks by car. On Hollywood Boulevard, they parked the car and walked along the Walk of the Stars holding hands. Gloria reminded him of a little girl as she excitedly called out the names on the stars in the pavement. She even put her hands and feet into some of the concrete impressions of the females. He finished off the rest of the film in the camera. As they got ready to leave, she surprised him by pulling his head down to hers and planting a long, passionate kiss on his lips.

"What was that for?" he asked.

"I just wanted to kiss you with all these stars around," she chuckled. "Thanks for bringing me."

He slowly shook his head. "Let's get back to the hotel. We've got a big day ahead of us tomorrow.

Broussard and Salazar were playing cards when Townsend and Gloria entered the room. Gloria rushed over and gave both men a kiss on the top of their heads. "I brought you guys a souvenir." She handed each man a keychain with the image of the Hollywood Sign.

"Thanks, Gloria," Salazar said.

"Yeah, thanks. Looks like you got some sun, Glory," Broussard remarked, surveying her red skin. "Did you have a good time?"

"Oh, yes. I loved the beach. Jeff has a beautiful family. And we walked on the stars in Hollywood. I just wish you and Henry would have been able to go."

"When I get well, maybe we can all go down to Florida. The beaches in North Florida are very nice. The sand looks like sugar," Broussard stated.

"That sounds nice. How about you Henry? Are you in?" Gloria asked.

"I don't like the water," he answered.

"You can sit on the shore with a cooler of iced down beer and watch us have a good time," she said.

"Ok."

Broussard went to the refrigerator and returned with four beers. "Brad, what's the game plan for tomorrow."

Townsend took a sip of beer. "Well, in the morning I'm going to rent a van and pick up a few things for our trip to Vegas. I will also pick up a mattress to put in the back."

Broussard put his beer on the table. "I don't need a mattress. I can sit up in the seat."

"No, you won't," Gloria quickly corrected him. "That four-hour trip can open up that wound. In fact, let me have a look at it now." She walked over and removed the bandage. "Oh, Paul. You need to have a doctor take a look at it. I told you that you should have been laying down rather than moving around so much and drinking."

"You know I can't have a doctor look at it here. He would have to report it to the police. Ain't that right, Brad?" Townsend nodded with a concerned look on his face. "Tell you what. I have a doctor friend in New Orleans who knows how to keep his mouth shut. I'll see him as soon as I get back."

This was another kink in his plan, but Townsend was more concerned for Broussard's health. "I'll charter a Learjet and you and Gloria can fly down tonight." The others were impressed with Townsend's concern and ability to think fast on his feet.

Broussard was really touched by his offer. No wonder Gloria was crazy about him...this man is truly class, he thought. "I appreciate the offer, Brad. But I think I can hold on for one more day."

Townsend looked at Gloria for her opinion. She nodded slightly. "All right. Gloria, work your magic on him. But there is going to be a change in plans. We are not going to take commercial flights to New Orleans. I am still going to charter that Learjet, and we will fly down right after the exchange is made. Paul will get home quicker for treatment, and we will not have to worry about getting all that money through the airports."

Gloria led Broussard into the bedroom where she treated his wound. "Paul, I want you to promise me that you will follow my instructions, and that you will see that doctor as soon as possible."

Broussard appreciated her concern for him. He knew that although Townsend was the man in her life now, their close relationship was still there. "Ok, I promise."

Gloria gave him a little kiss on the lips. "Now, lay back and rest that wound." She returned to the living room and picked up her beer.

"How's Paul?" Townsend asked.

"He's resting. I cleaned his wound really good, so he should be ok until he sees that doctor. Also, I gave him something to help him sleep."

The three drank another beer before settling in for the night. Townsend gave Gloria his bed and crashed in the living room with Salazar on one of the two sofas. In the middle of the night, he quietly made his way into the bedroom and slipped into the bed with Gloria. She was so tired she didn't even notice until morning.

Chapter 56

Townsend got up early and took a taxi to the car rental agency. He picked up the cargo van and made a few stops before heading to Taylor's house. As he pulled into the drive, he thought about how it was just two weeks ago since he was last here. A lot had happened to him in that short period of time: he pulled off a daring heist, had been shot at, seen at least six men die, and was on the verge of falling in love.

Suzy met him at the front door. "Come in on, Brad. You're just in time for breakfast. You must have smelled my biscuits," she teased. She hugged him as he went inside.

"This day is starting out great. A hug from a beautiful lady and homemade biscuits."

"Hey, Brad," Taylor called out from the kitchen. "There's someone in here who wants to see you."

"Hi, Uncle Brad," Scotty greeted him.

"Hi, to you. Did you have a good time yesterday?"

"I sure did."

After breakfast Scotty showed Townsend his model aircraft collection. He listened very intently as Townsend told him all about his favorite one—the Huey. Jeff and Suzy were pleased at how well the two hit it off.

"Brad, we had better get going," Taylor reminded him. He hated to break up their time together, but it was already after nine o'clock.

Townsend looked at his watch. "Oh, you're right. Time seems to fly when you are having fun," he said. "Bye, Scotty."

"Bye, Uncle Brad. Will you come back and see me again?"

"You bet, Tiger." The boy liked Townsend's new nickname for him. Scotty ran over and gave him a hug.

Suzy kissed Townsend on the cheek. "Thanks for bringing him back to me," she whispered in his ear.

"I had to keep my promise to you," he said.

Taylor kissed his wife. "I will see you later this evening."

Chapter 57

During the drive to the hotel, Townsend informed his friend about Gloria's idea of donating some of the money to the refugees. "Fine with me," Taylor stated.

"I figured it would be, based on what you told me the other day about your feelings for the refugees."

"Seeing all their misery makes me thankful for what I have," Taylor related. Townsend nodded in agreement.

Gloria was outside when they arrived in the van.

"Hi," Townsend said as he walked over and kissed her. "Where are the guys?"

"They are upstairs guarding the loot."

"Hi, Gloria," Taylor greeted her as he unloaded several boxes from the van.

"How is Paul?" Townsend asked.

"He's all right, but he still needs to see the doctor as soon as we get back to New Orleans," she informed him.

"Let's go get them and head to Las Vegas," Townsend suggested. He placed his arm around her waist and escorted her to the room. Broussard and Salazar were sitting at the table sipping coffee when he walked in. "

"Henry, are you ready to see Vegas?" Townsend asked.

"*Si.*"

"Paul, how are you feeling?"

"I'm ready to get back to the Big Easy," he said.

"Ok. Let's go and finish this thing!"

Chapter 58

Townsend turned onto Las Vegas Boulevard and headed toward for the hotel room he had reserved. For the last four hours he had played the finale of the plan in his head over and over, trying to anticipate any possible snags that may occur, and developing contingencies to meet them. Although he felt good about the impending conclusion to this venture, he was too superstitious to become overconfident—a trait he had acquired during his combat days. "Welcome to Sin City," he announced.

Salazar looked in awe as they passed one casino after another. "Wow, I bet this place is really something to see at night."

"It's like a neon canyon. Hopefully, we will be back in New Orleans before dark. But you will have plenty of money to make a return visit."

"I will definitely be back...and I'll probably bring Maria. She would love it."

"Jeff, you have been pretty quiet. What's on your mind?" Townsend asked.

"Do you think the Chinaman's men will come after us?"

Townsend considered his question for a moment. "I don't think so. Van Tat was a secretive kind of guy. He shared just what was necessary to get a job done. The less others knew, the less he had to worry about. Chang seemed to be the second in command and he is dead too. The only other one who knew our names is Deng, and, according to the Chinaman, Chang took care of him. Those two guys at Three Pagodas Pass were just hired to refuel us. Chang probably killed them too so they would not have to be paid."

"How do you know that Chinese man is dead? He could have survived with treatment," Gloria informed him.

Townsend looked over at Taylor and smiled. He turned to Gloria. "Do you remember that gunshot when we were leaving the warehouse?"

"Yes. You mean Jimmy shot him?"

"No. It was that policeman. He was just making sure that the Chinaman did not buy his way out of things again. Van Tat and Chang were not only responsible for killing Jimmy's sister, they also had something to do with the death of the policeman's daughter."

"Oh," she said. "You mean the policeman executed him?"

"No. Jimmy said the Chinaman had concealed a pistol and was about to kill the cop. Good thing we left him with his service revolver. It was self-defense." Among the many things Townsend liked about Gloria was her big heart and genuine concern for human life and the suffering of others. Hopefully, these personality traits would rub off on him and make him an even more caring person.

Townsend pulled to the side of the hotel. Taylor and Salazar helped Broussard into the wheelchair. "We will come up to the room after you check in," he informed Gloria.

"I'll be right back," she responded. She then pushed Broussard's wheelchair into the lobby. A few minutes later, she came out and gave them the room number. "See you in a few minutes."

Salazar went up first. Townsend and Taylor followed shortly afterwards carrying the jewels. Townsend was maintaining his notion of minimizing team member association down to the end.

Chapter 59

Townsend looked at his watch. The meeting was in less than an hour. He took a quick shower and put on the business suit he purchased that morning.

"Ooo, check out Mr. High Roller," Gloria said as he walked back in the bedroom. "Nice. You look very handsome," she complimented him. She walked around him pretending to check out the fit. "When I heard that water running, I wanted to jump in with you," she whispered.

"Those are some nice duds, Brad. This is one of the few times I have seen you in a suit," Taylor commented.

"Thanks. I think you will like the one I got for you too. It's over there. Try it on."

Taylor took the suit out of the bag. "Hey, this is nice."

"My bodyguard has to look good as well. We don't want to go in there looking bush league," he laughed. "I also picked up some other items," he pointed to a box on the bed."

Taylor walked over and opened it. "Hey, what is all this?" He pulled out a wig. "Who is this for?"

"Oh, that's yours. Mine is the darker shade," he smiled. "There are also some glasses and mustaches for disguises...and fake scars and tattoos. The bushy beard is for Henry since he already has hair over his lip."

"Boy, you plan for everything, don't you?"

"Just trying to be extra careful by making it harder to identify us, if it comes to that."

"Are you going to carry a gun?" Taylor asked.

"No. You take one and Henry will carry the other while he is waiting in the van."

"Hey, don't I get one of those sharp outfits?" Salazar joked.

"We don't need a well-dressed wheel man," Broussard said.

"Yeah, Henry. Besides, if you put on a suit, these Vegas women would be all over you, and we don't need to attract any attention," Gloria teased.

"Maybe you are right," he grinned.

"Gloria, can you help us with the disguises?" Townsend asked.

"It would be a pleasure," she chuckled.

Salazar dropped off Townsend and Taylor on the side of the bank and searched for a parking place that would give him a view of the front entrance. After circling the block a couple of times, he managed to find the desired spot. He put the .357 magnum in his belt and covered it with his shirt tail, settling in for his duty as lookout—and getaway driver should things deviate from plan.

Taylor, carrying his smaller pistol in a shoulder holster and a forged concealed weapon permit, served as bodyguard and escort to Townsend. After entering the bank, the receptionist directed them to the conference room the bank had set aside for the meeting. Townsend checked his watch: three minutes early. Outside the designated room, a large, well-toned man was stationed at the door. "I am Sanford," Townsend said. The man opened the door and allowed him in. When Taylor tried to pass, the man held out his hand, preventing his entry. "It's ok. Wait for me here," Townsend directed.

As Townsend approached the table, the man seated arose. "I am Pieter Van Zandt."

"Hello, Mr. Van Zandt. I am William Sanford," Townsend returned.

"It is a pleasure to meet you Mr. Sanford. Please, take a seat."

Townsend placed the attaché case on the table. Making sure there were no cameras, he took a small device from his pocket and walked around the room scanning for bugs. Satisfied there were none, he took a seat at the table.

"I see you are a cautious man too, Mr. Sanford. But this room is free of surveillance equipment. My associate outside and I have already checked."

"Well, one can never be too safe, especially with the stakes we are talking about," Townsend informed him.

"Speaking of the stakes, may I see the jewels?"

"Of course." Townsend opened the case and carefully spread the gems on a black cloth. He noticed the look on Van Zandt's face. There was no need to ask if he liked what he saw, his eyes had already given him the answer.

"There are more than I imagined." Van Zandt took out his loupe and began methodically examining the gems, starting with the larger diamonds and working down to the smaller ones. Once the diamonds were done, he began looking at the emeralds. It took him almost an hour to complete the task.

"So, what do you think?" Townsend asked.

"The diamonds are very nice and should be easily cut. I am surprised at the number that exceed ten karats...several over twenty-five karats. And the emeralds are exquisite. Several appear to be flawless."

"I've always heard that a flawless emerald is worth more than a flawless diamond of the same weight," Townsend commented.

"Perhaps. But there are other factors to consider as well." He laid the loupe on the table. "I will pay you 1.5 million dollars for everything."

Townsend liked what he heard. That was the minimum he had hope for. But he also picked up something in Van Zandt's behavior that caused him to play a hunch. "I was told that I would be paid fifty percent of their value. Well, I had them appraised at least four million dollars conservatively and as high as five million dollars."

Van Zandt looked like a kid who had been caught in a lie. He started to perspire. "You must realize that these jewels are very hot right now. I will have to sit on them for a while before I can start to release them and get a return on my investment."

"Mr. Van Zandt, the only market that would be affected is Singapore. New York, London, Cape Town, as well as Antwerp and Amsterdam can easily handle these stones. Because they are raw and undocumented, it would be impossible to trace them. All you have to do is cut them and sell them."

"My offer is 1.5 million dollars."

Townsend decided to press Van Zandt. A feeling in his gut told him the Dutchman was more than a courier. He was the buyer or at least a principle with authority to make a deal. And he wanted those stones really bad. "Well, in that case, it looks like we do not have a deal. Sorry you had to fly all the way from Amsterdam for nothing." Townsend put the jewels in the case and started to walk out.

"Wait, Mr. Sanford. I think I can increase my offer, but I will have to call Amsterdam."

"Make the call." Townsend was impressed with himself at how effective a negotiator he was.

Van Zandt left the room for five minutes. When he came

back in, he was smiling. "I have been authorized to pay you 1.7 million American dollars. Is that acceptable?"

Unknown to the Dutchman, Townsend would have accepted the original offer, but his acumen added another $200,000 to the pot. He strained to keep his elation in check. "I suppose, if that is your final offer."

"It is," Van Zandt informed him. He walked to the door and spoke with his associate. A few minutes later the other man came in with a small suitcase. "Here is your money, Mr. Sanford. I must say you have really done your homework, as they say in America."

"Thanks. Now if you don't mind, I would like to look at the money."

"Of course," he answered.

Townsend produced a small object from the attaché case. He took a random bill from several of the stacks.

"What is that?" Van Zandt asked.

"It is an ultraviolet lamp."

"Do you think we would give you counterfeit money?"

"Of course not. This is just to make sure that the banks have not marked the bills. They do that sometimes on large sums of money in the event a courier is robbed, then it will make it easier to identify the money. This is for your protection as well as mine."

Van Zandt looked impressed. "Very ingenious. I never thought of that."

"The money appears to be ok. This concludes our business." Townsend closed the suitcase and extended his hand to Van Zandt. Nice meeting you. Have a safe flight home."

"It is a pleasure doing business with you, Mr. Sanford. Perhaps we will have further business in the future."

"Who knows?" he said. He picked up the suitcase and walked away.

Taylor was waiting by the door as Townsend exited the room. He knew by the grin flashed by his friend that the deal went down. It took great discipline, but he was able to contain his excitement. Townsend handed him the suitcase. "Wow! This is heavy," he whispered.

The vice-president of the bank walked over to Townsend and handed him an aluminum brief case containing the nine hundred thousand dollars wired from Geneva. Townsend led the bank official into the conference room where he had just conducted his business with Van Zandt. He removed the stacks of bills and placed them neatly on the table and repeated the procedure with the ultraviolet lamp. Satisfied the bills were clean, he placed the money back in the case and signed the receipt. The vice-president, who remained silent during the transaction, thanked Townsend and followed him out of the room.

"Let's get out of here," Townsend said as Taylor escorted him out of the bank, ever vigilant of their surroundings.

As Salazar began to pull out of his parking space, he noticed a flashing light in his side mirror. His heart raced as the police car pulled beside the van. He sat motionless with his clammy hands glued to the steering wheel. The officer gave him a chiding glare for almost pulling into the path of his cruiser. Salazar acknowledged his error with a nod. The officer said something he couldn't understand before continuing on his call. After breathing a sigh of relief, he picked up Townsend and Taylor.

"What was all that about with the cop?" Taylor asked.

"I almost pulled out in his way. He gave me a dirty look, mumbled something, and then went on," Henry reported.

Townsend could not hold back his ecstatic grin. "In Vegas vernacular, we hit the jackpot. Let's get back to the hotel. But be careful. The last thing we need is to be stopped by the cops for a traffic violation."

Chapter 60

Gloria met Townsend at the door of the hotel room. "What happened?" she asked excitedly.

"We scored big. That's what happened." She threw her arms around his neck and kissed him. He placed the suitcase on the table and opened it. Gloria gasped at the sight of all the green bills.

"What was the take, Brad?" Broussard asked.

"Yeah. Did we get the million-five?" Salazar added.

"Well, not exactly," Townsend responded trying to keep a straight face. "I played a hunch...we got 1.7 million!"

"What?" Gloria screamed as she jumped in the air. She went around the room hugging everyone.

"What's the next step?" Taylor asked.

"First, let's double check this money. Afterwards, we'll pack up and you can take us to the airport," Townsend responded. "I'm going to find a phone and check on our jet. Why don't you guys go ahead and split the loot?"

As he walked through the hotel, the ringing of the slot machines reminded him of all the people who came to this city in search of a quick fortune. Most went home with a lot less than they came with. He and his friends were lucky—they would be going home with a small fortune. Outside the hotel, a steady stream of dreamers strolled the boulevard, appearing to be completely oblivious to the fact that the odds of taking some of the casinos' money were stacked against them. But that was what Las Vegas was all about—illusion and fantasy. What awaited him back in the hotel room was real, and so was the money.

When Townsend returned to the room, his eyes were immediately drawn to six stacks of cash on the table. One stack was larger than the other five. "What's this?" he asked, referring to the larger pile of bills.

Taylor placed his hand on it. "Brad, this is your share. We have decided that you should take anything over two million dollars. That still leaves us with four hundred thousand dollars each...and I'm sure that Jimmy is with us on this."

"That would make my share six hundred thousand. I thought we agreed to split six ways," he reminded them.

"But you did the planning, put in countless hours, and invested your life savings," Taylor continued.

"I was just one in a team of six. The job could not have been done without each of you."

"But this is what we want," Broussard said.

Townsend looked at Salazar. "And you?"

"*Si.*"

He turned to Gloria. "Yes," she said before he could ask.

"Thanks, guys. I appreciate all of you and your efforts...and your generosity." Townsend was touched. "Don't forget that Jim Lee is still holding about a hundred thousand in gems for us."

"We didn't forget. This is just how we want it," Broussard answered.

"Okay. That's settled," Taylor announced.

"What are you going to do with your share, Brad?" Salazar asked.

"I'm not sure. Originally, I have thought of starting a helicopter charter service in south Louisiana to shuttle workers to offshore oil platforms. But now, I'm thinking about opening a bar in the French Quarter." He looked at Broussard. "I'm beginning to see what Paul and Gloria see in that place."

Broussard smiled and nodded. I think I can help you out. "I've got several pieces of property there."

"What are your plans, Henry?" Townsend asked.

"I am going to put most of it in a safe deposit box, like you said. Then, I am going to just take it easy and party for a while. And after I get through partying, I may look you up and help you run that bar." He turned to Broussard. "What are you going to do with yours, Paul?"

"I don't know," he shrugged.

"Well, I know what I am going to do with mine," Gloria cut in. "I'm going to buy back my daddy's house in the Garden District." Broussard smiled at her. He knew getting the house was a goal she had dreamed of for years.

"Jeff, how about you?" Salazar asked.

"I'm going to pay off as many bills as I can without raising suspicion. Then, I'm going to quit my second job so I can spend more time with my family. I'd like to take my wife on a little getaway. We might come here to Vegas. Henry, we may even meet up with you and Maria."

"What about the refugees? How much should we give them?" Gloria asked.

"Fifty thousand each," Salazar answered. "Three hundred thousand dollars will buy a lot of rice."

She shook her head. "That's not enough."

"How about one million dollars?" Townsend suggested. Gloria and Salazar had surprised looks on their faces, but Broussard was not phased by his statement. "Each person puts in $150,000. That will be $900,000, and I will kick in the extra $100,000 since you guys gave me a bonus. That will leave all of you with a quarter of a million dollars each. I'm sure that Jimmy will agree. He was going to donate most of his take to them anyway." He made a silent survey of his accomplices. Each one silently approved the proposal with a head nod. "Now that the amount is settled, let's pack up, wipe this place down, and head for the airport."

Taylor retrieved a bottle of Champaign he had stashed. "But first, I think this calls for a celebration. He filled the five glasses and passed them around. "To good friends and great times," he toasted. They clinked glasses and completed the toast by downing the bubbly.

"Brad, I've been thinking. I have an apartment in the Quarter. If you and Glory want it, it's yours...rent free," Broussard offered.

Townsend looked over at Gloria. "Are you sure, Paul?"

"Of course, I'm sure, or I would not have made the offer."

"Yeah. That would be great. At least until Gloria gets her house back. Thanks." Townsend took his offer to confirm what he said earlier that he was ok with Gloria being with him.

"Come on, Paul, let me change your dressing. She led him into the bedroom. As she gathered her medical supplies, Gloria had a strange feeling—a kind of restlessness. She wasn't sure if it was from the independence and power the contents of her share represented, or if it was the anxiety brought about by wondering what her future with Townsend would be. She just wanted to get back to New Orleans and have Townsend there with her.

"Something bothering you, Glory?" Broussard asked.

"I guess being around all that money has me a little nervous."

Broussard knew it was more than the money. "Are you sure that's all it is?" he teased.

"Oh, be quiet and let me check your wound." She opened his shirt. There was a dried bloodstain on the bandage. She cut it off, cleaned the entrance and exit holes, and applied a fresh bandage. "All done. But you need to hold your moving around to a minimum."

"Thanks."

"You're welcome," she said with a kiss to the top of his head.

After performing her nursing duties, she went into Townsend's bedroom. She had been waiting for the opportunity to be alone with him. He watched her as she slowly moved toward him with a naughty look on her face. She placed her arms around his neck. "Oh, I want you so bad," she moaned as she pressed her lips against his. As they kissed, her hand made its way to his groin. "Mmm. I see you want me too."

"Tomorrow, I will show you just how much." The sound of his name being called out interrupted their clench. "Hold that thought," he told her.

"We're ready," Taylor announced. Townsend picked up the suitcase carrying his and Jim Lee's shares and walked out the door followed by Gloria pushing Broussard in the wheel chair. Taylor and Salazar carried the rest of the money with their bags.

The small jet was on the tarmac when they arrived at the airport. Townsend went into the office to complete the paperwork and ensure his other flight requests were met. Satisfied they were, he paid for the charter in cash.

"Looks like you hit the jackpot," the office manager remarked.

He smiled. "I guess you could say that."

The other team members were chatting with Taylor at the steps of the aircraft when Townsend walked up. "Ok. You guys ready to head south?"

Salazar shook Taylor's hand. "Let's keep in touch, Jeff. Maybe we can persuade Suzy and Maria to come back to Vegas with us later.

"Yeah, or all of us meet up in New Orleans," Broussard

added, with his hand grasping Taylor's.

Gloria stepped over and hugged Taylor. "Paul's right. I want you, Suzy, and Scotty to come and visit me after I get my house in the Garden District." She then gave him a peck on the lips, leaving him with a slight tingling sensation.

After the others were aboard, Taylor leaned over and softly said in Townsend's ear, "Brad, we did it. We really did it."

"Yes, we did," Townsend answered. "We got the tears of the Emerald Princess."

"Be careful."

"Roger that. I have food and booze on board that should keep them occupied for the next three hours. Give Suzy and Scotty a hug for me."

Taylor nodded. "T-N-T?" he offered as he put out his clasped hand.

"T-N-T," Townsend returned as their fists tapped.

They hugged and traded slaps on the back. Then, Townsend quickly climbed the steps and entered the cabin.

Taylor watched as the door closed and the aircraft began to taxi. He remained on the tarmac until he saw the Learjet carrying his fellow adventurers disappear into the clear desert sky.

THE END

www.ingramcontent.com/pod-product-compliance
Lightning Source LLC
Chambersburg PA
CBHW050735230626
47052CB00002BA/196